Praise for
Helen Hath No Fury

"Cleverly written, classically plotted, Pepper's latest lively adventure culminates in a confrontation both scary and comical."
　　　　　　　—*Portsmouth Herald*

"Very literate . . . The humor, insight, and rich range of allusion you hope for in a Gillian Roberts book are all there, waiting to be savored."
　　　　　　　—*I Love a Mystery*

"An entertaining read full of likable characters . . . Roberts has salted her text with the clues to the solution to Helen's death. The alert reader has a fair chance at playing detective right along with Amanda Pepper."
　　　　　　　—*Tip World*

"Roberts skillfully negotiates some rather tricky emotional waters in this new addition to a series notable for its smooth mix of traditional mystery conventions with the darker underpinnings of modern crime fiction."
　　　　　　　—*Publishers Weekly*

"Like a favorite blanket on a cold winter's day, this novel is warm and comfortable: a familiar story peopled by fresh and eminently likable characters."
　　　　　　　—*Booklist*

*Please turn the page
for more reviews. . . .*

HOW I SPENT MY SUMMER VACATION
"Roberts concocts colorful and on-the-mark scenes."
—*Los Angeles Times*

IN THE DEAD OF SUMMER
"Tart-tongued, warmhearted Amanda's sixth case is as engaging as her others, and here she gets to do more detection than usual."
—*Kirkus Reviews*

THE MUMMERS' CURSE
"[A] funny Philly puzzler for schoolteacher Amanda Pepper."
—*Publishers Weekly*

THE BLUEST BLOOD
"I'm not convinced that anyone offers better one-liners than those delivered by Amanda Pepper."
—*Alfred Hitchcock Mystery Magazine*

ADAM AND EVIL
"Another lively addition to the series."
—*Library Journal*

By Gillian Roberts

HELEN HATH NO FURY

AN AMANDA PEPPER MYSTERY

Gillian Roberts

FAWCETT BOOKS • NEW YORK

A Fawcett Book
Published by The Ballantine Publishing Group

Copyright © 2000 by Judith Greber

All rights reserved under International and Pan-American Copyright Conventions. Published in the United States by The Ballantine Publishing Group, a division of Random House, Inc., New York, and simultaneously in Canada by Random House of Canada Limited, Toronto.

Fawcett is a registered trademark and the Fawcett colophon is a trademark of Random House, Inc.

www.ballantinebooks.com

ISBN 0-345-42932-X

Manufactured in the United States of America

First Hardcover Edition: July 2000
First Fawcett Edition: October 2001

10 9 8 7 6 5 4 3 2 1

Special thanks to Marilyn Wallace, for invaluable and instantaneous feedback when desperately needed; to Dr. Ann Rivo, Evelyn Spritz, and Bert Strieb for doing research that saved the day for me; and, as always, to the best team a writer could have: Jean Naggar, my agent, and Joe Blades, my editor.

One

"HAVE SEX AND DIE." HELEN COULTER BARELY PAUSED for breath. "That's what she's saying."

Helen's words produced the heavy silence of a collective held breath. Etiquette had been breached. My book group had been discussing Kate Chopin's *The Awakening*. More accurately, we'd been listening to another member discuss the research she'd done on the book and author when Helen charged in.

My teacher muscles twitched, ready to chastise Helen for interrupting. I reminded myself that this wasn't a classroom, it was a living room, and its occupants, all ten of us, were adults.

Helen filled the lull she'd created. "I'm sick of that literary staple—dark-haired women who lust and die." Helen tossed her own sleek cap of brown-black hair like one of those vixen heroines of old B movies. "Why was suicide her only option? Suicide is *cowardly*, too *easy*. She had her own house, her painting, friends like the piano teacher, her children—why do such a thing? No wonder the critics hated it."

"Not because of that." Denise was the one who'd been interrupted. "They considered it pornography." Denise had a sheaf of printouts on her lap, and although she was being polite about being interrupted and misrepresented, she kept smoothing her skirt in a compulsive manner

1

that suggested how much she wanted to do the same thing to the discussion.

"Well, it makes *this* critic sick, too," Helen said. "Maybe a woman wrote it, but she's echoing all the men through history who decided that if a woman steps across *their* line in the sand—sexually—she has to be punished."

At this, Denise stopped pressing her skirt and sat up, on alert, sensing a slur on her husband, Roy Stanton Harris, state legislator, candidate for Congress, and energetic advocate of "family values." In my family, values meant really good buys—low rates for strip steak or telephone calls—but it didn't mean that to him.

Denise was a fairly recent bride. She'd retained her maiden and professional name since marrying Roy Stanton, as she always referred to him, but she'd merged identity and opinions with him and had become the perfect political wife.

"Sorry," Helen said, not sounding at all sorry. "But that's how I feel. Sick and tired of men telling women what to do with their bodies."

Denise looked on the verge of snapping back, but only for the smallest interval. And then her composed expression returned. "Could we talk about the book? About Kate Chopin's book?" she asked quietly. "About Edna Pontellier and her world?"

In response, a chorus of voices. After a year in the group, I've given up wishing we'd be coherent or stay on track. We've twice voted down the idea of a formal leader, and instead take turns leading sessions. We are noisy and opinionated, sometimes chaotic, but I appreciate the emotion that's behind the clamor. A love of books propelled me into teaching, then made the job frustrating, because I can so seldom transfer my passion for words and stories to my students. So it was a treat to gather with literate women to whom ideas mattered, women who savored books the way they might fine meals. Or savaged them if they found them rancid, because their quality mattered to them.

"Don't blondes also lust and die?" Clary Oliver asked. She was Helen's business partner and best friend, and together, they produced high-end children's clothing. Now she adopted a challenging stance and raised her eyebrows. "Hath not a blonde a sex drive?" she asked. Her own head sported a unique and expensive shade of beige.

Her sister and shadow, Louisa, also blonde, laughed with a harsh "Ha!" that I was sure was supposed to convey lots of meaning, but Louisa's meanings were generally not worth figuring out.

"Sorry, Clary," Helen told her partner, "but think about those famous sex-and-suicide girls—Emma Bovary, Anna Karenina, and Edna, too. Not a single blonde."

Susan Hileman, whose red hair and freckles could have been borrowed from Raggedy Ann, spoke up. "I read somewhere it goes back to the blonde Anglo-Saxons. The invading barbarians, the baddies, were dark, and we all know wild, sexy women are bad, right? So they're dark, too. Angels and babies are blonde, the pure and the innocent, unless the woman's a platinum blonde—an obvious fake, and thereby corrupt."

Susan had been a lit major with me at Penn, and a year ago was my conduit into this long-established book group. She worked for a PR firm, tweaking images. But that was, she insisted, only her day job. Her true calling was as a writer, and she had a mystery in progress.

There had been several earlier mysteries in progress. I wasn't sure she'd ever finished any of them.

"Renegade blondes," she continued, "the obviously bleached kind—they drive a *man* to his destruction by making him kill for her. Except for Marilyn Monroe, who was perfect, because she was bleached but squooshy. Corrupt, but compliant." Susan pointed at her springy red curls. "As for me, my literary or film role is doomed to be as the sexless best friend."

I wondered if there really was a pattern, and where my own brown hair—I like to think of it as chestnut, but really, it depends on the light—fit into the spectrum. Undoubtedly not in the province of heroines, and not even of sexy villainesses, more's the pity.

"Edna killed herself," Tess said, quietly pulling us back to the subject at hand. "Drowning was certainly not her only option." Tess was a psychologist with short no-nonsense brown hair. I just knew there weren't any myths about the two of us.

"Do you think society killed Edna?" I asked. "In the sense that it had no place for her. She had two affairs. She didn't much care about her kids. She no longer fit anywhere."

"Thank God times have changed," someone softly commented.

"Nothing's that changed," Helen said. "Because of the Ednas. Edna could have stood up for herself, lived a Bohemian life, defied them, but she didn't. That's the same today. Most people won't take a stand—a stand that might put them in a bad light."

"It was harder then." The incongruously babyish voice belonged to Helen's neighbor, Roxanne Parisi. Roxanne struck me as a woman reinventing herself, at least outwardly. Her current image seemed costumed rather than dressed, in gauzy layers and noisy jewelry, and all of it topped by hair dyed the color of fine Bordeaux. But her voice seemed left over from an earlier incarnation.

"It's hard now," Helen said. "Hard to take a stand. Be defiant."

"Don't you just love the ruined woman!" Susan said with her customary verve. "*Ruined!* As if we're pill bottles with warnings: Do not use if seal is broken—contents may have been tampered with."

"How come you can't ruin a man?" somebody muttered.

"Can we get back to this book?" Poor Denise. She had assiduously prepared for the evening, and here we were, being especially unruly.

"What about her children?" Helen demanded. "Didn't she have an obligation to them?"

"She didn't really like them all that much."

"The art! Everybody's forgetting the art and the piano teacher—Madame—what's her name?—remember how independent—"

"The book's a hundred years old—you have to remember the cultural context—Victorian, for God's sake—against which—"

"That's right—why aren't we looking at her as a woman of her times and her specific world?"

We were into the verbal free-for-alls that drove us crazy but never stopped.

"After all, the book was banned, libraries wouldn't take it, Chopin never published another book—"

"I guess the book is relevant," Helen said. "Because it's so pathetically predictable. Women having sex voluntarily. Men deciding what to do about it. And one hundred years later, nothing's changed except the language of it."

The chorus swelled, disagreeing, agreeing, addressing the group, herself, the woman next to her, as many verdicts as voices.

"What about her affairs?" Clary asked. "Aren't they relevant? What about her morality? Does everybody here think what she did is all right?"

"You're right—the book's about marriage, isn't it? About how oppressive and confining it is."

"Was."

"Hah!"

Half the time, the married members proselytized for marriage. One of us was a young widow, two were divorced—one who'd already run through three husbands, another two—and yet another had been engaged for ten years. And then there was me. I. Amanda Pepper, spinster teacher. I didn't have an ex and I didn't have long-term commitments with the man I lived with. I was therefore the focus of their missionary zeal. As if my mother had trained them.

They never seemed to notice that when they weren't touting that hallowed institution, they were trashing it, but I did.

"Wouldn't you have an affair if you were married to that man?"

"The book's called *The Awakening*, after all—"

"I think it means more than sexual awakening. I think it means—"

In the din, the only voices we could hear were our own. It was one of those moments when you don't want the male of the species to happen by our "discussion" and have his every disgusting macho prejudice confirmed.

But no man was likely to stroll by. Helen's husband, Ivan, was out of town, in Cleveland, foraging for shopping centers, parking lots, and office buildings. I don't completely understand what he does, but I do understand that it's lucrative, as witness the house he and Helen had been renovating for nearly a year.

Philadelphia's Delancey Street where Helen lived is interesting. The blocks alternate between large homes and huge homes. It's said that originally one block was for the wealthy, the next, meant to house their servants. I'm not sure that's completely true, but Helen's house was definitely of the lord-of-the-manor variation with four stories of spacious high-ceilinged rooms, plus a solarium and roof garden currently being installed as a finishing touch. I wondered if the small family of three ever crossed paths in the enormous house.

Earlier, we'd toured the renovations, oohed and aahed over the new fireplace in the master bedroom, the Jacuzzi tub, the supersleek and expanded kitchen, the brick patio behind the house, the enlarged rear window, the skylighted bathroom. We'd even done anticipatory oohing at the potential roof garden, at the chicken-wire fencing, the bags of dirt, and stacks of bricks. I could imagine the solarium, the flower garden, the bricks turned into a privacy wall. It was going to be magical up there on a summer's night.

"She was a baby-making ornament." The voice brought me back to the living room and poor drowned dark-haired Edna Pontellier.

"Think that's so different from half the marriages you know today? She was an early trophy wife, is all."

Nobody looked at Denise, who was our closest thing to a trophy wife. She was twenty years younger than Roy Stanton and quite beautiful. But I had a sense that her ambition was as fierce and powerful as his. Maybe he was the trophy.

"What about my question?" Clary asked. "Having an affair doesn't change anything."

"Except the quality of the sex. That's not chopped liver."

"See—here—I'll find it, I'm sure." Susan shook her red curls and flipped pages, then put the book back down. "I mean, Mademoiselle Reisz is part of what 'awakens' Edna. The piano music makes her aware of passion and beauty. I wanted her to continue with her art, be like Mademoiselle Reisz, an interesting outsider."

"She would have been ostracized!"

Good books are like Rorschach tests. What each person finds on the page depends on what she's brought along with her. I know very little about the daily lives of these women. I see most only once a month, but I feel as if I know more about their values and concerns, more of what matters to them and who they are, than I do about many of my longtime friends. All of that is via the books we read, the ideas that fill our monthly meetings.

Think about it: we were ten adults squabbling about a woman who lived—fictionally—a century ago, in a vastly different culture. It was delicious. It was fun. It was amazing that we could care that much about Edna's suicide and what led to it.

I'd once had a student whose mother was Vietnamese, a woman who spent her childhood trying to survive, not perusing Western classics. She'd married a U.S. soldier and moved to Philadelphia with him, and now, she was catching up on U.S. culture via her children's assignments. So when her daughter's class read *Romeo and Juliet*, so did she. And she was heartbroken by its ending, had expected, her daughter told me, that "they would work things out and move to a nice house in the suburbs."

But the women in this luxurious living room were not immigrants who'd never before seen works of Western literature. And in truth, we weren't arguing about Edna's decision to drown herself or Kate Chopin's writing style or about Victorian social systems, no matter the words whirling around the room. We were talking about our systems of belief, our confusions, and our blind spots.

We munched away as the discussion went on. Helen was an exemplary hostess. Tonight, even while she spoke, she simultaneously refilled wine glasses and passed platters holding cheeses, miniature calzone, and fruit.

Someone once again mentioned Edna's suicide, and once again, Helen exploded. Something was gnawing at her tonight. Maybe it was the stress of remodeling for more than half a year. "Suicide was a cop-out!" she said. "A way for Chopin to end the book. But it's stupid. If you're going to die—literally or metaphorically—might as well go down in flames, not do yourself in. Stand up for something—*fight* for something."

"Fight for what?"

"What she believed in. What she wanted! Confront the hypocrites. Do something for change! Then she could have *left* if she was so unhappy. Gone off the way her lover did, to a new country where things are different. Or stayed and defied them all. Maybe even said hello to her kids once in a while."

"Can we slow down, back up, and talk about the *book*?" Denise asked. "I have reviews and commentary."

"We *are* talking about the book." Helen surprised me with the chill that had entered her voice.

"I don't see what's wrong about discussing our reactions," Tess said. "It obviously struck nerves, so maybe—"

"But Denise did all this work—" Clary tried.

In their partnership, Helen leaned toward the visionary end of the spectrum, the designs and fabrics, and Clary was the one who handled the cold, hard facts of doing business. It was in character that Helen would declaim and Clary would try to get us back on track.

It was in character for us that her attempts had no effect.

Helen looked at her partner with unfocused eyes, as if all she'd registered was noise, not words. "Nothing's changed, either," she said. "No offense, Denise, but politicians preaching hypocritical family values are as oppressive to women as Edna's society was. Why aren't any of them saying 'impregnate a woman, go to jail'? It's all about punishing females men have treated rottenly."

"This isn't about today's value systems," Denise said. "Edna's personal was not the political."

"But it was; it is! It always is!" Helen said.

"Really, Helen," Clary murmured. "Can't we listen to—"

"Can't you see it yourself? That's what it's about! Men looking for women to blame through the centuries. And they still are. But what if Edna had spoken up instead, let other women hear new ideas? I wanted her to be brave." She sipped her wine and seemed to visibly cool down. "Sorry," she said. "Some things infuriate me."

Denise smiled brightly at me. "You're quiet tonight."

I hadn't realized how much of an observer rather than participant I'd been until she mentioned it. "I was thinking about what Helen said. One of my classes is reading *The Scarlet Letter*, so that idea of looking for a woman to blame through centuries—"

"*The Scarlet Letter.*" Susan interrupted me with enormous authority. "The Colonial variation on the theme—but Hester didn't die. She went to live in Europe and got rich, didn't she? So there goes your theory, Helen. And then there's Polly Baker."

At mention of the name, all side conversations stopped for universal groaning.

Susan looked stunned, but she shouldn't have. Last meeting, she'd told us much more than anybody wanted to know about Polly Baker, the heroine of a practical joke once played by Benjamin Franklin. Polly supposedly was a Colonial woman tried for fornication after the birth of her fifth illegitimate child. At her trial, she spoke on her own behalf so eloquently that one of her judges married her. Together, they produced fifteen more children.

People took Polly seriously for nearly two centuries,

and now she supposedly had an important role in Susan's unfinished mystery.

"You told us about her. We listened. And listened. Don't start!" Although Roxanne delivered the lines in humorous fashion, it was obvious she meant it. We all meant it.

"But she's relevant!" Susan said. "Love outside of marriage, punishment—except she triumphed."

"Susan, she never existed."

"I say we rename our group the Polly Baker Memorial Reading Circle and be done with it," Tess said, provoking applause. "I mean what else do we have in common?"

"Well, some of you have workmen in common," I said with a smile, hoping to get us off a debate about Polly Baker. The flagstone for Helen's solarium hadn't arrived, so the contractor had moved his crew to Tess's house, where they were enclosing and insulating a porch. I was aware of such details because they made me aware of how different my life felt from some of my book-club mates'. Mine was free of building materials. That felt significant.

"No, seriously," Tess said. "We're different ages, different jobs, different lifestyles, different tastes in reading and men and politics—but we all always have Polly. Apparently."

"You're making fun, but I like it," Susan said, head high. "We could have pins and T-shirts made. She'd be our mascot."

"If you'd finish the book."

"Can we please talk about *this* book?" Denise asked. Her eternal politician's-wife politeness was wearing thin. "Let's get back to Edna."

By now, interest was lagging. Two women examined the fabric on the newly re-covered sofas. Susan and

Clary looked annoyed; Tess, who worked with the mentally unstable and was therefore comfortable with uncontrollable groups, looked bemused; and Denise kept checking her watch.

At which point, Helen sighed and had another hearty dose of white wine. "I'm glad I don't have to drive anywhere tonight," she said. "And I apologize for taking the floor or the soapbox and ruining the discussion. How about if I get coffee and dessert while you all talk? Without me in the room, there's a chance you'll get to hear all that stuff Denise prepared."

I offered to help. The house was so large, the kitchen seemed a commuter-train ride away. A long way to carry ten coffee cups and, if Helen was true to form, almost as many varieties of sweets. Susan also joined us.

"You girls," Denise said. "The Three Musketeers."

Which we were not, but earlier in the evening when we'd been up on the roof, Susan had made a comment—I couldn't even remember it now—that made Helen and me laugh. And Denise had commented about that, too, as if we were a clique. "Right back," I said, and followed Helen through a series of gorgeous rooms.

From then on, we did actually talk about the book. Sometimes even in turn. And listened to Denise's research about Kate Chopin's life and philosophy plus critiques of this work—the damning ones when it was first published and the reconsiderations eighty years later when the work was rediscovered. And then we talked again about personal reactions to Edna's comfortable but closed-tight world, her short climb out of it, and then her downward spiral.

Finally, we planned the next meeting. We were reading the newest Barbara Kingsolver, in which I was pretty sure nobody killed herself for the sin of having had sex.

The evening nearly over, Helen's mood grew less dark.

She lifted her coffee cup in a toast. "Here's a promise," she said. "Next meeting, I will not get on my hobby-horse, whatever horse that might be. I promise that I won't say a word."

Unfortunately, she kept her promise.

Two

I WAS HAVING THE SORT OF DREAM WE ONLY DREAM OF having. I was at a picnic beside a light-sparked lake. I wore a long white summer dress. My feet floated above the lush grass, and I was being discreetly adored by a man with deep, dark eyes.

I was Edna at the start of her romantic dream. Edna, thrilling to new love, to music overheard, unaware of the dark edges of the picture, innocent of how her story would end.

A discordant blare rocketed me from Edna's world to mine.

Nobody I would accept as a friend would call at this hour. It had to be the champion of dawn chatterers, my mother, and I definitely did not feel like an early-morning session with her. It was possible that I'd had too much wine the night before at book club.

Nothing like getting depressed before you're fully awake.

The noise had stopped. Mackenzie must have picked it up.

Couldn't be my mother, I remembered. She had talked my couch-potato father into joining her on a cruise. He'd agreed, because having your hotel float along with you was as close to not-traveling as traveling got.

But ship-to-shore phone calls had to be prohibitively

expensive. Plus, there currently wasn't even a major nagging issue. We'd reached détente. She'd finally understood that I was neither leaving Mackenzie—in pursuit of further education or further men—nor, in her terms, "moving forward" with him. And most heretical—that I was not upset about the status quo.

"Mom," I'd said in desperation, "I'm *happy* with my life. Happy teaching. Happy with Mackenzie. Happy single." And I was. After much upheaval and blithering, life felt balanced, in place, and quite fine, thank you. Mirabile dictu, she heard me.

Unfortunately, hearing it shorted out her hardwiring. She was programmed so that all circuits led to marriage, all roads (after she dusted, resurfaced, and decorated them) to the altar, the sole location of Happy Endings. All else was prologue, not the story itself. At a loss as to what happened next, she set out to sea.

I put the pillow over my head, a signal to Mackenzie that no matter who was on that line, I wasn't taking calls at this hour.

He didn't ask. I opened my eyes and saw the man sitting on my side of the bed. His bright blue eyes were a shock—a part of me was still in that humid dream with the dark-eyed man.

"Time to get up," he said. "You heard that alarm." He placed a mug of coffee on the night table. He looked great, as fine an image of a paramour as had been the dark-eyed dream man. White suit or white terry towel-wrap, it's all the same if they provide coffee in the morning.

"Delicious," I said after a sip. "My thanks and compliments to the chef." I relaxed into real life.

"Have a good time last night?" he asked, standing up. "Sorry I couldn't wait up. I was wiped out."

I summarized the evening's highlights while I watched

him dress, put on his public persona. "Helen seemed odd," I said. "Overly agitated about what Edna should or shouldn't have done."

"Did you remind her it was fiction?"

"Interesting what buttons fiction can press," I murmured. He was moving close to warp speed. "In a rush?" I asked.

"Pretty much."

"Then I'll see you tonight. I'll be home. Book club meets but once a month."

He bent and kissed my forehead. "Bad timing. I promised to meet an old buddy for dinner. Used to work together, but he quit and went to law school."

That was something Mackenzie had once talked about doing.

"He just got married."

That was not something Mackenzie talked about doing.

"Remarried. Re-remarried. This is his third."

"What an optimist."

"For a smart guy, he's incredibly stupid."

"I take that to mean you know his new wife."

Mackenzie shook his head. "But neither does he. He never does, till it's too late. He did this last time, too. Meets somebody and goes gaga. She says she wants to get married right away, he signs on, and then all the stuff he would have learned by dating her, he gets to learn about in divorce court. Incredibly expensive. But here he's done it again."

"I hope you won't let him know how you feel about this marriage." About any marriage. The word had hardly ever been spoken in this household, except by my mother, and then only via long distance. We'd surely never had an actual discussion of the institution, and *till death do us part* meant he'd stay with me until another homicide made him rush off.

"This is the third wedding gift. Luckily, his wives keep stripping him of all his earthly possessions, so I can keep on giving the same thing." Another nose-tip kiss. "You're not upset about tonight, are you? It was the only time he had. I didn't want to make it couples, because I'm not eager to meet this one. I've met the other two—both pretty, needy, not the brightest bulbs, clingy, and twenty-two. This new one's twenty-two, as well, and I'm sure all the rest is the same, too. He's a devotee of the if-at-first-you-don't-succeed, try, try-again theory."

"No problem." I liked that we each had autonomy, that there was no guilt in having our own schedules, friends we saw on our own. The status quo was a pleasant, undemanding, in fact consoling, equilibrium we'd reached after a few years of ups and downs about where our relationship was headed, how it was doing, and whether it should exist at all.

My mother's face, her expression doubtful, hovered above the bed. I blinked, and she was gone.

"You're the greatest," Mackenzie said.

I don't trust that phrase. In general, I've found it to mean I've been tolerating something I shouldn't have been.

He sat down on the side of the bed again and took my hand, studying it as if it were a brand new artifact. "I've been thinking."

It's odd about thinking. It's a good thing to do, and hearing that someone we care about has been doing it should fill us with joy, but it does not. Instead, it combines with being "the greatest" and produces tensed neck muscles and a sense of imminent doom.

Mackenzie saw my expression change and laughed. "Nothing bad! In the light of Tom's wives, I'm grateful you're nothing like them. That you're you. I'm happy

we're . . . well, we're here. Where we are. Together. *Easy.*
Nobody pushing for anything else, anybody else. You
and me, the way we are—this is good." He stood again.
"I won't be late. Maybe I can fast-forward him through
the courtship and wedding details. I've heard it all before." And then he did, indeed, leave.

I sat drinking my coffee and digesting my early-morning
compliments, wondering why the latter stuck in my throat.

Why was Mackenzie so deliriously happy with my reluctance to be married? With our nondiscussions of it?
He was happy because I didn't push or nag him into his
friend Tom's follies. Happy because I wasn't the idiot
girls Tom kept marrying.

It wasn't great being terrific in comparison to ninnies,
it wasn't ego gratifying being the greatest out of a field of
wretched non-greats, but it was nice that Mackenzie was
a happy man. Happy with me. That we were a happy
twosome, because I was happy, too. I had what I wanted,
too. I knew that because I had told my mother just that
countless times.

I was happy!

Nonetheless, thoughts about my—our—his happiness
made me first uncomfortable and peeved, and finally, totally, inexplicably, disgruntled.

How could he say such a thing? Feel such a thing?

It was one thing to consider our arrangement satisfac-
tory, to be contented with it. But it felt like a whole other
thing—an infuriating thing—to *think* about it and become *ecstatic* about not being married to me!

Happy.

Which he so obviously was.

What a lousy thing to wake up to.

Three

PERVERSITY WAS OBVIOUSLY THE THEME OF THE DAY. Perversity and annoyance.

My annoyance with Mackenzie fed right into my annoyance with my students' low-keyed behavior, particularly my fourth-period class, the one right before lunch. Their stifled yawns and mechanical responses to all remarks about *The Scarlet Letter* made me yearn for the noisy babble that had irritated me the night before at my book club. Enthusiasm, even when slightly berserk, was preferable to apathy, even if, as now, the indifference is good-natured and tolerant.

I should have been grateful for that. It was spring, the semester was running out, they could have raised all manner of hell and gotten away with it, but that wasn't their mood today. But instead of gratitude, I rankled at their expressions.

The most interest they showed was when the PA system squawked its way into the middle of what I was saying, and a boy whose voice broke almost each syllable asked the swim team to meet in the front hall immediately after school.

I wished the swim team would take the PA system along with them and drown it.

None of my class was on the team. We didn't need to hear the annoyingly blurry blast of sound. It wasn't much of a team anyway, but Maurice Havermeyer, head-master of Philly Prep, was determined to boost our school's athletic reputation. "Go, Philly," the pathetic adolescent said in a voice with no inflection, except when it cracked. "The office wants to remind you this year, every grade level's outstanding athlete will receive a special Philly Prep trophy. Remember Dr. Havermeyer's new school motto: '*Mens Sana in Corpore Sano*.' Which means 'a sound mind in a sound body.' Thank you." We heard him say, "Where's the switch? How do I turn it off?" He wasn't going to last long as an office aide, even though he had pronounced the Latin relatively well.

Should I tell the kids the motto wasn't Havermeyer's and wasn't new? I looked at my motley crew. Perhaps, having given up on the sound minds, Havermeyer was settling for relatively functioning bodies.

The kid found the off switch. End of excitement in the classroom.

I couldn't understand their not liking *The Scarlet Letter*. It wasn't difficult going and it was surely a story of passion and civic wrath—a story with sex at its core—that should appeal to a teen. But sometimes I wonder whether the kids I teach are capable of empathy. Too often, they are the diametric opposite of my book group. They're unwilling to venture into another person's psyche, particularly if the person is, to them, "foreign" in age, situation, or historical period. This doesn't bode well for the future of the world.

Poor Hester Prynne. As if it weren't bad enough that the Puritans treated her like dirt, so did my contemporary kids. Bubbling with hormones and longings themselves, they nonetheless dismissed Hester, not as a sinner, but as worse—irrelevant. "That was then and this is now," their uninvolved response said. "Why should anybody care?"

The weather wasn't helping, either. My classroom windows were open, so that full-strength eau de spring encircled each and every student. Me, too, I admit. Thinking was difficult in the sweet, druggy atmosphere, and if any of it was going on behind those glazed faces, it most surely wasn't about the effect of Puritan mores on an unfortunate young married woman.

I wondered what—or who—filled each mind in front of me. Times like now, as I looked at a room's worth of faces, or if I paused in a hallway between classes, I became aware of how many lives and stories were crammed between the walls that defined us, how everyone's separate trajectory crisscrossed the others' in an endless emotional cat's cradle.

And each hour, teachers like me tried to weave all those strings into a single tapestry featuring Hester Prynne or algebraic theorems. As if *Philly Prep Student* were a species, with each member having the same qualities. No wonder the attempt so seldom worked.

Spring whispered tolerance—on my part, too. Teenagers and seasons were what they were, and what sense would making a ruckus about it be?

We successfully lurched through the hour, and only once did I backslide and wonder whether a single word, let alone idea, had gotten through to 90 percent of the class.

As they stampeded out, I marked my book where we'd ended the discussion today and made notes of topics to reintroduce. Nothing like false optimism to get one through her days.

I gradually became aware that a student was still in her seat, dawdling with her book bag. "Any problem?" I asked. I smiled and waited, briefcase in hand.

She flushed. "I'm sorry. I'll be . . . I'm just . . ."

"Take your time." Her flustering confused me. This

was not Petra Yates as I knew her. She was a pretty youngster, and unlike most of her classmates, she seemed to accept the idea that she was attractive. Not that she'd say so, of course, but she wasn't scrunched and bowed and hangdoggy the way too many of her classmates were, hiding their bodies and faces. Nor did she flaunt the many charms nature had bestowed, but there was a whiff of general, all-purpose defiance that made me sure it was a lot easier being her teacher than her parent. Except for now.

She dropped her pocketbook, a lumpy fabric sling that clunked to the ground, sounding as if it contained scrap metal. "Sorry!" she said, "I'm such a . . . I keep . . . I don't know what's wrong with me!" She looked perilously near tears.

I tried to lighten the atmosphere even though I couldn't imagine how it had gotten so dense—was I that much of an ogre? "Better hurry or you'll miss lunch," I said mildly.

"Could I stay here instead? I won't touch anything. Please? I don't feel like being with . . . I feel . . . I just need to . . ." I thought she might have just crossed the line between looking near tears and producing them, but while her bottom lids glittered, she made no move to swipe away the moisture.

I looked more closely. Aside from her nose, which had become rosy, she was pale and drawn, with dark circles under swimmy eyes. Several of my students had that look now—the pollen count was way up. But Petra wasn't sniffling. "Something *is* wrong, isn't it? How do you feel? Are you well?"

She backed off a step. "I'm fine," she mumbled before gulping three times, then inhaling deeply, letting the air slowly escape.

"I'm not so sure of that. Maybe the flu? How about you have the nurse check you out. I'll walk you."

"I'm fine. Tired. Please, could I sit here during lunch?"

The day before, I'd had to wake her up at the end of class. Unfortunately, that wasn't sufficiently unusual, especially in spring, to have made it stand out in my mind until now. The point was, she'd been lethargic for a while.

"If not the nurse, then promise me your family doctor."

She rummaged in her oversize bag for a tissue, with which she blew her nose and wiped at her eyes. "Sure," she said. "But really, I'm fine."

"I don't think so. You've been groggy in class lately."

"Spring," she whispered, but not as if she truly believed that was a reason.

"You're not—" I stopped myself.

Her eyes widened. "Not what?"

"Taking anything? Some ... substance that might make you sleepy?"

"You think I'm on drugs? Or alcohol?" she said. "In the morning? In your class?"

I had, but now I grabbed for a face-saver. "Antihistamines," I said. "Some of them make you drowsy."

"I'm fine," she repeated, but she looked almost too tired to utter the words.

"Maybe you're not eating enough. Are you dieting? Maybe that's what's dragging you down. Skipping lunch and all."

"I'll leave," she said. "Sorry I asked." She headed for the door, feet dragging.

"Petra, listen to me. You're not yourself. Your parents must be concerned, too." Not enough, I thought. Why weren't they keeping their child home, getting her whatever medications she needed? It had taken me too long to see that she was ill, but I could understand my being slow on the uptake. I had over a hundred teens to monitor, and I saw them for less than an hour a day.

"Don't bother my parents about this. Please?"

"If you're this way at home, I wouldn't think anybody else would have to tell them a thing."

Petra's mother had died ten years earlier, and her father had married a woman who accompanied him to school conferences, but I felt she did so for reasons other than Petra's welfare. She'd corrected me when I referred to "their" daughter. "Petra is Bill's daughter by his first marriage," she'd said crisply, interrupting me. It seemed clear she'd married him, not his children, even though they'd been about five and three at the time. But in truth, that moment's roughness had been the only unpleasant impression I'd gotten. An ordinary couple, at least one of them sufficiently concerned with Petra's welfare to show up at every open house and school night. And here was the girl, blue-ringed eyes wide with fear at the prospect of "bothering" them, telling them she was ill, as if this were something she'd caused—

It hit me from all directions that perhaps she *had* caused the situation.

Her paleness and exhaustion.

Her expression when I mentioned the cafeteria or lunch.

Her emotional distress about Hester Prynne.

"Oh, Petra," I whispered, "are you? . . ."

She didn't answer, but looked me in the eyes, so that her answer was clear. "Please," she whispered. "I can't . . . they can't know."

I had hoped that I was wrong, that I had jumped to conclusions. But her expression told all. It wasn't my misconception. It was, quite literally, hers.

"What am I going to do?" Her eyes welled over. "I can't . . . I don't . . ."

I put my hand on her shoulder and guided her back to the desks. "Let's sit down." She looked likely to faint otherwise, even though I didn't think women did that anymore. On the other hand, Petra wasn't a woman. She was fifteen years old. A schoolchild. A pregnant one.

From our desks, we stared at each other. I sighed. I felt part of a sad but ancient ritual. How many women had sat like this through history?

"I wish I were dead." Her voice sounded hollow.

"No! Oh, please, don't think that way. Don't let yourself think that—"

"Everybody would be better off."

"Petra, that isn't at all true, and this isn't the end of the world. There are—"

"That's what you think! What am I supposed to do—be a Hester Prynne?"

"This isn't the seventeenth century. We aren't Puritans."

"I'm fifteen." It was more moan than words.

"Are you positive about this?"

"I bought a kit. I bought two kits. They both said I was."

"And you haven't told your parents."

"My father would kill me."

I remembered the quiet, soft-spoken insurance broker. "Oh, Petra, of course he wouldn't."

She looked directly at me now, her eyelashes wet with tears but her expression grim. "He said he would. He said it a hundred times. He said young people today have no morals and if any daughter of his—"

"It's an expression, that's all. Your father didn't mean it literally."

She looked at me and said nothing for a long while, and when she finally spoke, her voice was honed to a bleak edge, devoid of hope. She would explain her situation because I'd made it necessary, not because explanations could make anything better. "He says if my sister or me, if we ever . . . he said if we couldn't control ourselves, if we . . . with boys before we're out of his house, then he'd throw us out of his house altogether. That we'd have to live with my grandmother, his mother, up in the Poconos. He says he wouldn't have any more to do with us."

"Do you think he meant that?"

"I know he did, because Valerie would love getting rid of my sister and me, having my dad all to herself and her kids, so don't think she'd stop him. And my grandmother—I'd rather die than live with her. She hates Patsy and me. Particularly me. Says my mother was a . . . a . . . that she trapped my father into marrying her and that we inherited her badness. She's always quarreling with my dad about us, and then afterwards, when we're home again, he gets into one of his fits about how we had better not prove her right, do we understand? My sister and me, we went there once for the summer—guess what, it was Valerie's idea. It was the worst time of my life—she was always screaming about straightening us out, hitting us with belts and sticks because we were wild. My father didn't discipline us properly, she said."

"Did you tell your father?"

Petra's expression was polite, but distant. "He said we must have deserved it. He never contradicts her even if he gets angry about what she says to him. He never contradicts Valerie, either." She laid her head on the desk.

"How long ago do you think this happened?" She was wearing a baggy shirt and baggier jeans, and I had no idea what her contours looked like.

She sat back up. "I don't *think*, I *know*!"

It took me a beat to realize I'd implied that she was constantly sexually active, and she obviously wasn't. I

felt old-fashioned, but still reassured and irrationally relieved. "March," she muttered. "March third."

Two months ago. "You haven't mentioned the . . . the
father." I could barely shape that last when I knew it
most likely applied to somebody who himself hadn't finished growing.

She shrugged. "He doesn't go here."

"His school wasn't what I was getting at."

"Why? You think I should get married? I'm fifteen! He
won't care, anyway—he has a girlfriend, he goes to college. He doesn't know me! I was at a party. Somebody
brought whiskey. He was there without his girlfriend. I
don't know why or how things started and then . . . they
kept going. I was sick later on. I thought . . . I hoped that
maybe that meant nothing could have happened. I never
saw him again. I just want to forget all about that night!"

I didn't say any of the obvious responses, especially
that forgetting was the one option she did not have. We
sat, or I sat and she slumped, in silence. I could not think
of what should happen next.

What a sadly appropriate name she had. Petra. Stone.
For a girl caught between the proverbial rock and hard
place.

Petra could remain silent, the way other girls had done.
Starve herself and wear ever looser garments. And then
what? No one could forget the news stories of young
girls giving birth in motels and at proms, then killing the
babies.

Or Petra could seek adult help. She could find a safe
place for the pregnancy and find adoptive parents, although I wondered what the cover story would be to her
father. It isn't easy finding an alibi for being missing four
or five months.

Or Petra could tell her father what was going on, and

he'd banish her to her grandmother's. I could even understand why he'd believe that the best course, although his daughter considered it justification for suicide.

But if Petra didn't tell her father or her stepmother—who, she believed, wanted only to have her out of the house and gone—and get parental consent, then despite the laws of the land, the laws of Pennsylvania wouldn't permit her to terminate this pregnancy, if that was what she wanted.

"I wish I were dead!" she said. Again.

That was twice. It didn't feel like teen histrionics of the passing kind. Besides, I would never take a teen's death threats lightly for a myriad of reasons, at the head of which was the memory of Addie Winters, an eleventh grader who last year had been thought to be posturing, overdramatizing her miseries. Until she drank half a bottle of vodka, took the family car, and rammed it at ninety miles an hour into a wall.

However stupid their adolescent reasons for ending it all seemed, they were their reasons.

"If I were dead, they'd be sorry. Even Valerie."

"No. Bad, bad idea." I took her hands. "This is serious, Petra, but it's not the end of the line. This has happened to countless millions of girls. Life goes on."

"Like my mother. I'll be just like my mother." She laid her head back on the desktop.

I could hear the received hate she now conveyed, and how their history had been told to Petra and her sister. Not with love or compassion or understanding, it sounded like.

Of course, Petra could run away to a more accommodating state like New York. But where? It was an enormous state, and as for the city—it didn't feel savory, sending a frightened fifteen-year-old pregnant girl alone to that massive and overpowering place. But accompanying her without her parents' permission would land somebody like me in jail as a criminal. It had happened already, made the headlines, made its point.

We were back to the rock. And the hard place.

"Petra."

She pulled herself out of a near trance, but I saw that was about as much action as she was capable of taking. She had no more fuel, no more resources.

"Promise me one thing and then I'll leave you, and you rest here as long as you like."

She didn't even raise her head from the desk, merely rolled it so that she watched me with one eye.

"Promise you won't make any decisions about this—*none*—until tomorrow. Nothing will be worse tomorrow, so give me that time to think about all your options. To come up with a workable solution. Give it twenty-four hours. Promise me that."

The eye, gray-green and prehistoric looking, did not blink.

"Promise."

She exhaled in a frustrated-sounding sigh, then, still not raising her head, said, "Okay."

"That's for real?"

She closed her eyes and it felt like a door had slammed.

That was about as much as I knew how to do at the moment. I wished there was a tribal council waiting under a tree in the village. A council of elder women, good and hardened souls who'd have accumulated more wisdom than I, who together would know things about the world and how this powerless girl could fit into it and save herself.

The closest thing I could imagine to that village council was my book group, with all its good-natured disagreements and detours that lay atop years of hard-won knowledge about how it was to be a woman. They'd laugh at the image of themselves as fonts of wisdom, but they'd nonetheless know—after lots of simultaneous thinking out loud—what a girl in this oldest of stories and dilemmas should do. They'd have a dozen solutions and opinions as to what should happen next.

But we weren't meeting till another month was gone. That would be too late to ask.

Four

THE GOOD AND BAD NEWS ABOUT A HIGH SCHOOL IS that it's like life—one damn thing after another. There is no time for real reflection, for dwelling on any one class or event, so once lunch was over, my fears for Petra were pushed to the back of the bus by the next mass of humanity to enter my classroom. Almost immediately, I had to direct my antennae to whether Patrick's jitteriness was due to hormones or controlled substances; what I was going to do if Nonnie Carter continued to lie about having given me her essay; and whether the shaky, immature-looking handwriting on Brett's excuse note was really his mother's, or his.

After that class, another with its own set of concerns and amazements. A lot of hair issues that hour: Baby John, for so he insisted on being called, had sculpted his into a checkerboard pattern, and Cara had dyed strands of hers to replicate, she explained, what you see through a prism.

Of course, hairstyles aren't actual problems—not when they aren't mine—but the distraction and comments Baby John's and Cara's heads engendered were.

At times, I understand why conservative Muslims insist on the chador. Cover everything except slits for the eyes so nobody trips and falls. Only thing is, I'd want it on boys as well as girls.

31

And, of course, there were always and ever the semi-intelligible notices from the principal to his staff, notices that had an ever more pronounced edge of hysteria as summer approached. And there was always the glower and stare of Helga the Office Witch, with whom I had to deal at end of day because I wanted a word puzzle duplicated. Helga frowned, pulled her cardigan tighter across her front, and seemed affronted by the request. Helga considered the marks teachers put on her pristine paper pedagogical graffiti that defaced her stock and insulted her aesthetic sense.

"I need it for Thursday," I said. Two days' notice to press one button—we dangerous, vandalizing teachers were not permitted to use the copy machine ourselves.

"I don't know . . ." She let her sentence drift off into an imaginary world of incredibly weighty duties. "You need how many copies?"

"Twenty." I controlled the urge to grab back the master sheet and say that I'd do the copying myself, at a commercial spot. I'd done that too often already. That's her master plan as she accumulates the world's largest blank-paper collection.

She shrugged and sighed. You'd think I had asked her to carve the twenty sets in stone.

It was a further slide downhill with the journalism club after school. The *Ink Wire*'s current editor in chief was an elfin creature named Cinnamon Stickley, a name I thought cruel, but she apparently enjoyed. Cinnamon also emphatically wanted our final issue of the year to be completely devoted to "Philly Phashions," detailed descriptions of what each student was wearing to the prom. This would be beneath even our lax standards.

Today was our second round of discussions about it.

"This is a student-run paper, isn't it, Ms. Pepper?" Cinnamon's gamine smile didn't begin to hide the steel behind it. She was going to be one formidable whatever it was she intended to be. I was, in fact, suggesting topics like that—life beyond the prom and graduation—but apparently I was the only one aware that there was such a thing.

"A student paper with a faculty adviser," I reminded her. "As in one who'd give advice. And I'm that one."

"Advice is a suggestion, right? Not like *law* or anything."

A smart cookie with a stripper's name. That combination would spell doom for a whole lot of people in her future.

"So while we're all so glad for your input," she said, gesturing toward the various other editors who were playing "yes, Cinnamon," "we don't agree."

I had a sense of déjà vu. I'd been through this—or something sufficiently close to this—before. Last spring, in fact. Or the spring before. Maybe déjà déjà vuvuvu.

We wasted two perfectly good hours in further democratic student-involved discussion. There are times dictatorship sounds irresistible, but at least we found a midground in which student plans and aspirations would be recorded, along with news of summer programs and a roundup of the year just past. I could live with that.

IT WAS RAINING, AND I DIDN'T HAVE MY RAINCOAT.

Which, I suddenly realized, I hadn't brought home last night. I raced around behind the school to my car. Then, damp and disheartened, I sat there listening to the motor, too lethargic to move on.

Every day, as I settle into the car alone, in that adolescent-free moment, I feel like I've just competed in an Olympic event. I am drained, exhausted, and stunned. Only the elation's missing.

Going to Helen's, stopping the car, finding parking, and retrieving my raincoat felt overwhelmingly difficult.

I told myself that as I was already damp, there was no point getting the raincoat now. Closing the barn door after, et cetera. Next outing, I'd bring along an umbrella and that would do the trick. And I'd stop at Helen's when I had more energy.

Which was stupid, I answered. Really bad time management.

I hated these arguments I had with myself. Since I took both sides, I always lost. I put the car in gear and headed for Helen's, which was at most four blocks away.

By now, Petra had become a thin glaze of worry atop whatever else had happened. I'd asked for twenty-four hours while I came up with a decent idea. Several of those hours were already gone, and I still saw only bad choices for her.

Helen's street is one-way. I had to go past her block on a parallel street, so I could turn back in the right direction. Traffic was its usual late-afternoon clog, and with every stop and start, I regretted the decision to retrieve the coat. Naturally, as I crept along, the rain dwindled to near nothingness.

But finally I was there. Ahead of me on the opposite corner, I saw the short side of the yellow Dumpster that had become her "annex." She said it had been there so long she was getting it its own address.

A patrolman was on the corner, and as I made my turn, I saw another one near Helen's front door. Both wore slickers and plastic covers for their hats. Neither was doing anything in particular.

My first thought was that with them there, I couldn't park illegally on the pavement, which had been my plan.

My second thought was slightly less self-centered. Something bad had happened.

My third was back to me and ridiculous. My raincoat had been stolen! As if my raincoat would be a prize in a house that was a treasure trove.

A block and a half away, I found a space that was at least 75 percent legal, and I hustled back toward Helen's. As I approached, the front-door sentry straightened up. I smiled and pointed at the door. "I left my raincoat here last night," I said. "I'm here to pick it up."

He smiled. I must have been a pathetic sight, rain running off my hair into my eyes. But not sufficiently pathetic to let him bend the rules. "Sorry, ma'am," he said. "This wouldn't be a good time."

There was no better time for a raincoat than when it was raining, but I didn't point that out. "Should I wait?" I asked.

"No, ma'am." His smile looked painful, the grimace of a man trying to appear good-natured when he is not. He remained planted at the base of the three marble steps leading to Helen's front door.

"Then could somebody else retrieve it for me? It's in the hall closet." I had no idea how I'd describe my tan raincoat in a way that singled it out from the Coulters' undoubtedly tan raincoats. By the amount of crumpled tissues in the pockets?

"Sorry." He didn't sound sorry.

"Could you tell me what's happened here?"

"No." He didn't even pretend to be sorry about that one.

I didn't know what to say. I had a million questions, of course, but there was no point in offering them up to this man. "Well, then . . . thanks." I expected him to say, "For what? I haven't done a damn thing to help you," but amazingly, he didn't.

I was halfway down the block when I heard, "Hey, hey, you!"

I looked back toward the policeman.

"Not there, here! My house, my house! Don't make me shout!" She was across the street, huddled on the top step of an entryway, wrapped in an afghan, holding an umbrella. Had she not been adamant about the "my house!" business, and had not Delancey Street short shrift for squatters, I would have assumed she was homeless.

She waved me in to her, closer. "I saw it."

I crossed the street. How lovely that even Helen's most elegant of streets had its resident busybody. That's what I'd like as my next career. And on a great street like Helen's.

"Yes?" I said again.

"Up there at that house? On the corner?"

I nodded.

"She fell." The woman was tiny, shrunken looking, and her face—the half I could see under the umbrella— was seared with wrinkles. She could have been pulled from a fairy tale, except for the orange and purple afghan. "I was going to the store, and I reached that corner and saw it happen. Like that."

"Fell? Who? Where? Like what?"

"Like that." She angled one hand down, fingers pointing to the street. "Boom. The lady of the house, they say. I couldn't tell."

I could see so little of her except for her umbrella, that I felt as if I were talking to a toadstool. "When was this?" It felt long ago the way this woman was telling it.

Her mouth turned down. "The police asked me, too, like I would know the very minute. I don't go by watches, I go by my stomach. I was going to the store to get bread. My son's wife, she knows I like a sandwich for my lunch, but she leaves for work and never remembers to buy my bread."

"The police—why are they . . . was she badly hurt? Did she break a bone? Did you see her trip? Was it down the front steps?"

"Slow down, Missy. I don't hear so good anymore." And then she spoke as if I were the deaf one, slowly, each word overenunciated. "She. Fell. Off. The. Roof."

"My God!" I looked up at the rooflines stories above my head. I was beginning to understand the police entourage, but I didn't want to believe what this woman was saying.

The umbrella she held shook from left to right and back again. "Fell into her own Dumpster. I didn't go over, was too afraid. Besides, what could I have done? I'm old. I screamed, nobody came, big surprise, so I went to the store two blocks away and called the police from there. And bought bread for my sandwich while I was at it."

"Is she . . . please, do you know if she's . . . all right?" The one thing I knew for certain was that she wasn't "all right"—but I couldn't make my mouth say either *alive* or *dead*. Those words were too freighted.

"All right? She fell three stories—or I think her house is four—into a Dumpster! Probably hit it coming down, because there was blood on the sidewalk—even I could see it when I went up there later, and my eyes aren't too good."

I was glad I hadn't walked around the corner, hadn't seen more than a blur from the car when I turned. "Is she . . . alive?" I whispered.

Nothing. I wondered if she knew it wasn't raining anymore.

"Is she alive?" I repeated, more clearly.

She tilted her umbrella back so that she could look up at me more directly, and her maze of wrinkles rerouted themselves into a combination of incredulity and annoyance.

"Was that a stupid question?" I muttered.

"I sure think so," she said, keeping the umbrella tilted as she studied me. She must have caught something in my expression. "Oh," she said. "Oh, dear. You know her?"

I nodded.

"Then what would I know? I'm just an old lady sitting on her steps. She's probably getting all better right now in the hospital. Don't you worry yourself." She stood laboriously, cataloguing what parts of her didn't work "so good" anymore, folded her umbrella, said good-bye, and unlocked her front door.

I stood there, afraid to walk, because doing so would mean I'd accepted what I'd just heard, that it was real, that I was pulling it in and making it just one more piece of my life, and then, moving on.

But the old woman turned just before she entered her house, looked at me. Her crackled old voice grew soft at the edges. "Best get going, dearie," she said. "I've lived a long time and what I know is that's what you have to do. There isn't any other choice. One foot in front of the other, again and again. It's the only way."

Five

THE LOFT DID NOT FEEL WELCOMING WHEN I FINALLY reached it. In fact, it felt cavernous and stale, and I resolved to fully furnish it. It needed its sharp corners and soaring ceilings softened by homely, homey objects, especially at a time like this. Now, in its large emptiness, I too clearly understood vulnerability and loneliness.

I made myself tea with honey, as if I were ill, and then I glanced at the mail I'd brought up with me. Nothing much in the way of companionship there. Bills, circulars, a coupon mailer, and a postcard of a generic palm tree and sandy beach from my parents. As my father had undoubtedly already muttered, just out of ear range of my mother, the scene might have been of Florida where they live rather than whatever port this was.

I turned on the TV for the sound of a human voice, but the voice I heard identified itself as Roy Stanton Harris, champion of some mythical patriarchal paradise. "Okay, girlies," he said. "You brainless females, I know what's best for you."

Okay, that wasn't what his ad actually said, but that's what I heard. Even though he spoke with such charm and was so attractive, he infuriated me.

I turned off the set, but I still needed to talk to somebody. Not sure precisely who that would be—I hated

bothering Mackenzie, assuming he'd even be reachable—
I lifted the receiver.

It beeped. I keep forgetting to check for messages these
days, now that we no longer have a machine with a light
that blinks a *yoo-hoo*! Now messages are secretly stored
inside the phone. All a person needs to do is lift and
check.

This person forgets more often than not.

There was one message. Susan Hileman, sounding un-
naturally subdued and taciturn. "Call me as soon as you
can. I'm at the office."

She knew. Susan's normal tone is as bouncy as her red
curls. This tone said she had bad news she didn't want to
leave on a machine. Besides, as with most of the other
book group members, I had little contact with Susan outside the monthly meetings. She'd probably never left me
a message that didn't have to do with what we were
reading or where we were meeting.

She picked up while the phone was still on the first
ring, and when I identified myself, she exhaled so emphatically, it was a sonic boom in the earpiece. "Thank
God! I've been—well, I've just been. I thought teachers
got home early! Listen, I'm glad you called back before I
had to leave, because—"

"I know."

"Who told you? We made a chain, like for book
group, and you were my call, so who—"

I explained about my raincoat, about the police, the
old lady across the street. It was a rough sort of comfort
to have such mundane facts to relate, because it was impossible to talk about the real subject, to talk about
Helen.

I could feel the pitiable limits of responses available,
none of which felt as if it were up to the gravity of the
situation, of its meaning or meaninglessness. "I don't

know any details," I finally said. "Do you know what happened exactly? Or how?"

"The roof garden railing was temporary—chicken wire, remember? She kept us all away from it last night, so how could she forget today? But apparently, she leaned against it and fell. Four and a half stories."

"What was she doing up there?"

"Checking some work, as I understand it."

"But I thought no work was going on. The crew's at Tess's house." I stopped myself. "Sorry. I'm talking as if that matters. As if I'll explain why it isn't possible that happened, and then it will turn out that it didn't happen."

"Clary called me," Susan said after a pause. "She started a book group chain. Also other chains, for other parts of Helen's life."

I was impressed by Clary's efficiency, and I stifled thoughts that it might be cold of her. Unemotional. Untouched. Some people had businesslike habits ingrained, I reminded myself.

"You call Tess, she'll call Louisa, and that's it," Susan said. "This is awful, isn't it? I'm so upset, I keep crying. I mean I don't know what to do. This feels . . . impossible."

"Her poor daughter. And Ivan. He must be devastated!"

"Probably would be, if anybody could find and tell him."

"Meaning?"

"He isn't in Cleveland where he said he'd be. At least not at the hotel he said. Never had a reservation." She dropped the matter-of-fact, no-inflection tone she'd adopted. "Damn but I hope the explanation isn't as tawdry as it sounds like it's going to be."

"I'm sure it isn't. He dotes on her. Don't read things into this. There is undoubtedly a boring explanation. Somebody had the wrong information, or his plans changed and Helen knew but it wasn't worth repeating to anyone else. Not everything is suspicious, Susan. Not everything's mysterious. This is real life."

"I never said!"

"I'm sorry. I didn't mean to imply . . ." I did mean to. Susan's imagination is hyperactive and there's no Ritalin for that. I think the fertility of her brain is what keeps her from ending her books. She invents alternative scenarios, comes up with ever new options.

But that was neither here nor there. What was here was Helen, dead.

"What about Gretchen?" Susan asked. "She surely needs her father! She's with Clary, it isn't as if she's abandoned, but still . . . it's horrible, his not being reachable at a time like this."

"Poor girl. This is such a shame for her . . ."

We could as easily have said, "Whush, whush, whush." We were making noise to stave off that time when we'd have to hang up and be alone with our bad thoughts. Eventually we faced it and hung up.

I sat and thought about Helen. I could see almost any one of the rest of us becoming so distracted that we ignored the rickety temporary fence, but Helen was the least flibbertigibbety of us all. And she was intensely involved in every decision concerning the reconstruction of her house and was unlikely to lapse into sudden daydreaming while inspecting the work on the roof.

On the other hand, she hadn't been herself the night before. Preoccupied. Agitated. Antagonistic. Maybe she hadn't been thinking clearly.

I wished Mackenzie were home. Or anybody. Anything.

Actually, anything was, but the cat was completely occupied by his five P.M. nap and wasn't swayed by my need for companionship.

I remembered I was supposed to make a call as part of

the chain. Except I couldn't remember whether I called Tess or Louisa, and she was Clary's sister, so surely she already knew, even if I was supposed to call her.

I was making excuses. I decided that I'd call them both, starting with Tess. How woefully different I was from Clary Oliver, who'd efficiently organized the spreading of the sad news, who would have remembered who it was she was supposed to call. On the other hand, why hadn't she called her own sister? Maybe she disliked Louisa as much as I did.

After hearing my news, Tess said nothing for a long time. Then, her voice tight, she said, "I can't believe anybody could be so stupid as to put up a fence that weak."

I'd expected something more profound from a psychologist. "They assumed nobody would be up there till the brick wall was up," I said softly.

And then, as if she heard herself, she sighed loudly. "Sorry. I'm having trouble absorbing this. I guess I'm looking for somebody, something, anything, to blame. As if that would make it better."

"I wish I could think of anything that could."

We did some more of the whush-whush-whush platitudes, and then Tess seemed to regain her balance a bit. "I'll bet everybody's as lost about this as the two of us are," she said. "What if . . . it would be good if we got together—whoever wants to—to talk as soon as possible. The sooner the better. Tomorrow night seems good."

"Group therapy?" I wasn't sure about this idea. It sounded too . . . too something. Not Helen-ish at all. Not book-club-ish.

"We'll talk, remember her, deal with our feelings about this horrible accident. We all feel the impulse to make contact at times like these. We could help each other."

I certainly shared that need to communicate, make

some kind of contact with other people who would understand. I couldn't think of any objection to Tess's idea, and not only agreed, but offered the loft as the meeting space. We made rudimentary decisions about time and food—everybody would bring whatever she felt like, if anything at all. Funeral food. Folding chairs. Then we, too, hung up. I had a job now—I had to phone two people with the specific plan, which I then did, commiserating and repeating that time-filling talk.

I also had another job. I had to clean the place. It seemed frivolous and shallow to worry about such things now. But on the other hand, it beat thinking about Helen's death.

In fact, cleaning filled time and gave me purpose, which is, perhaps, why it used to be so popular an activity with my sex.

I plumped pillows, ran a dust cloth across the oak table, straightened a stack of unread magazines, dry-mopped the floor, polished the bathroom.

And then, I was out of steam and surfaces. I tried to mark papers, but couldn't focus on anything but Helen. That hideous fall. The way everything can change in an instant.

I tried to read a magazine. I turned pages, ripped out the cardboard inserts and ads so that the pages would lie more smoothly, and then I gave up on that, too.

When the phone rang, I grabbed it with unwholesome eagerness. I knew it was one of us—the book group woven tightly together because of this tragedy. It might even be somebody notifying me of what I'd already notified someone else. The circle would go round and round because so were we—spinning in the absolute confusion that follows having assumptions and expectations irrevocably snap.

This time, it was Louisa. I'd never called her, but she

knew. She sounded subdued and unlike herself. When Louisa speaks, it's generally in overlong, staccato bursts. Luckily, most of the time, she's silent. Louisa is Clary Oliver's younger sister, and I think that's the only reason she's in the group. She's like a dim copy of her sister, and it's possible she's spent her life being angry about that, because all her energy seems to go into grievance collecting and self-pity. She'd outdone her sister only once—by having three divorces to Clary's two. But Clary was a successful and self-supporting businesswoman, and Louisa had spun through half a dozen fizzled career plans. She was currently a consultant to nonprofits, but I had heard Helen once refer to Louisa herself as a nonprofit and, another time, as a business liability. It was assumed by everyone that Clary supported her and her children, and it was further rumored that Helen resented the time, energy, and resources given over to Clary's younger sister.

"Did you hear?" she asked. "About Helen?"

This was late to be asking, and I was surprised that she'd call me, consider me a possible source of comfort. "It's dreadful."

"My sister is sick about this. Do you believe it, though?"

"Believe what?"

There was a moment's missed beat. Then Louisa spoke again, even more slowly. "Then you didn't hear. You don't know."

She paused. She paused longer. She knew something I didn't, and she had to be sure that was perfectly clear. Her need to establish tiny footholds of power wherever, however she could was one of the many reasons I didn't like Louisa.

"Okay," I said. "Obviously, I don't. What is it that I don't know?"

She cleared her throat. "Helen's death," she said. "It wasn't an accident. She did it on purpose. Helen committed suicide."

Six

Louisa exhaled dramatically. I exclaimed, expressed shock, horror, confusion. Louisa exhaled again. I could almost smell her cigarette's smoke through the receiver. Despite the horrible and somewhat urgent nature of her call's content, she was going to insist on being begged.

I obliged her. "Why would you say that? Helen seemed the last person who'd—that roof garden was unfinished. Remember how she kept us away from the fencing last night?"

"Which only shows that she knew it was dangerous, don't you see that? So why would she go out onto it today—"

"Because she was working with—wait a minute. You think she committed suicide because she went up there knowing it was unfinished?" That made no sense.

"That's not what I'm saying at all!"

"Then say what you're saying, Louisa. Please. And why you're saying it."

"I'm saying it because it's true. Helen left a note. Clary found a notebook in her desk. A little loose-leaf thing she used like a scratch pad. Recipes, notes to herself, lists. And this long thing about shame and disgrace—"

"This thing—she wrote it or was she quoting it?"

"It wasn't like she had quotes around it or anything,

or Clary would have said. It said about how what she was going to do would upset her family and how she hated to do it, but she had to hope they'd come to understand that she had no other choice."

"No other choice?" The worst of all possible short sentences.

"That's exactly the way I heard it. No other choice."

I was dumbfounded. I pictured Helen last night, so alive, so charged up. "But she . . . Helen was upset last night about Edna's suicide in the book."

"I think that was because the author made her do it— a plot device, that's what annoyed her," Louisa said.

I suddenly couldn't remember clearly what precisely Helen had said, and then I thought, and almost convinced myself, that maybe she overreacted to what Edna Pontellier chose to do because she herself was becoming obsessed with the same act.

"Don't act like I'm making this stuff up, Amanda! Clary *told* me!" The hysteria-edged staccato was back. "That's what Helen's own handwriting said, unless you're calling my sister a liar."

I really didn't like Louisa, and her reactions were off center. I didn't dignify her stupid challenge with an answer. "Whatever that writing meant—would a person work all morning, looking normal—"

"We don't know if she was. Maybe she was upset all morning, too."

"Anybody say so?"

"I don't know if anybody's asked. I only know what I told you. I thought I was doing you a favor, telling you. Why all these questions?"

"Still and all—it seems too . . . to go to work, then take a lunch break to go home and leap off the roof?" I asked her to repeat what she remembered of the message. "In a notebook," I said. "That isn't the same as leaving a note."

"Who *cares* what it's in? What it says is what matters. I'm *sick* about this," she said. "Yesterday afternoon, Helen and I had a major . . . she'd just about ruined my life. She's—she was on the board of the preschool and my Jared was not admitted and I'm sure she had a hand in that because she was angry about a loan I had to get from Clary, and—"

"Please," I said. "Please." Who cared right now about Jared's preschool choice? How could she go on this way?

"It isn't my fault if my ex hasn't come up with one support payment in the last—"

Louisa actually had two topics. Her children *and* how badly every person she'd ever met had treated her. She emitted another smoky sigh, and I pictured her staring ceilingward, watching her exhalation trail up and around the room. "I could see how upset Helen was last night. She wasn't herself, and I felt bad about causing it, but a mother has to protect her children, doesn't she?"

"Thanks for calling me," I said, eager to be rid of her. "I'm sorry it was such awful news, but—"

"But the thing is," she said, "it was a fairly . . . it wasn't a . . . I was furious, Amanda. You can understand. I may have gone overboard, said things . . . ." She let out a small wail. "He's my *child*! This is about his entire *future*! Her vindictive power play . . . but even so, what if I *drove* her to this? This level of despair?"

This was another of the many reasons I didn't like Louisa. She was the absolute center of the solar system and everything was about her, even somebody else's suicide.

"I'm sure you didn't drive her to anything. Whatever happened has nothing to do with—"

"I hated how we'd left it," Louisa said. "So I called her

this morning, and I'm sorry, but my temper got the best of me again. I said some bad things. I . . . shouldn't have, I know. Repeated rumors. I should have kept my mouth shut."

"Rumors?"

"About her personal life. I'm not going to make the same mistake and repeat them again."

Ivan, I thought. Ivan who wasn't where he was supposed to be. Ivan. His name in that context felt like a deadweight, pulling me down.

"I just . . . I made things worse. And then, three hours later, she did this horrible thing! We never got to make peace, to set things right. This is on my conscience forever and—"

"You need closure," I said, although in normal circumstances I wouldn't have used that term, that idea, except for doors. "That's exactly the sort of thing Tess is hoping for from tomorrow night's get-together. It'll be good for you, and I'll see you then."

I hung up and pushed Louisa from my mind. There wasn't any room for her anyway, only for Helen, who was ballooning into every crevasse, pushing against my skull—white noise, white light everywhere, but nothing I could identify or hold on to.

Was this possible? Could a woman's will to live so suddenly give way?

What did we know about anyone, if something like this could happen the day after we'd been together, exchanging ideas?

I was standing in a large, safe room in the waning light of afternoon. All the walls and windows were intact and sealed against the outside world, and my feet were planted on solid ground, but I braced myself against the side of the range, held on to its edge because if I let go, I was sure I was going to slide across the floor and become what I kept seeing in front of my eyes—a body hurtling through space.

I couldn't stop thinking of Helen. I hadn't known her well, but I'd admired what I knew of her. She had competency—a rare and undervalued commodity. She made her life fit, turning her artistic bent into a successful commercial venture while raising her daughter and maintaining a solid marriage.

A seemingly solid marriage. I hoped somebody had located Ivan by now, and I hoped still more fervently that his mysterious whereabouts had turned out to be innocuous.

But Helen. Helen had juggled home and career—hers and his, to some extent, hostessing for Ivan's business events as well as for her own. She was attractive, fit, and always wonderfully put together. She'd organized the book group, years before I joined it, because she made time for books, she'd said with an embarrassed smile— rising extra early so that she could read for pleasure every day—at five A.M. That in itself was proof enough for me of exceptional qualities.

I couldn't believe any of what I'd perceived was an act. She was a woman trying hard—and mostly succeeding— at taking on the world on her terms. This was not in any way my picture of a suicide in the making.

And she'd *hated* Edna's suicide. Not just as a literary device, a way of ending a book. She'd had contempt for the woman, or at least for the author who'd allowed such an end to pretend to be a solution—but no matter how visceral Helen's reaction had seemed, how from her heart, even I could hear how weak an argument that would sound like. That was fiction. This was real life.

Helen was dead. It hurt to think it.

I made myself dinner and it sat in front of me, cooling and coagulating while I stared at a TV show I couldn't have described two minutes later to save my life except that there were people roughly my age, looking like they were having a lot more fun than I was even though they were complaining that they should have been having a lot more fun than they already were.

I sat, curled into myself on the sofa, until Mackenzie bounded into the loft. I'd been waiting for him, so consumed with the miserable events of the day that I was stunned by his ebullient greetings, how hyperalive he seemed, wired and thoroughly enjoying life.

"Am I ever glad to see you!" he said. "I have just heard the chronicles of hell, the fleecing and emotional torture of Tom the Man, although, of course, that's all in the past, says he. This bride is 'a little bit immature' but she makes him feel 'alive.'" He flopped down on the sofa next to me and leaned close.

It seemed too cruel, too inappropriate to tap his shoulder and say, "Excuse me, I have news of a rather more serious character." There should be some protocol for that, some early-warning system. But if there is, I didn't know it, and so instead, I let him ramble on.

"I never had the heart to suggest that he'd said the same thing about the recently shedded missus. I felt like a secret hoarder in the war of the sexes—I knew I'd go home to somebody wonderful, somebody who was nothing at all like Tom's women. Not any of them."

"Damned with faint praise," I said.

"I didn't mean it that way."

I knew he hadn't, and I was flattered and glad to have him go on. I just couldn't seem to express that sort of feeling right now or tell him why I couldn't express those feelings right now, tell him about Helen. Helen alive, Helen hurtling, Helen gone.

"A guy who can't live with or by himself. He said as much." By now, Mackenzie was doing his sofa stretch, legs straight out to the ground and arms above his head, hands clasped. It's an almost unconscious end-of-day routine for him, as if he's shucking the accumulated tensions and irritants of the day, physically expanding until there's no room for them in his system. It stretches just about every muscle, and normally even gives the viewer— when the viewer feels normal—a small lust-lurch, because it provides a full and unimpeded view of his excellent physique.

But there are few things as incomprehensible as a happy person when you yourself are miserable, and so my peevishness turned his stretch into flaunting himself. And worse, releasing his day's tensions while I held mine inside like an undigestible hair ball.

"Mackenzie," I said. "Listen up. I'm glad you're in such a great mood, but—"

"I do go on, don't I?" He straightened himself back into a sitting position. "Your turn. How was your day?"

I felt like a rain cloud about to dump its contents on poor C. K. Mackenzie's undeserving head. "I've had some horrible news."

He was all contrition. "I'm so sorry! What happened? To whom? What?"

I have to say that his ability to listen when so requested was perfectly honed.

I took him through Helen's story stage by stage, including meeting the old woman who had witnessed Helen's fall. And finally, I told him about Louisa's call and the latest announcement, that Helen had been a suicide.

He nodded, he actively listened, he looked concerned and upset and whatever else I would have wanted, and I should have been able to relax, but I couldn't. Instead, tension gripped a clenched fist on the nape of my neck.

I knew why.

I didn't buy Louisa's explanation, no matter what notes Helen had written. But I also knew how Mackenzie was going to react to my saying so. If I did. Which I would, because keeping my mouth shut is not one of my more practiced skills. "I can't believe it," I blurted out.

"No wonder. It's staggering news. A friend, somebody you saw last night—"

"I mean it literally. I can't believe it."

"Believe what?"

I shook my head. "Everything I know about people— about anybody—makes it impossible to believe either idea. She shouldn't have been up there. Her work crew was at Tess's, not at her house. Why leave work to go up there? And suicide doesn't fit. I saw her furious that even a fictional woman would try to solve a problem by suicide. She was so emphatic that she seemed silly—a woman beating a dead Edna, if you'll pardon me for what I was thinking. But given her abhorrence for what the woman in the novel did, it's impossible to believe that the very next day she'd think it was a good idea."

"So you're sayin' it couldn't have been an accident, and it couldn't have been suicide, despite the note."

"The so-called note was in a notebook—a three-ring notebook. Who knows who it was for or what it meant?"

He nodded. "Despite that."

"Guess so," I said. "Or . . ."

His expression was suddenly hard edged. "You suggesting foul play?"

Now he'd tell me I was a fool, that the police know best. I waited, ready to pounce when he warned me off from the world of thinking.

Except he didn't. What he did was wait, along with me.

"If I did . . . you seem as if you aren't . . . well, aren't you going to tell me I'm being crazy, or ridiculous?" I finally asked.

"Why would I? I haven't even heard your complete reasoning process yet."

"You always do."

"A man can learn," he said gently. "You've been right before."

The planet shifted gears. "You're—you're making fun of me, aren't you?"

"You're paranoid."

I looked directly at him.

He smiled. "I'm waitin'," he said. "I'm listenin'."

For once, I was speechless.

Seven

By morning, I remembered Petra.

There is nothing quite as miserable as going to school when you're the teacher and you haven't done your homework. When you haven't kept your word. I wanted to hide at home rather than face Petra with nothing except sympathy and concern.

I assured myself that given the profound shocks of the preceding day, there had been no time, no reservoir of psychic energy to give over to my student's problems. I reminded myself that I was human, that a friend had died violently the day before. I explored every guilt-assuaging alleyway I could imagine, but I still knew I was letting Petra—and therefore myself—down.

I slowly entered the building and made the obligatory stop at the office to empty my cubby of the daily directives and ads from textbook companies. Next to me, Shelly Traynor, who also taught English, read a message and sighed.

"What's up?" I asked softly.

"Oh," she said. "I didn't mean to . . . it's this note about Gretchen Coulter. She won't be in for a while. Her mother . . . it's awful. She—"

"I know." Poor, poor Gretchen. I wondered if her father had surfaced yet.

"She has learning problems as it is, with the dyslexia."

56

Shelly sighed again. "Turned off to school because of them, and I thought we were making real progress that she could hold on to over the summer, but now I don't know what to do, how to help her."

She wasn't the only one grappling with those very words, and I couldn't think of any instant solution that wouldn't further intrude on Gretchen's troubles. I shook my head sympathetically, wished her well, and trudged up to my room.

The closer the end of term comes, the more thoroughly I tend to plan out a week's lessons. This is not done out of competency, but pure terror of what else might fill the yawning vacuum of summer-hungry adolescents. Luckily for me, the week was mostly in place, and nobody noticed—or at least commented upon—my robot-like behavior or the irony of teaching a unit on clear communication while I broke my silence with a mumble, and that, only now and then.

Yesterday, they'd each been given the picture of a complex quilting pattern and had written a description of what they saw. Today, their descriptions, minus the pictures, had been redistributed, and the class was trying to follow their classmates' written directions. The results were entertaining and exotic patterns that had nothing to do with the originals. A lesson in miscommunication, but with good humor. There were occasional groans, but more often giggles.

Only a small part of my mind awaited the results of the exercise. The rest, most of it, was divided between Helen's plunge from her roof and the thought of Petra arriving and finding me without answers.

My second-period class was also midway through a writing project. Theirs was called Abnormal Psychology. They'd recalled or invented vignettes of odd behavior, which they first described on paper and then for the class. We had many raised eyebrows, laughs, and nods of recognition—every family has someone who'd qualify— but after a discussion yesterday, the class was moving on from thinking of these people as merely "weird." Now, they were to describe the behavior and then "analyze" its causes. They were making up histories and situations for their characters, and they seemed fairly captivated by the process. Except, of course, when interrupted by the PA system.

This time, the urgent! flash! stop the presses! interrupt every single room in the building! message was that Littering Was Bad.

My jaw clenched painfully, but it took all that pressure to keep me from saying what I wished I could say about the interruptions.

Dr. Havermeyer and his mouthpiece Helga lacked all impulse control. He had a thought—littering is bad—and boom! He had to announce it to the world. In the head, out the mouth. He must have been a joy of a student.

Then it was time for Petra's class. They arrived, but she did not. I stood in my doorway, hoping to see her race in, and fearing it at the same time.

While I stood there, a girl came to my classroom door and, with no expression on her face, scanned the room.

"Can I help you?" I asked.

She pressed her lips together, looked at me sideways, then tilted her head in an attitude of consideration, started to shake her head, stopped, and bit her bottom lip. I wondered how my last class would have described and analyzed her behavior.

"You're Miss Pepper," she said.

I already knew that.

"I'm Bonnie Kramer. Petra's friend."

"Do you expect her?"

She shrugged. "Not exactly. Well, I wish, actually, I

wish, but I thought she might be here, that's why I came over, but—"

"She isn't."

Bonnie half turned. "Well, then, I guess I'd better be—"

"What's going on?"

Bonnie looked at me appraisingly. "She told me that you know. That she talked to you. Told you. That you would help her."

"Where is she? She promised not to do anything till we talked," I said. "Please, tell me what's going on."

"I went there this morning, like always. I live around the corner, and she's nearer the bus, so I always stop and ring the bell and we take the bus together, but this morning, Mrs. Yates answered the door and asked me why I was there. I didn't know what she meant—I go there every day, and I said so. And Mrs. Yates goes, 'She said she was sleeping at your house.' And I realized I just made a real mess, so I tried to make it better. I said sure, she was at my house but she forgot her notebook, and could I get it. I couldn't think of anything good." Bonnie blinked back tears.

"It's okay."

"No, it's not. She's screaming, 'That little bitch, where did she really go?' and 'I wonder how many other times she's lied to us' and on and on, and I made everything really bad. What'll happen to her if she ever comes back, and if she doesn't, then what'll happen to her? Where would she live? What would she do?"

"Back up, could you? You spoke to her yesterday. You knew she'd spoken to me, right?"

Bonnie nodded. Inside the room, the herd had realized that nothing was stalking them. That in fact, I was rooted at the doorway, my attention elsewhere. And so they had begun gamboling in the meadow. "Excuse me," I said. "Wait here. I'll be a sec."

"I have math now."

"I'll write a note. Please."

It was my sad duty to put a damper on the merriment. I stood in front of them, my roll book and a notepad clutched against me, and I reinflicted Hester Prynne on them, an essay about which characters in the novel were or weren't moral. And then I hurried back to Bonnie, one eye still on them as they moaned, groaned, and settled in to writing. It was all an interesting charade since I knew these papers weren't going to count for much, if anything, and I also knew that they knew it. And, I suspected—they knew that I knew that they knew.

But with a collective sigh, we played our roles. "Now," I said to Bonnie. "You were talking. In person? On the phone?"

"On the way home. And when she came over, we talked more."

That seemed to constitute a full report for Bonnie. I prompted. "And? How was she? What was her mental state? Did you think she might run away? Did you say anything that would hint where she might have gone?"

Bonnie shook her head. "She told me about talking to you. She was sort of glad she had, and sort of sorry? I remember she said that. And she told me about questions you asked, and that she told you about her grandmother who is *awful*—I once went up there with her and her sister. She was afraid you were going to make her tell her parents."

I didn't know how to respond. I hadn't even known what I'd say to Petra. I'd been so worried about saying the wrong thing. But this sudden flight had me stymied. Without doing a thing beyond offering to help her sort things out, I'd managed to make her more desperate. "Were you there? At that party?"

Bonnie's eyes widened, and I got the feeling that she

thought if she made them large enough, they'd hide her confusion while she decided whether to tell me the truth or not. Finally, with another tightening of her lips—the girl was going to have purse strings around her mouth way before her time—she nodded. "But I didn't . . . I don't like to drink. I didn't know what was going on with her until weeks later when she . . . found out."

"Did you know the other people there? The . . . boy she was with?"

A head shake. I couldn't tell if that was true.

"You have no idea where she'd go?"

Another head shake. "I can't believe you can know somebody that well—my best friend! And then they disappear. Like you didn't even know them at all."

I thought about Helen, secretly suicidal, and I wondered how many times in life we had to keep learning and relearning the basic truth that everyone is a mystery.

"She wouldn't go to her grandmother's," Bonnie said, "and her other grandparents live out in California so where would she go? I think she ran *away*. Just *away*."

I pictured the girl on the street, in a shelter. I pictured her in too many situations, all of them bad and bound to get worse. There are, in fact, fates worse than death. "She may get in touch with you," I said. "And if she does, please tell her to come back, to—"

"But that's it! I've ruined everything. Her parents know she didn't sleep at my house. They know she lied. They'll go nuts! I'd have to tell her, warn her, wouldn't I? That her parents know and they're furious—and if I told her—then she'd never, ever come back!" Bonnie's eyes flooded and she shook her head, angrily. "I did the worst thing. I did just the worst thing," she said. "All day long that's all I can think about, what I did."

"You stopped at her house. There's nothing to berate yourself about. If she gets in touch, tell her to call me."

The words came out of my mouth of their own volition. I hadn't known I was going to say them. And once I had— and they took on supernatural quality, floating over to Bonnie who then looked at me through moist and suddenly adoring eyes, as if I possessed special wisdom, the ability to save, to heal the sick, and to work miracles—I was the one who felt sick. I was the one who thought I'd just done the worst thing.

Bonnie was too young and naive to ask what I'd do when and if Petra called. She simply accepted. I was about to fail two girls, instead of just one.

"Here," I said, ripping a page from my notepad. "I'll write you a late note for your math teacher. But take this, too—" And I wrote on a second sheet. "—my home phone."

It shouldn't be like this, was all I could think of as I watched Bonnie walk away. Nobody should have to run away from home. Nobody should have a home so terrifying and cold. Stone, they'd named her. Petra, stone. Maybe it was wishful thinking on their part, the hope that she'd be just like them.

Eight

OUR IMMEDIATE IMPULSE HAD BEEN TO HUDDLE TO-
gether, shield ourselves against the specter of Helen's
death. But twenty-four hours later, when the book club
members emerged from the elevator into the loft, each
hesitantly bearing a casserole or covered bowl, facial expressions and body language said, "Why are we doing
this? What did we have in mind?"

With death instead of a book to discuss, we lost all our
self-assurance. It was so much easier dealing from the in-
tellect than from the heart, which has no language. We
were sheepish and tongue-tied. Why we'd thought that
by congregating we'd come up with the wisdom and
comforts we craved, I don't know. Through history,
people have searched in vain for what to say about, what
to make of death. Revelations weren't likely to occur just
because my group was grieving.

Judging by expressions and uncomfortable silences
and the overfussing with the dishes they'd brought, I
knew I wasn't the only one feeling inadequate because I
didn't know what to say and do. In another culture, it
would have been easier. We would have fallen upon each
other and sobbed, wailed, keened. That used to seem
primitive to me. I now recognized it as astoundingly
pragmatic, perceptive, and wise.

Our awkwardness wasn't only about Helen's death or

Helen. It was also about how afraid we are to admit we're afraid. For all our grown-up status, for all the things we do and all the roles we play in life, the knowledge that we aren't in charge of a whole lot that's important is terrifying—and not something we like to let out of the bag. So we smiled and put our collective sustenance on the table, where I'd set out plates and forks and napkins. And we eddied around, making small talk like people at a dreadful cocktail party.

The feeling persisted that I should do something, that I was the hostess—although that wasn't exactly true. I was more the venue provider, which sounded so chilly and distant that it didn't even serve as something I could tell myself for reassurance, so I hostessed up, urging everyone to help herself to food, and with heaping platters balanced on knees, we settled around the room on the borrowed folding chairs.

Mackenzie emerged from where he'd been holed up in the bedroom. "Won't bother you ladies," he said in his soft bayou-edged voice. "Wanted to express condolences. From all I heard, Helen was an impressive woman, and I'm sure everybody feels her loss and will for a long time." He poured himself a glass of wine and, after much urging and waitressing by the group, amassed a plateful of offerings and retreated to the bedroom.

"He's *gorgeous*," Roxanne said the second the bedroom door shut. "And, oh, that Southern *accent*." There was much agreement and further embellishments about his hunkiness and my luckiness.

I appreciated the sentiments, although I admit the hungry expressions on some of my dear friends' faces worried me. I believe Louisa Traverso, she of the three failed marriages, actually drooled.

The accolades continued. I was glad the awkward silence had been broken, although I found this effusiveness excessive. No need to be so very effusive in their praise, or to so lovingly catalogue his fine attributes.

They made him seem like a great purchase I'd made, a clever investment. Or an especially adorable pet.

And then, just as abruptly as it had begun, it ended, and the stilted silence returned. This time, it felt like shame in new attire. We weren't supposed to be ogling a handsome man; we were supposed to be mourning, eulogizing, doing something about a dead friend.

"What we have just witnessed, ladies, is the life force in action," Tess said, putting us back on course. "Isn't it nice to know that despite how sad and rotten and upset we are about Helen, it hasn't extinguished our pilot lights altogether? I say hooray for it."

It is good to have a shrink around.

"I'm so upset," Roxanne said, breaking the ice in which we'd set the dead woman. "And shocked. I've known her forever, but I must not have known her at all. That frightens me. I don't know what it means." She looked down at her fingernails, ticking one tip against the other. We waited. She made her tick, tick noises. Then she lifted her head again and spoke more forcibly. "I'm sorry, but she did not seem depressed Monday night."

There was a round of murmurs, all agreeing. "Not depressed," was repeated softly. "Not suicidal!" more loudly.

I was glad to hear my gut impressions seconded. Nobody had found Helen quite herself Monday, but nobody thought that a tirade against suicide dovetailed into committing suicide the next day. Nobody suggested that Helen had felt irresistibly drawn to replicate Edna's actions.

My suspicions surfaced again, but this did not seem

the time to broach them, since nobody else was moving from disbelief toward what I thought was believable.

"But there was a note," Tess said. "This is so difficult to absorb or believe, but then there's the fact of the note."

"She wasn't depressed, but she wasn't herself either on Monday," Clary said. "She was so *jumpy*!" She stopped, her eyes growing first wide, and then overflowing. "I didn't mean—how could I have said that word! I didn't mean . . ." She shook her head and bent over to find tissue in her bag.

"Please," Tess said. "It was just a word. And she did seem hyped up, overly upset about the book and Edna's behavior."

Clary cleared her throat and seemed to have almost regained her composure. "Listen, I meant to say . . . the truth is, I can only stay awhile," she said. "Ivan's devastated, and I promised I'd—"

So Helen's husband was back. Clary didn't offer an explanation for where he'd been and nobody asked. At least not out loud.

A polite cough broke the brief silence. "I can't stay either," Denise said. "I wanted to be a part of this, but in truth, I shouldn't be here at all. I'm supposedly out in Villanova with Roy Stanton, but I said I'd be late. Zack's at the helm." As she said her stepson's name, a fleeting frown, very fleeting—Denise seldom showed even slight displeasure—darkened her expression.

I was continually surprised by what a political animal she was. Being arm candy, a professional smiler for an ambitious man, sounds appalling to me. I hadn't known her before her marriage, but people said she'd been strongly committed to women's rights. Now, her expressed beliefs were cloned from her husband's, so far to the right and so antifeminist that it was incredible she tolerated, let alone embraced such notions. Apparently, she'd vowed to love, honor, and adopt his driving ambition as her own.

None of us, including Denise herself, talked much about Roy Stanton or his campaign in book group. One night a month, etiquette trumped politics.

"Zack's very take-charge, very enthusiastic, but still, he's new to it, and young. I shouldn't stay long." This time, Denise managed not to grimace as she said her stepson's name.

I'm not sure I could have been as noncommittal about Zachary Harris. *Aimless* has become an old-fashioned word, but it described the obnoxious young man wandering through life with only the enormous chip on his shoulder as company. His mother had died right before he entered Philly Prep, and a whole lot of slack had been cut for the grieving child, so much that for six years, he used that slack as a hammock in which to sulkily doze away his days. And when he wasn't aimless, he was aimed in the wrong direction, involved, I'd heard, in petty crime and unsavory pursuits.

But now, five years after high school, he'd turned around. He'd been infected by the same congressional lust as his father, for whose campaign he now worked. According to Denise, suddenly and completely, he'd found his place in life. Some discover religion. Others discover politics. Whatever works, works.

"What I meant," Clary said, "was would everybody mind if we more or less . . . discussed whatever it is that we came for? I mean . . . Helen. Now?"

Her sister, Louisa, sat picking at her cuticles. Sooner or later she'd find a way to turn this into a this-is-all-about-me session, but for now, she was quiet, which was good for everything except her cuticles.

"How's Gretchen?" Tess asked.

Clary shrugged. "Exactly as you'd assume—devastated,

stunned, bereft, needy—and afraid she provoked this. Apparently, she'd been nagging for some computer system—I'm not sure what. And Helen had really gotten mad. Told her that she had no idea how hard life was, and what a bad time they were going through. Gretchen didn't know what Helen meant. I assured her that all marriages hit speed bumps, that things were tense at work, and that she, Gretchen, had nothing to do with what her mother chose to do." Clary gulped, put her hands up, signaling that she was empty now, that she'd said all she knew, and her chin was out pugnaciously, as if daring us to contradict her, or to mention her glittering eyes.

I had a mental image of Gretchen, the child in pain, and saw her blur and be Petra, as well. It hurt even imagining what either of them was feeling. I redirected attention to Helen, not her child. Not anybody's child. "Clary?" I asked. "How about you? You see her every day. Did you have any inkling she was suicidal? Did you see her that morning?"

Clary sighed. "I wasn't there that morning. I had an appointment in Jersey. She was gone by the time I got back." She frowned. "I mean she'd left the office."

"Would it be horribly wrong to ask whether business problems could have overwhelmed her?" Denise leaned forward, earnest and worried.

I love questions like that. If it *was* horribly wrong to ask that, then how should we react? By shouting "yes!" and stomping out? Punishing her with silence or the dunking stool? The question was awkward, given that Helen's business partner was not apt to reveal serious problems.

Clary obviously also felt stymied. She cocked her head, looked to the distance, and said only, "I can't imagine why."

A nonanswer.

When nobody followed up on that, Clary burst into tears. "Sorry," she said. "Sorry. This isn't like—I just can't—"

My own eyes stung and I looked down, as well. The entire room grew quiet, but this time, it felt appropriate, like a meditation, a necessary one.

Clary sighed raggedly. Then she dabbed at her eyes and looked at Susan. "Know what? Helen was a fan of yours. In her book—the book that had the note also had a lot about your Polly Baker story."

"Polly? Really?" Susan looked delighted.

Clary nodded. "Helen must really have loved it. I mean writing it down, wanting to remember it."

"Speaking of writing things down," Tess said. "I thought of something we could do, something that would be nice. I'm assuming we're all concerned about Helen's daughter, and that I'm not the only one who feels useless in a situation like this. Gretchen doesn't know me well, and she'd be uncomfortable if I went to talk to her or spend time. But a letter might be different. My mother died when I was around Gretchen's age, and a few of her friends wrote down their memories of her. It doesn't sound like much, but there have been so many times I reread those letters. . . ." She let the sentence dangle.

"Well, but—" Louisa was expert at objecting.

"I'll find a pretty scrapbook," Tess said, interrupting her. "We can put all the letters in it. Just write on one side of the page, is all. Whoever wants to—no obligations, but if you're going to do it, do it as soon as possible. I think Gretchen could use immediate gestures of kindness."

"What kind of things do you want in it?" Louisa sounded put-upon. "I'm not exactly a writer, you know."

Tess was the calmest person I knew. I don't know if this was part of her professional training, or if it came naturally, but where others rush to fill silence and say anything—and by *others*, I mean myself, of course— Tess waited while you could almost hear her thinking. What I found amazing is that almost always, her listeners were patient and did not themselves rush in to fill that space. "An anecdote," she now said. "An opinion, an appreciation, a thought about life, why you'll miss her, a photo. Whatever good things her memory triggers in you. Gretchen's an adolescent; she lives in another country. Someday she'll want to know her mother better as a person. She'll want to see her with adult eyes. That's all—we share our perceptions."

"I didn't know her that well," Louisa said. Louisa probably didn't waste her mental storage space on good or happy memories. She needed all of it for her world-class collection of grievances. "I saw her once a month at book club. And at my sister's social events. And felt her presence, because of the preschool board she was on." She pursed her mouth, and to her probable dismay, nobody encouraged her to talk about the heartache of not getting her kid into the right preschool. I knew she wanted to begin a sentence with, "I don't mean to speak ill of the dead, but—"

"Can we have the memories, the letters, in by the weekend?" I asked. "I'll be glad to help out, Tess."

"What do we do?"

I shrugged. "We should have a central collection point. It could be Tess—"

"We're at the shore," Tess said. "Have to get the house ready for summer. Replace the rusted and the rotting." She smiled at the mess she implied she would find. "However," she continued, "I could get the scrapbook and my letter here before we leave Friday, and if you wanted to, the whole shebang could be ready by Monday."

"That's when they're talking about a memorial service," Clary said. "If the body's released by then, which it should be."

Two people suddenly realized they were leaving town the next day and wouldn't be able to get anything down on paper beforehand. It looked as if Tess's idea was going to be stillborn.

"Wait a minute," Louisa said. "Just one minute. Forget the book."

"But—"

"Let's say it. A collective memorial. Right now. All together. We don't need a scrapbook. Do you have a tape recorder? We could get it all down—"

I was horrified to acknowledge that a decent idea had come out of Louisa.

"I know how to splice tape," I said. "Edit it. My class did a sort of radio play, and I learned how. So say whatever you like. Revise, don't be inhibited. We can always edit it out."

This was a pleasant, well-meaning plan.

It was also quite sad, because here we were, women who'd missed signs of imminent suicide, who hadn't a clue as to why Helen jumped, convincing ourselves we could produce meaningful memories Gretchen could use to help define her mother, a woman we obviously hadn't known at all.

Nine

LIKE MAKING THE SCATTERED PIECES OF A JIGSAW puzzle fit, we were to fuse a portrait of Helen for her daughter, for her daughter's future. We had preliminary discussions about abiding by very un-book-club-like behavior, such as speaking in turn. We tested and retested the tape recorder, found it fine, made a large pot of coffee, and did everything possible to delay a project we were set on even though we knew it was futile.

"Might I go first?" Denise pointed at her watch face.

I suspect that most if not all the women were as delighted as I to have somebody take the lead and give this amorphous project a shape and direction.

Denise did so with her usual calm self-confidence. She identified herself to the tape and spoke softly. "I only knew Helen through the book group, so what most impressed me was what she had to say about life through the books we read. More than anything, I'll remember her values, her ethical sense. She looked for the moral underpinnings of the story, to see if they were sound. I didn't always agree 100 percent, but I respected her for her fine values."

Denise sounded ready to launch into one of her husband's campaign speeches about morality. Next we'd get to family values and how Helen exemplified them, even though Helen had been last seen ranting against men telling women what to do with their lives. But I caught my knee in midjerk and realized that Denise was right. Helen always looked below the plot for the underlying ethics and meaning. That's what had gotten to her about *The Awakening*. Helen was a firebrand, crusading for causes she felt were in the right and looking for reflections of them in everything, on the page or off.

Denise smiled, said that was about it, and left to rejoin her husband's campaign.

"Two things for starters," Roxanne said next. "First, Helen was a good friend. I don't just mean to me." She leaned closer to the tape. "I mean to whomever she was a friend. You could rely on her. You could trust her. You could have fun with her or be serious with her. That's pretty special and much rarer than it should be." Roxanne's sweet little-girl voice felt just right at that moment, soothing and kind. "And second, I want to describe meeting your mother for the first time," she continued. "She looked like she had a lamp inside her— she gave out light from some invisible source. That sounds crazy, but it was true. Every boy's eyes were on her and that radiance that night, and, Gretchen, when I look at you, I see that light turning itself on, too."

That was kind and selfless, given that Roxanne had been Ivan Coulter's college love, dumped after he met the shining Helen. Of course, that was long ago. Nowadays, Roxanne was married to an oil-company engineer and was the Coulters' neighbor and friend.

"Of course, Gretchen," Clary began with no ceremony, "you know how close I was with your mom. Maybe too close to describe her. At first, in college, I was almost put off by her. She was so pretty, so smart, and so popular. Everybody loved her, and she dated half the campus. We once joked about her having dated every Tom, Dick, and Harry—except it wasn't a joke. She was madly in love with a Harry right then. I didn't know who it was, but I was sure he existed because I did personally know guys she'd dated named Tom Lester and Tom Peters and Tom O'Hara, and Dick Burton and Dick—you probably catch my drift. I think it was literally true.

"So there's that. But so much more that I can't describe—can't even see clearly. Like when you look too closely at a newspaper photo and all you see are the dots that make it up, not what the picture's of? She's too complicated and maybe we have too long a history and it'd take too long for this tape, for sure." Clary snapped off the tape and blew her nose and wiped at her eyes. She sat blinking and inhaling for a brief while, her finger held up as a signal she'd begin again soon. Finally, she cleared her throat and started the tape again. "We've been through rough times and good times. But what comes to my mind first was how decent a person she was, how good-hearted. Sometimes I guess I thought of her—and maybe you did, too—as being a worrywart or even sometimes as, well, a meddler. But it was concern that did it, a sense of fairness, a desire to make things right. I don't want this to sound too goody-goody, because it wasn't, necessarily. That trait didn't always work well for making business decisions, but—" Clary inhaled and seemed to be choosing her words carefully. "—it was a good way to be a human being." And Clary, whose motions were always quick, stood up, said "Gotta run, sorry," and was gone.

"Listen, Gretchen," Tess said into the tape, "your mother's beginning to sound too much like a plaster saint and just a bit unbelievable, so I want to say that while everything everybody else said is true, she could be a real pain in the butt, too. She was human is what I'm saying. Which means that if you're beginning to think that we're all making stuff up that sounds good—now you know that isn't true. Believe what we say.

"For me, I've seen your mother sad and upset and angry, but my personal mental photo, if you asked for one, would be of her laughing. Lots of times, lots of laughing. I remember when you were born, and, oh, how she'd laugh with pure joy just because you existed. So I think I'd add that to the picture of her, plus bravery. There were lots of times she stuck her neck out, when she believed in a cause and went for it. Do you remember her marching against the Gulf War—when she turned out to be the only person who showed up? Well, it was the wrong day, in fact, but march on she did. And then laughed at herself, too. That's what I hold on to and you should, too, no matter what." Tess sighed heavily, then grimaced.

I nodded to show that I'd cut that sorrowful sigh out, but I was controlling a sigh of my own. Her "no matter what" meant she accepted the idea that Helen had committed suicide.

"I admire your mother's spunk." Wendy Loeb had a self-assured, warm tone. As she spoke, she fiddled with the impressive engagement ring she'd worn for a decade. "She had guts. I met her years ago, through Ivan. The three of us were a partnership. We were going to build apartments in Devon and get stinking rich. But the project went kerplooey, and we got really poor instead, and in debt, and that might have scared off most women from high-risk projects, but not Helen. She paired up with Clary and wound up making another risky business work. And I found my footing again, too, and it all has a happy ending." She stopped and put her hand to her mouth, eyes wide. I put my hands up to express, I hoped, that it was all right. An understandable slip of the tongue that no one would take to mean Helen's death was a happy ending.

But she shook her head and said, "Turn it off," and

when we did, she was crying. "Erase that. It sounds horrible, it sounds as if I thought—you know how it sounds. Just because we had that awful time with the project—Helen blew it, if you must know, and it set me back years. But then, look, things turned out economically for all of us, including Helen most of all, but that makes me sound . . . and it's all water under the bridge. It's the past; it's forgotten." She puffed out a hard exhale, then nodded. I turned the machine back on.

"I meant she had guts, like I said. In the best way. The courage of her convictions. Standing up for what she believed. Trust me, business partnerships that go sour aren't the best way to stay friends, but because of who she was and how she was, we did. I admired her, and I learned from her."

When it was my turn, I realized that I'd known Helen less than anyone else, having been with her only a dozen times, a year's worth of book club meetings. I said how smart I thought she was, and how thoughtful. "Maybe everybody else takes that for granted, because they knew her better than I did, but that's what stood out for me. I always wanted to hear what she had to say because it was always thoughtful and heartfelt and that's a pretty fine combination." Something like that.

Then, as if we'd primed the pump, people started remembering more, funny or moving anecdotes, and the tape went on until suddenly Louisa, who'd been silent the entire time, leaned forward and in a tense, flat voice, said, "Your mother was civic minded. That sounds . . . I know how that sounds, but everybody else has said all the other things, anyway. But I mean she cared about a lot of things that weren't just about her. The, ah, community. And—and I'm sure that she always did what she thought was best, no matter how it looked."

For a second, I thought she was offering consolation

for the suicide, but then I regained my senses. This was Louisa, and Louisa's only topic was Louisa. She meant Helen's possible role in not admitting Louisa's child to the nursery school. This was Louisa being generous of spirit.

Roxanne piped in again. "I liked the way she was always looking forward. A kind of innate optimism. And she was interesting. We had an appointment we never got to keep, for a story she wanted me to sell. Something about her business, but—and this is a confession— Gretchen, generally I don't find business, her business, all that interesting—but I knew she'd make the story interesting. She had that kind of a personality."

We took a break so that everybody could think about whether there was more to add.

"When were you supposed to meet with Helen?" I asked Roxanne.

"Yesterday. Five o'clock." Roxanne shrugged.

"She made an appointment." Susan spoke softly. "Isn't that odd?"

Roxanne looked confused by the comment. "Not really. We had the appointment for a few days. We were both at a party, and she asked me. I thought it was probably about her new program, which, to tell you the truth, was going to be next to impossible to get any space for in the paper. It's not that unique, but of course, we all think our stories are earth-shattering. She was wired about it. I didn't want to hurt her feelings."

"What was it about?" I asked.

"I think it was the internship program they're starting. She said, 'An announcement,' so it had to be something new. Look, I don't want to say anything bad about Helen, but the truth was, she acted like she was going to announce World War III. I like helping friends, but really . . . she didn't need that kind of PR. She was a wholesaler, but she didn't get it. She had that manic energy sometimes. Said this 'scoop'—I swear, she used that word—would help my career, but even though I knew it wouldn't, what are you going to do? Anyway, it's moot now."

"It makes it more confusing." Susan looked woeful. She searched each of our faces in turn, looking for something I don't think she found. "Listen," she said, "except for that note, there's nothing that indicates depression or suicide."

"Do you think it was really an accident?" I had shelved my suspicions as inappropriate. They had no solid base, and especially now, after hearing more about her, the idea of someone intentionally going after Helen seemed remote. But Susan had been looking peculiarly alert all evening, and I wondered. And I wondered what I'd do if she were the one who suggested foul play.

"Is it your professional opinion that it's possible to hide depression that well," she now asked Tess, "and then kill yourself like that?"

Tess nodded. "If she'd reached some inner calm—a decision that she was going to do that—then she might well appear pretty normal, as in fact she did."

"But she was anything but calm. She was ranting about Edna's suicide!" Susan said. "Not inner or outer calm."

"Edna's," I said, thinking out loud. "Maybe that was different. She felt Edna should have fought her society, stood up against it. Helen was a woman who did that, so maybe she just couldn't identify with Edna. Is that possible?"

This time, Tess sighed, lifted a shoulder, and said, "Anything's possible. But as I recall, she called Edna's suicide too easy."

"Listen to us," I said. "The only thing we've got, even now, even after putting together our impressions of

Helen, is confusion. A day ago, I'd have said I knew Helen. Not well, but I knew her. Not like Clary must have, or Roxanne, or maybe others of you, but what's obvious now is that I didn't know her at all, and I'm not getting the sense that anybody did. We saw her, we interacted, we shared opinions and bits and pieces of our lives, we ate her food and fed her ours, but nobody knew her."

"She had Ivan," Tess said. "He knew her. That's what husbands are for."

Ivan, I thought. Ivan, who'd been unaccountably not where he should have been. That wasn't what husbands were for.

Susan was the one who said it, finally. "The only thing that makes sense of this, that puts together the contradictory evidence, is if she didn't do this thing."

"You mean not on purpose?" Tess said. "You mean that she had an accident. But still . . . why did she leave her office and go home then?"

"A contractor?" Roxanne suggested.

"He was at my house," Tess said. "The entire crew was. Of all people, Helen knew that."

"That's what bothers me," Susan said. "It doesn't work as an accident if there's no reason for her to have gone home. And it doesn't work as a suicide either. The only thing that makes sense at all is that Helen Coulter was murdered."

Dead silence.

"Okay," I said softly. "I'll be the one to dare ask. Where was Ivan? What's going on?"

Apparently, no one knew. Clary probably did, but she'd gone.

Susan cocked her head in the direction of the bedroom. "His guys looking into this?"

I shook my head. "I think they assume it was accidental—or a suicide."

"So should we!" Roxanne flung out her arms so that gauze fluttered. "This gives me the creeps. Why even think that way, Susan? This isn't one of your mysteries, this is real life! Besides, who are we? There's nothing we could do about it anyway, so why even think such an awful thing?"

"Because even if we didn't really know her, we know her better than the police do," Susan said.

Louisa Traverso stood up. "What are you going to do, Susan?" she demanded. "Say your theory on the tape?"

"Of course not!"

"Good! You had me worried!" Louisa grinned as if she'd made a joke. "Then the recording session's over, right? I'm going home. No need to wash my dish, Mandy. I'll put it in my shopping bag. I hope the kid likes the tape."

After Louisa left, Susan stared at the closed door awhile before she spoke again. "While we were making the tape, I kept thinking that if I died in a way that surprised or confused my friends, I'd hope they didn't accept it the way we seem to be doing. I sure hope they'd push a little, that they'd wonder and ask. It's awful to think of disappearing, that so few people would have a clue as to who I am that something horrible could be done to me and nobody would notice."

I took a deep breath and jumped in. "I think that together we could do something. We could try to figure out what was going on in her life the last few days, or weeks. The sum would be lots greater than the parts."

"Maybe we could. We all seem to know a piece of the whole. If we put together our pieces. . . ?" Tess didn't look convinced of what she was saying.

"I don't know if we can," I said. "But I want to try. For

Gretchen. Having your mother kill herself is as bad as it gets. The ultimate rejection."

Tess nodded, her expression solemn.

"Living with that has to be hard," I continued. "But if you had to live with that and it wasn't true . . . that'd be . . . unthinkable. That's punishment Gretchen doesn't deserve."

"And don't forget," Susan said in a near whisper. "If that's true, there's a killer who gets away with it."

"All right," Roxanne said. "But what do we do? What do we actually do?"

We looked at each other, searching for the master plan. But none of us had it, certainly not me. "We pool knowledge," I said. "We ask questions and combine what we learn. Tell each other. We *try*," I said. "We try this, then that. We just try. And then, if we put together a portrait that feels convincing, that says this woman would not jump off her roof, had no reason to, we can go to the police. We can show them why they have to investigate."

And given no better idea, we nodded and called it a plan.

Ten

It wasn't raining the next day. Therefore, with important things to consider, and pressing obligations, I seized the least significant and most trivial item to do. Also the one that had a chance of being solved. At lunchtime, I called the Coulter household, to make sure I wouldn't be intruding when I retrieved my raincoat.

"Coulters," an accented feminine voice answered.

I explained who I was, what had happened to my raincoat, and what time I'd like to stop by and pick it up.

No response. I tried again, summarizing what I'd already said, and then I waited again. "No," the voice said. "*No es—*"

Damn. Studying Latin and French, as I had, has not proven useful. Half my non-English language skills apply to a long-gone culture, and the other half would be useful only if I could afford to travel.

"*Se habla inglés?*" I asked, stretching my Spanish to its futile limits, because when the person on the other end answered my question with a gush of non-inglés, I had no idea what she said. Except for the *no*. I decided I'd stop by and rely on body language and hand signals. Meanwhile, I heartily agreed to something, or several somethings, saying, "*Gracias, sí,*" and finally, "*adiós.*"

Once again I underlined *learn Spanish* on my mental to-do list and returned to the teachers' lunchroom.

When I first started at Philly Prep, I thought lunchtime and free-period discussions would concern, of all things, teaching. A few weeks into the year, I thought that they might now and then concern teaching. Nowadays, I was shocked if they ever touched on anything that had to do with school—except complaints. Therefore, when I sat down, I was shocked. Rachel Leary, the school counselor, and Flora Jones, our resident computer expert, were so engrossed in their discussion they didn't notice that I'd joined them. And they were talking about a student. My student, Petra Yates.

"If I ever have children," Flora was saying, "I will use Mr. and Mrs. Yates as examples of how not to be. They appear quite normal, even concerned. Even like good parents, but have you tried talking to them? I complimented Petra's skills—she did terrifically in my class." She shook her head, looking as weary as she could, which isn't very. Flora's engine is high-powered and fueled by something better than mine is. She's that supposedly impossible female icon, the one who has and does it all, except she's for real. She's finishing her MBA at Wharton and teaching computer skills part-time at Philly Prep, in her spare time she runs marathons, and once, when she stopped long enough to blink, she won the Miss Black Teenage something or other contest. It's a wonder I can stand her.

"No mystery why she ran away," Flora said.

"Any news?" I asked. Both women turned their heads. There was a moment's acknowledgment of my presence, and then both shook their heads.

"The police have been called in," Flora said. "But it's next to impossible to find a kid who doesn't want to be found. She could be in California by now. She could be any kid on any street in any city."

Any pregnant kid in any city, I thought. And beyond

that, I couldn't bear to think. I knew that none of this situation was of my making, and I hadn't even had time to fail to help it. But I'm a grown-up and Petra is not, and it always feels like a failure when neither I nor my peer group helps a kid in distress. That's our central job, isn't it, and more or less the baseline for survival of the species.

"Her parents stormed Havermeyer's office this morning, and of course, he handled it by storming mine," Rachel said. "Apparently, the school's to blame for their daughter's disappearance."

Flora speared the lettuce of her salad with a violence I was sure she was sparing the older Yateses. "Of all the moral hypocrites! That wife of his barely bothers to hide how much she hates his children. Her kids don't even go here, but when we had our parents' conference, they were all she wanted to talk about. She countered every good thing I said about Petra with something about her children, whom she identified that way. '*My* son won his eighth-grade science competition,' she'd say. I wanted to shake her. Or really, I wanted her husband to shake her, to remind her that we were talking about Petra. Does he have any idea what this is doing to his daughter?" She made a sweeping motion with her hand, ridding herself of the Yates family.

"By what odd logic is the school responsible?" I asked.

Rachel shrugged. "Apparently, we have a student body of less than sterling, all-American quality here."

A moment of silent despair. "They bring their problem kids to a school that specializes in them, then complain there are problem kids in the school? But if our school atmosphere encouraged Petra to run away, how come everybody else hasn't run away?"

"It's all bluster and show," Rachel said. "So we'll apologize—for what, I don't know—and look ashamed and make the Yateses feel better about their own failings. They had to know that their performance wouldn't solve a damn thing or bring their daughter back home sooner, or make her safer meanwhile. But all the same, they had to go through with their act."

I kept being on the brink of telling them what I knew about Petra's motives for fleeing, but I'd been entrusted with a secret, and until I knew for certain why I should break the trust, I wasn't going to. Small potatoes indeed, and cold ones, too—but it was one thing I could do.

Or maybe I could do something more, with Rachel's help. Make a plan—assuming Petra resurfaced—for an end run around the hateful stepmother and the fearsome grandmother. Maybe Mr. Yates had to be made aware that his home atmosphere was poisonous to his oldest daughter. Maybe—without breaking Petra's trust—we could shake him back to consciousness. He cared. There was material to work with.

Mr. Yates was worried about "family values." He was probably voting for Roy Stanton Harris, who also claimed to miss sleep worrying about whatever that really meant. I wished it meant valuing their families, but I knew it didn't.

All afternoon, while my classes more or less did their thing, I worked on the idea. Helen's supposed suicide prompted it. Petra had said she wished she were dead.

First, of course, we had to find Petra and know, please God, that she hadn't followed through on her suicidal threats.

And then, another workday was over. A beautiful day it had been, spring as we fantasize but seldom experience. The air had the charged texture of impending love, and I stood still, inhaling with my eyes closed, feeling sunshine on my lids, and for the first time that day, at one with the world.

"Er, ah, I don't want to bother you but ... Miss Pepper?"

For a sun-glazed moment, the forlorn, short girl didn't register.

"Bonnie," she said. "Petra's friend? I'm sorry if you were meditating or something. Were you?"

"Meditating?" Automatically, I shook my head, then reconsidered the blissful connection I'd felt to the day. "Maybe. In any case, have you heard from her?"

Bonnie lowered her gaze to the pavement. I was glad she wasn't looking at me and couldn't see the disappointment I was unable to hide.

Had she sought me out to tell me this nothing?

"I think about her all the time." Bonnie's voice was muffled as she directed her words to the paving. "I try to imagine her in a safe place, but I can't think of where it would be. She isn't . . . I don't know what to call it." She raised her eyes and looked at me intently. "Like she isn't dumb, but she isn't smart some ways, either. You wouldn't believe the stupid stuff she'll listen to, just because somebody says so. And she's afraid of a lot. Much more than I ever am, so how could she . . . ?"

"Oh, Bonnie, I don't know either. I'm worried, too."

"Some ways she's brave," Bonnie said, talking to herself, I thought. "Like stuff that would freak other people, like being hurt. Once last summer, I went to the country, to her grandmother's with her, and I saw her grandmother hit her with a wooden spoon. Petra said that once, she hit her with a broomstick."

I must have shown how appalled I was, and Bonnie nodded. "Petra's brave. She didn't even cry. It had to hurt—it turned all purple and yellow." She sighed. "Her grandmother's a witch, and you can't tell what'll make her mad." She shrugged. "Practically everything does."

We stood in silence. "Maybe she's found a place she

can wait this out," I said. "There are such places." I wondered how many. In my mother's time, maybe even my sister's, there were homes for unwed mothers all over the map. There was also a level of shame, of being "ruined" that necessitated hiding out. That was gone, and along with it, most sanctuaries.

Bonnie made her expression blank. "The look" I used to call it—silent teen-speak for "I cannot believe you said such an absolutely stupid thing."

I remembered how she'd prefaced our talk of Petra with "But" and then had grown silent. "Something else is on your mind about her, isn't there?" I asked softly.

Her attention flicked over my face, then to the ground, and then to the park across the street, where azaleas bloomed hot pink against the new greens of the trees. "I found out his name."

"His?"

"The boy. The one who—"

"The father?"

Bonnie winced. The term made her uncomfortable. I hoped it made the father uncomfortable, too. "Ethan Mueller."

"Petra said he didn't know."

"I think maybe she changed her mind and told him. I knew his friend, the one who brought us to the party, so I checked. Asked questions. I didn't say why. Or even who I was. I was afraid if his friend knew, he wouldn't tell me."

I nodded.

"But that wasn't true. In fact, he said Ethan must be quite the Romeo, because I was the second girl this week to call about him."

"Petra was the other one?"

"I have to think so. Anyway, I got Ethan's phone number, too."

"Good for you. That was clever."

"I thought maybe he'd know where she was. But he wasn't there. He was back at college, in D.C. Finals. His mother gave me his dorm number, but he wasn't in."

We stood on the pavement, our heads bowed, almost as if in prayer, or mourning the lost girl. Bonnie had sought me out in order to tell me that she knew no more of use than she'd known before. And yet I understood why it had felt imperative to share the nonnews. It was the same impulse that had brought my book group back together after Helen's death. Saying Petra's name, reinforcing her missingness, the fact of our worries, felt like something. Acknowledging the effort Bonnie had made to find her friend meant something.

But ultimately, our hands were still empty. "Thanks," I said. "It's good that you tried. His finals will soon be over, although it doesn't look like he'd know much, does it? I wish I could think of something else to do myself. And if you have any other ideas—tell me, all right? You still have my number?"

Bonnie nodded. I watched her as she walked to the bus stop, and I thought how sad it was that neither of us had mentioned Petra's parents as resources or people who needed to know whatever we did.

Eleven

I RANG THE COULTERS' DOORBELL AND WAITED. I DIDN'T want to intrude on their mourning, so I hoped I could easily get to the closet, claim my coat, and leave. I'd see the bereaved in a few days, whenever the memorial service was held.

That was my plan, and a simple one it was, but even so, it didn't work. A diminutive brown-skinned woman opened the door a crack, looked me up and down, then shouted, "Go 'way!"

Undoubtedly the woman I'd so miserably failed to talk to on the phone. Now I was miserably failing to talk to her in person. "Please," I said, "I only—"

"No! No—" Her eyes rolled upward, as if she were searching her brain, then she glared at me. "—No papers! No! No!"

"But I'm not—I don't have any—"

The door slammed shut. I stared at it, unwilling to believe that I had failed at this minuscule task, too. I might still be staring at the closed door, my mind equally slammed shut and unable to decide what to do next, had I not heard my name. I was still so involved in my failed storming of the Coulter house that I looked up, expecting to see a face peering out of a window.

At the second call of my name, I realized the voice was

behind me. Roxanne Parisi's voice, from across the street.

She rushed over. "I was just running to the cleaners," she said. "But I *thought* it was you. Everything okay?"

I walked down the front steps and shrugged. "Sure. I left my raincoat here Monday, and I don't know how to explain it to the housekeeper."

Roxanne made a dismissive gesture. "She's impossible. Means well, but she gets things backwards. Besides, they've been deluged by the less tactful members of my profession."

I tended to forget that Roxanne was a journalist, because she seemed so lackadaisical about it, as if it were a game.

"Ivan, understandably, told her not to open the door unless she knew the person." Roxanne's Bordeaux hair fell in haphazard waves to her shoulders. She was fond of emphasizing her words with a toss of the mane, which, along with her flowing garments, suggested a more bohemian lifestyle than she actually possessed.

"It's not the dim housekeeper's fault," she said with a wide smile. "I think she was one of Helen's many kindnesses." Roxanne was a pretty, likable woman in her early forties, and I'd have felt more comfortable if I didn't feel she was overly aware of herself, on stage all the time, performing for all of us. "It's not anybody's fault," she said. "It's been dreadful."

I understood all that, but that didn't reconcile me to the loss of my raincoat.

"Actually," Roxanne said. She slurred out the syllables, and I shivered. That *actually* meant our civilities, however brief, had been only a prequel. The time and location of this encounter might have been fortuitous, but Roxanne had an agenda and she would have made this happen.

I suspected that I wasn't going to be overly happy with whatever was on her mind. And finally, it meant that Roxanne wasn't going to be interested in retrieving my raincoat for me.

"Actually," she repeated, "I'm glad you happened by. Convenient for me." She smiled. I didn't. "I was going to get in touch. I feel bad about last night."

We paused at the corner—or I did, and Roxanne was forced to do the same. My car was two streets over, and I couldn't think why I should go out of my way to accompany Roxanne to the dry cleaners. Particularly with this anticipatory bad taste in my mouth. "About the taping?" I asked. "Why?"

She studied a sapling at the curb. "I wasn't totally honest." She bit her top lip and kept her eyes on the baby tree's one budding limb. "And now it's apparent that people don't think she jumped."

"Helen," I said, feeling a need to give the dead woman her name. "Well, we don't understand it. I thought that included you."

Roxanne sighed. "I had a couple of things I didn't want to say last night. Not for the tape, not even off the tape. After all, Clary was there." Her expression begged that I intuit her real meaning.

Lacking paranormal powers along with a raincoat, I set her straight. "You probably think I'm following your train of thought, but I'm about three stations back, Roxanne."

She reverted to the look-everywhere-but-at-me eye movements. Over the tree—it wasn't much to study for long. Down to the ground, eyes sweeping from left of my feet to the Dumpster—Helen's first coffin—and then quickly away. I didn't blame her; the Dumpster was a hideous reminder of what had happened, but there it sat, dominating the sidewalk around the corner.

Roxanne sighed, and for a minute I was afraid she wasn't going to say anything more, but then I reconsidered. People who say *actually* the way Roxanne had deliver the message that prompted it.

"Look, I know some people think that I . . . that just because my husband's away so much . . . that something was going on between Ivan and me," she said at a suddenly rapid clip. "That's why I didn't bring this up last night. Couldn't handle whatever . . ."

I was obviously outside the gossip loop. Roxanne and Ivan. What a dreadful spin that put on everything. And Roxanne was probably lonely. Her husband did something in Saudi Arabia connected with the oil business, and he did it for months at a stretch.

"It isn't true."

"Okay," I said. "It's clear."

"You believe me, don't you?"

I nodded. I wasn't sure if I did, but agreeing seemed the only way to get her to the point.

"Good." She looked excessively relieved, as if I'd just eradicated the rumors. "Helen and Ivan—the thing is, they'd been going through a bad time."

"Because of . . . ?"

Roxanne's forehead furrowed. "To tell the truth, you know how you listen for the idea—your friend's upset— but you don't pay enough attention to the details right away? Something was giving her a hard time. Maybe her business. Maybe that affected her home life. Maybe that's why she wanted me to do the article, put a positive spin on the company? Makes sense, doesn't it? But I didn't want to say that last night with her partner and supposed best friend sitting right there."

Supposed? Why *supposed*? But I didn't feel like asking. There were altogether too many maybes in Roxanne's theory. "You sure?"

Roxanne shook her head, bouncing her purply waves. "If I were sure, I would have said so last night. Or told the police. All I know is she said she was going through a difficult time."

She now. Not they. Maybe business. Maybe home. I had to be careful not to let Roxanne tilt whatever she knew into something else altogether. I had to consider her motives, why she was telling me this. I wished she hadn't mentioned the gossip I was to ignore, because now I couldn't get it out of my head.

"She was freaking about money and was really on Ivan's case. Ivan had a chance to become a partner in a big development plan in Jersey. The one Wendy's working on. Major money involved. Huge potential. It was more or less a done deal, and then Helen put the kibosh on it. I don't know what precisely she did to prevent it, but he dropped out, just like that."

I know how it is for a hapless bug bungling into a spider's web. Too many sticky strands encased me. Helen and Ivan and Roxanne and Wendy and even Clary.

Wendy Loeb was involved in real estate development. Ivan Coulter was a developer. They'd worked together once; Wendy had said so last night. But it ended badly, even though time had apparently healed all old injuries. Now, another failure because of Helen's interference?

On the other hand, Helen might well have objected because Wendy Loeb's ten-year engagement was to a man reputed to be "connected." Somebody like Helen—somebody like me—might well object to being connected to those connections.

If Wendy was sufficiently upset or economically injured by this pullout, would her friends help out by tossing Helen over a roof ledge?

"Did you see anything that day?" I asked. "Anybody? I mean living right across the street . . ." And where were *you*? I wished I could ask. Helen would have gone up on the roof with a friend. And the deed done, the friend and neighbor could saunter home. Nobody would notice, and it could have been done in seconds.

Roxanne shook her head. "I had a lunch date on Nineteenth. Left around a quarter of. When I think hard, which I've been doing, I think I remember somebody in white overalls, you know those things they wear. And a hard hat. I told the police, but I don't know if I really saw him or am just remembering a year's worth of men in overalls floating around that house."

A weak-enough alibi. She could have done it, and then she could be with Ivan Coulter, her long-lost college love, because now I did half believe the rumors. "I'm not sure I'm clear what precisely you're suggesting." Well, I was, but I needed to hear it from her.

She had oversize features, a great face for a caricaturist, and now she opened her large eyes as if stunned that I hadn't gotten it. "Mandy," she said. "Isn't it obvious? Helen was under siege. In trouble with her business, maybe in trouble with the law. Consequently, in trouble in her marriage, as well. Think of the expenses going on in that house lately—and her financial crisis and . . ." She sighed heavily, and her mouth twisted down at the corners. "It seems obvious to me," she said. "Helen jumped. Helen committed suicide. Hope you don't mind my saying so, or suggesting that you—"

"I accept reality?" I smiled.

"More or less." She nodded and looked at her wrist—as if there was a watch there, which there was not—and said, "Gotta run." And she proceeded up Delancey.

I felt sprayed with debris. I'd have to sort through the bits and pieces she'd tossed at me.

I crossed the street and turned the corner, walking toward my car, and realized I was shaking my head, trying in vain to get rid of the unsettling barrage of confusing, and possibly doubtful, data.

Ah, Helen, I thought. What's really the truth? Almost involuntarily, I looked back at her house. So impressive and substantial. You'd think misery couldn't find a way in.

My breath, sympathy, and thoughts froze as I looked directly at the Dumpster, Helen's early tomb. I'd seen only the far edge earlier, but now I saw it full-on and saw a message that had not been there when Helen lived, or when Helen died.

In oversize red and dripping letters was sprayed: R.I.P. LIAR.

I stared for the longest time, fearful and apprehensive, trying to decipher the message behind the message. Was this mean-spirited but essentially meaningless graffiti—or a new form of the writing on the wall?

Twelve

MACKENZIE SPRAWLED ON THE SOFA, BUZZ BISSINGER'S book about the city open on his lap. He marked his spot with a finger, looked up, and smiled. Permission to interrupt.

"Business must be slow," I said, and then I remembered that he'd told me he'd be home early. I was on mental overload and forgetting basic things. "Good book?" I quickly added.

"Very, and how was your day?"

"It's not one I'm going to press into my scrapbook." I made tea for both of us and sat beside him. "It's getting so that I don't trust anybody."

"Know the feelin'."

I looked at him. I always enjoyed that. I liked where three and a half decades had etched lines. I liked the way his hair was prematurely salt and maturely pepper. If I'd designed him, I'd pretty much have come up with what was presented to me. It relaxed me to be with him, and I knew I could speak my mind. He felt like home.

I told him about the day, about Petra's continued disappearance, and he was adequately distressed, though not at all hopeful of finding her until she wanted finding. And then I told him what Roxanne had said, and my concerns. Her. Helen. Ivan. Wendy.

He advised against basing theories on rumors and

gently reminded me that what seemed the case most often was the case. Things seldom were as convoluted as, perhaps, I was making Helen's death out to be.

He never said murder was an impossibility, but neither did he encourage the idea. Still, he seemed troubled by the writing on the Dumpster and suggested I call the police to point it out, in case they'd missed it.

"You know," he said, apropos of the rumors Roxanne had hoped to dispel, "the ladies of your book group make a pretty poor argument for marriage."

Before I could even say "huh?" which is what *I'd* have said, my mother spoke. She was on a cruise, far away, but it was her voice I heard in my brain. *What is wrong with this man? Why is he so obsessively antimarriage? What does he have against it?*

My mother was haunting me.

Or I was becoming my mother, which was a much more terrifying prospect.

"There are ten of you, right?" Mackenzie asked.

I nodded.

"All of an age to marry or to have married, correct again?"

I resented his need for verification.

"So Faith—the one who works at city hall?"

"I know who Faith is."

"She's a widow, and Wendy has been engaged since Queen Victoria was on the throne. Two more are divorced—Clary and Louisa, correct? And Louisa's been married what, three times?"

I was impressed by his ability to remember those names and their marital status—and then, of course, I wondered why that data had registered so powerfully on him. And again, Mama boogied in, whispering this time, but a stage whisper, inescapable: *What is wrong with this man?*

"Denise?"

I nodded. "Her first, his second. He was a widower."

"Tess and Susan, also married. That's it, correct?"

"Helen. She was married, or don't you count her now that she's dead?"

He looked surprised. "Testy, are you? Why?"

I did not choose to answer. If he'd listened really clearly, he would have heard my mother questioning his psychological stability. "You forgot me, too," I said.

"Never."

"You did. One more single."

"Right."

A totally unsatisfactory response. I thought he'd either compliment me on my liberated free self or make his meaning clear.

"Anyway," he went on, "now you're saying that Roxanne, one of the married ones, is probably messing with Helen's husband."

"Mackenzie, what is the point of these calculations?"

"Thinking about it, is all. I mean, does it frighten you seein' Louisa with her three marriages and a kid from each? Or Clary? You told me they were bitter divorces."

"I don't see what relevance their lives and mistakes have with my choices."

"Really?"

"Really!" I snapped. *This is not a normal, healthy set of questions,* my mother said. *The man is pathologically afraid of marriage. Or of something.* "Shut up," I muttered.

"What?"

"Talking to myself."

I OFTEN DAYDREAM ABOUT A LIFE THAT'S LIKE A LINEAR narrative. A story that moves from A to B without a detour, sidetrack, interruption, or distraction, that starts at the beginning and moves forward to a conclusion.

That sounds elegant and purposeful, clean and straightforward.

It might be boring, but there are long periods of time when boring sounds irresistible. I'd love the chance to try it out.

The next morning wasn't my chance. Before I was out of bed, I felt consumed by sorrow. Petra and Helen had been with me all night, both asking for something I didn't know how to provide.

And on a much more mundane level, nor did I know how to dress. I dragged myself out of bed, but overnight, the contents of my closet had turned to ill-fitting rags. My blue slacks, which would have been acceptable, were still at the cleaners, and my white linen blouse was missing a button, and I couldn't make any other objects in my wardrobe coordinate.

My hair was having an even worse day than I was, and every spray and goop and pomade I applied only intensified its problems.

When I turned on the radio to get a weather forecast, I heard yet another ad for the overfunded jerk Roy Stanton talking about the good old days. I snapped it off.

I realized with dismay that I hadn't finished—actually, I hadn't even begun going over a homework assignment on found poems that should have been handed back today. I knew the class had enjoyed the project and some were quite proud of their work, but I'd wasted a lot of time the night before wondering if I was, indeed, turning into my mother.

Instead, I was turning into a failure at everything. At teaching, at dressing, and at being a human being, a friend, a helper.

I couldn't even boost my energy, if not my spirits, with a cup of coffee. Our state-of-the-art coffeemaker went belly up with a blue shot of light and a stench that didn't change the downhill direction of the morning. It left a scorch mark on the butcher-block surface. I left home.

En route to school, the heavens sprung a leak. Were I a nineteenth-century poet, I might think they were sympathizing with my sad state. But I was a twentieth-century teacher without a raincoat, so I knew this was happening simply to spite me. Or perhaps, to further punish me.

Nothing improved with my arrival at Philly Prep. Before I entered the school, in the hundred feet or so outside the building, I had two confrontations with students, one of whom had made a bad situation worse, and the other of whom believed that I had done precisely the same thing.

Bonnie must have been waiting near where I always park my car, because I yelped as she all but leapt out at me. "I wanted to be sure and catch you!" she said.

"You've heard from Petra?" Maybe the day was looking up, then, despite the misty rain slowly soaking my hair.

She shook her head. "Ethan."

Forgive me. I hadn't had my daily infusion of caffeine. My head was still wet outside, but still half-asleep inside. I must have looked blank.

"You know, Petra's . . . you know. The guy."

"He got in touch with you?"

She nodded solemnly. She wore a slicker and a cute waterproof hat I envied. "Last night. He called from college. His mother gave him my number. So at first he was okay." She shrugged. "Like he thought maybe I'd called him up to invite him somewhere. Then I said I was a friend of Petra Yates, did he know who she was, and he got weird. He knew who I meant." That seemed the end of her tale, as far as she saw it.

"And?" A drizzlette dropped off my eyebrow. Bonnie

was frightened and needed contact, but that didn't mean we had to do it in the rain.

She kept her eyes away from mine, looked slightly to the left of me, and when she spoke, her voice was hesitant and low. "He hollered at me. Said I was harassing him. Said he'd done all he was going to do about Petra. I said, Ha! I knew what he'd done and I knew what had happened because of what he'd done, and he said he was hanging up but that his father was a lawyer and he'd take legal action to stop me if I didn't stop pestering him and calling his mother, and I said . . . I said . . ." And again, the head shaking and eyes everywhere on the horizon except at me.

"Said what?"

"He made me mad. I wasn't pestering him or anything! I just thought maybe, maybe she'd called him, that he knew what she was doing, or something, that was all."

I nodded, waiting. What could she have done?

"I told him she had disappeared and the police knew about it and they knew what he'd done because I'd given them his name and they suspected foul play."

"Tell me you're kidding."

She wouldn't look at me.

"It isn't like that anymore," I said. "People don't kill girls just because they're—"

"If they're desperate, they could. If they have Petra's parents and if they're in college and this underage girl's father would kill him . . . Okay. Maybe I shouldn't have said it, but I was *mad*. I'm scared about her and he should have been, too. So I told him everybody knew she was dead and he was the prime suspect."

I closed my eyes, as if that would erase what she was saying.

"I said he should expect official visitors. Soon."

Only now did she look up at me. Her expression—a bit belatedly, thought I—was anxious.

I couldn't think of what to say. Mostly I wanted to shake her, to ask why she'd behaved like an idiot, escalating something already bad into all manner of hideous possibilities.

I was worried for her. I was already worried for Petra. But I now was worried for myself, as well. As with, for starters, the avenging lawyer father who found out that I was Petra's confidante. I was in this, and I shouldn't have been—according to the law, I absolutely shouldn't have been because I was not Petra's parent.

But what was the point of further agitating Bonnie? What would that make better? I tried soothing her instead, floating meaningless syllables that seemed sufficiently like English. ". . . frightened him . . . surely he won't . . . your anger may have . . . no cause to worry about . . . apparently he doesn't know . . . not to worry unduly if . . ."

"I'm afraid he'll call my parents. Then I'll be in trouble and so will Petra."

Petra already was in trouble in the old-fashioned sense. And, I feared, also in a more contemporary all-purpose sense.

Worse, except for having produced one very frightened and furious young undergrad, we hadn't moved one inch closer to finding Petra.

I took a deep breath. "It'll be all right, Bonnie," I said. "You'll see. If I were you, I'd keep this between us. The police are looking for her, and it doesn't seem as if this boy knows anything." I wondered if I meant what I was saying. Could the unthinkable have happened? A millennial replay of *An American Tragedy*? What else could so violently shake young people besides the idea that their futures and dreams had been canceled by an accidental pregnancy? But that was then. My mother's generation, not mine, and not Petra's or Ethan's. The good old days, as Roy Stanton and few women would say.

Still, until Bonnie had said that, I hadn't considered the idea that Petra might have come to harm—except for the harm she would be doing herself on the streets or as a runaway. Now, the idea was there, as improbable as it still seemed. I told myself that this boy had simply been rattled, and that Bonnie had behaved ludicrously, over-dramatically, and it all added up to nothing. "Can you keep this our secret for a while?"

She nodded.

I had to think, but didn't feel capable of doing so because all thoughts led to dead ends. I couldn't picture what would be improved by bringing Ethan into the mix, or telling Petra's parents or the police about him. I thought it would only increase the potential for hysteria, punishment, and retaliation.

Or was I simply not thinking, and would, perhaps, things be worse because of not doing so?

I wished that once, just once, I'd have a clear sense of what I was supposed to do.

Thirteen

I WAS BARELY INTO THE SCHOOL, STILL IN THE FRONT entry, when I spotted Gretchen Coulter outside, looking dislocated and uncomfortable. I walked down and over to her, surprised to see her.

I couldn't tell if she was glad or further upset by my approach. "Gretchen," I said. "I want to say how terribly sorry I am—everybody is—about your mother. It's so sad. My sympathy."

She looked suspicious of my words and motives.

"If there's anything I can do—"

"I didn't know what to do at home, anymore," she said.

I nodded. "It's good to be with other people." I hoped I wasn't as inane as I thought I was.

"Miss Pepper," she said when we were back at the school's entryway. "There is something."

"Yes. What? Anything!"

"Please don't be angry, but I know what you're doing, what you think, and I wish you'd stop. You're making everything worse."

"But I—what? What do you mean?"

"About my *mother*." Gretchen was a pretty child, with much of her mother visible in her face and personality. Because of her dyslexia, she'd had a dreadful time in a competitive elementary school, and now was with us. Once she began coping with her disability, she showed signs of becoming the firebrand that Helen had been. Today she was understandably subdued, but I still saw a spark of that other self as she said the word *mother*.

"I know you think you're being helpful, but you aren't. My father's really upset and you're making him more upset. He's—please just stop!"

I took a deep breath. "What, precisely, am I doing?" I hadn't, as far as I could tell, done one damn thing. Except notify the police about the Dumpster, which hardly seemed something to further disrupt the Coulters.

She eyed me coldly. "You know. Saying my mother didn't . . . you know." She looked down, twisted her lowered head to an odd angle, as if trying to avoid seeing everything that surrounded her. "Didn't . . . do it on purpose," she finally said. "*Investigating* as if . . . somebody . . . even as if my father . . ."

"How—why—where did you hear this?"

"Mrs. Parisi."

Roxanne? Why on earth would any well-meaning adult trouble this child with such— "She shouldn't have—"

"I made her. I was looking out my window, I saw you. I heard you ring the bell, and then I saw you talking. I asked her what it was about, and she told me."

Nobody had made Roxanne tell this child anything. Roxanne wanted to, and now I wanted to know why.

"Did you even know my mother?" Gretchen asked me. "Why do you think that way?"

"There's no way that I think, Gretchen. Not yet. Only that we should be absolutely sure before we make up—"

"We? Who does that mean? My father and me, we're sure. And I don't know why her book group should even care, should even think about it. They weren't so nice to her."

"What are you talking about? Who wasn't?"

She shrugged. "That day, before the meeting at our house. My mother told me that maybe she wasn't going to stay in the book group. That she didn't feel comfortable there anymore, that she didn't like being around this one person, and that if I ever felt like I didn't want to be around somebody, be somewhere I didn't feel good about, I should know that I could leave it." Her voice, driven by anger and possibly grief, had regained its usual animation and force. "So it's none of any of your business! And you're making my father crazy!"

"Me?" It was almost a whisper. "Why?"

"He said it wasn't as if we didn't already have enough problems, that you and the other women were pawing over my mother's life, like . . ." She blinked rapidly and pulled her lips in.

"Oh, Gretchen. Forgive me. The last thing I meant to do was add to your pain. I'm really sorry."

Her shoulders slumped. "Whatever." She turned and went into the school.

Luckily, there was no chance to say more, because I'd have had to lie. For all my dismay at having created more problems for the remaining family, I still needed to know who Helen Coulter had been so that then I could know if I believed she killed herself. I still wanted to know what had really happened to Helen Coulter, largely for Gretchen's sake. The child couldn't say the words *suicide* or *jump*. I'd seen how those ideas seared her insides. But now, I also wanted to know why thinking of other scenarios so infuriated Ivan Coulter—the man who had been missing the day of Helen's death. And why Roxanne had felt compelled to inform father and daughter of what should have remained quiet, nonintrusive speculation.

Surely by now the family had noticed the Dumpster graffiti. What did they make of that?

I walked into the building feeling pounds heavier than

I had just ten minutes earlier, wondering what any of this meant.

THE DAY, WHICH HADN'T BEGUN WELL, DID NOT IM-prove. My tenth-grade class had been stricken with mass amnesia. No one had ever heard of a part of speech or suspected that there could be such a thing, let alone felt capable of defining such difficult concepts as *noun*. Instead, a hoarsely disguised voice called out from the back of the class, "I know, I know! 'Four score and twenty.' Period. That's a part of a speech!"

"Yeah—'ask not what.' That's another part of a speech."

"How about 'Romeo, Romeo, wherefore'?"

I never said my kids lacked humor of a sort. But course content, things that had been repeated and reinforced since September—that, I do say, they lacked.

In truth, I was impressed they'd known bits of the Gettysburg Address, JFK's inaugural, and Juliet's soliloquy. They shared the great cultural heritage of the U.S. And we'd all been so needlessly worried in recent years about the loss of that basic core.

It had been such a clever, well-planned lesson, too, based on actual examples from their work. I thought they were getting the idea why "He told him that if he hit him, he'd feel even worse," a direct quote from one of my student-writers, was not sufficiently clear. But that was when they decided that they had no idea what a pronoun was. Or any other part of speech. Or an antecedent. Or, for that matter, clarity.

My next class was somewhat intrigued by—emphasis on *somewhat*—and somewhat participated in—again, emphasis on *somewhat*—a discussion of Hawthorne's observation that love and hate are the same things at bottom, both requiring "a high degree of intimacy and

heart-knowledge," each making the person dependent
on the other for his spiritual life. For once, they were
roused—somewhat—from the ravages of spring fever,
but while that should have gladdened my heart, I kept
thinking about their missing class member, wondering
when or if we'd get news of Petra, and whether I should
be telling what I knew, and to whom. I wondered how
avidly her parents were trying to find her, and tried to
stifle a sick fear that they might be willing to leave things
as they were—that after a feeble show of interest, they'd
"accept" the status quo and go on with a post-Petra life.

A child could be unwanted at any point along the way,
and most bitter of all was being unwanted long after
birth, as Petra seemed to be.

Finally, the day redeemed itself by ending. Almost. Because as I repacked my briefcase, my editor in chief approached, her face in a self-satisfied smirk that made me
immediately suspicious. Cinnamon waved a translucent
lime plastic envelope.

I love things like that envelope. Love stationery. Con-
tainers for pens, desk organizers, lovely creations for the
most mundane of objects. I promised myself a half dozen
of these shiny, slick objects as my reward for this dismal
day. I'd put each class's papers in a different colored one
and my entire life would turn around and be serene. Organized. Linear.

"We've reached a consensus." Cinnamon waved the
lime envelope. Lines of type showed through its front.
She smiled broadly. "Consensus. Good word, huh?"

I nodded and walked alongside her. "We don't have
journalism today," I reminded her.

"Right. Correct. I know that."

This was very fast, this new material. An entire newspaper's worth overnight? "Did you write this yourself?"

"No, Ms. Pepper. That would be wrong. It's not my

paper, it's the students' paper. I called a special emergency meeting last night. To make the coverage more comprehensive, the way you said. My staff and I were up half the night."

I glanced at her to see if she was amusing herself, but apparently, she took her role seriously, although not seriously enough to have informed me that the suddenly avid journalists of Philly Prep had held a meeting.

"I realized that we should have called you—and in fact, I did call you, but you were out. Your machine answered, so I hung up. What was the point?"

I considered dragging myself through an explanation of the point, or stating that I had indeed been home and I knew she was lying, but I was exhausted, and poorly dressed, and had bad hair. I merely said, "Next time . . ." Of course, as we both knew, there'd be no next time. This was the final issue of the year.

"Oh, sure. But for now, it's done. Just what you wanted. The spectrum has widened and it's not just prom fashions anymore. We have goals, and we have what people are doing next year, and we have columns of memories like you suggested. Lots of new things. We talked through all your points, and I think you'll be happy. We sure are."

"So quickly! I'm amazed by your speed," I said.

"They may need editing, I'm not saying they wouldn't, but we are in *essence* done. Ready to put the paper to bed!" She held her shiny lime envelope aloft as if it were a trophy.

Her high spirits wedged under my mood and lifted it. I wished I could track Cinnamon through her life, see what she did, how she behaved. I often have those wishes, and when I'm dictator of the world, there'll be a law about this, too. Students who expect teachers to invest time, energy, wisdom, knowledge, and their very souls in the student's life and welfare would be obliged once a year to report back on how all that effort panned out.

"And pretty much everybody's in it, too, so that's great. Nobody hurt. No bad feelings for the last issue. That's what I think."

I had no argument with that. I was amazed by—and suspicious of—Cinnamon Stickley's easy, complete, and speedy concession. I was also relieved that without my throwing a pedagogical fit, our final issue wouldn't be 100 percent devoted to "Philly Phashions."

"Want to go over this with me now?" I asked.

"Would love to, but I can't. Got to run. Have a fitting. My prom dress, Ms. Pepper! Time's running out. Happy reading! You chaperoning this year?"

I shook my head, pretending solemn regret. C. K. and I had done it last year and felt we'd served our time. It was fun seeing them in their finery. For a while. Then the gray zone between participant and police person became onerous and endless.

"Ooooh, too bad. I wanted you to see my gown. We'll miss you!" She looked crestfallen—another charade—and was off.

Once in my car, while going through the familiar end-of-day malaise, I untwisted the white thread looped around the envelope's button clasp, and pulled out the revised copy. I was indeed amazed by how industrious, productive, and swift the staff had been about shifting gears from the stupid "Phashion" issue.

Until I read the first "new" and "comprehensive" article. I then quickly thumbed through the thirty or forty remaining pages.

In fairness, the articles now did have a wider scope—Cinnamon style. The issue of what followed high school had been addressed—Cinnamon style. Ambitions and dreams had been included—Cinnamon style. So now, a typical in-depth, broad-focus article read:

"Marsha Malloy, who hopes to attend Community College next year to become an international lawyer, will be wearing a bare-shouldered, shape-defining café-au-lait silk sheath with an overlay of silk organza, with contoured yet thin straps made of black Spanish lace with a floral motif. This lace is repeated at the hemline, which is scalloped . . ."

In case you're wondering, Marsha Malloy's black extremely high-heeled sandals were by an Italian designer, Mediterranean in spirit, and pleasantly accented by a thin strip of mirror inserted into the back of the heel.

And her wrap? A cashmere shawl in the same café-au-lait as the dress, should you think the journalism had been shoddy or incomplete.

One of the touted new features was a special Philly Phashion Awards for nonprom clothes of distinction.

And another was "Phashion Phailures": a "clothes we wish we hadn't worn" trip-down-memory-lane column.

Score: Cinnamon, ten; me, zip. How had I been so easily flummoxed?

I dreaded the battles ahead because they'd be so necessary, so tedious, and to so little point. I repacked the pages, started my car, then wondered where to go.

I was reluctant to go into the empty loft, but I couldn't think of anyplace I had to go and I lacked the imagination to spontaneously invent a destination. Briefly, I considered another raincoat run, but remembering Gretchen's anguished expression and the pain I'd inadvertently caused her—and was probably going to continue causing—I vetoed the idea.

A lot about Ivan Coulter troubled me. I didn't know why he, of all people, should want to believe Helen committed suicide. Or more precisely, I could think of a reason why, but I didn't want to. I didn't want Gretchen to lose both her parents, one to death, the other to prison.

All I was trying to do was find out who Helen had been. Round out the picture so that we could possibly present some ideas to the police about the suicide. Or the accident. Or the murder.

Why should that bother anyone except a murderer? If there was one.

I didn't want an empty house. I wanted people. Happy people, wherever I could find them. A make-believe community. Were I another variety of person, I'd head for a department store or mall, but I wasn't a shopper, not even when vaguely agitated, as now. However, it was a beautiful day that made walking a pleasure, and it even made the idea of cooking dinner sound enjoyable. It was a day on which everything should be dreamy and perfect—so I headed to Reading Terminal Market. Food shopping was in a special category of its own. Infinitely easier than finding the right dress, or gift, or pair of shoes. And people were happy contemplating an abundance of food.

Maybe the bustling market would fill me up with itself, and for a few minutes, I could stop obsessing about the two lost women: Helen and Petra.

Maybe. It was certainly worth a try.

Fourteen

PHILADELPHIA IS REALLY A COLLECTION OF SMALL TOWNS called neighborhoods, and my village in the heart of the city is no exception.

And when you further narrow the population to middle-class women who don't have to worry about where their next meal is coming from—aside from the sense of which store will deliver or produce it—the odds are actually in favor of meeting someone you know when you're in a public space devoted to food.

So it wasn't peculiar or even unusual, and it surely wasn't an omen or a sign of anything that I bumped into another villager at the Market.

I'd wandered through the aisles, cheered by the Market's very existence. I walked as quickly as possible past the Lancaster farmers and their sticky buns, shoofly pie, and freshly baked pretzels. I felt irresistibly drawn to Iovine Brothers Produce, to orderly piles of vegetables blazing in crayon colors. If I couldn't have that straight-ahead life, I could have healthy. At that moment, I believed that if I ate only primary colors and shapes, circles and ovals, my life would take on the purity of what I ingested.

History suggested that by the time I got home and began chopping and steaming, I'd have lost my enthusiasm—I've had these fits before—and, often, my very appetite for vegetables. Didn't matter.

None of that stopped me ogling everything plump and perishable, the better for it to die a slow death at the back of my refrigerator.

I stood in front of exotic mushrooms—amazed by hedgehogs and red-skinned lobsters, chanterelles, black trumpets—and decided on a wild mushroom sauce on pasta that evening. Maybe mushrooms and eggplant. And peppers? I swooned into a delirious vegetable reverie.

"Mandy!"

My name ruptured my happy cocoon and mood. I was not meant to meditate, not even about pasta toppings.

My fellow forager was Wendy Loeb, who smiled and waved a hand holding a bunch of asparagus. The engagement ring that had been worn for ten years sparked and glittered with each motion. I mentally added tender spring tips to my mushroom medley, but left a five-carat diamond off the shopping list. "One sec!" she called.

Wendy was a cheery woman who preferred the sunny side of the street, which is possibly why she was able to overlook the duration of her engagement and her fiancé's less-than-savory reputation.

She may have been shopping for asparagus, but she'd already invested in handmade chocolates. "I should not have bought these," she said as she bustled over. "I swore that God could strike me dead if I ate even one piece. It's for company, I told myself, and I knew I was lying even as I said it. If just once that lightning bolt would come through the window like my mother promised, I'd change my ways. For now, I'll stop weighing myself, is all."

She was short and round and it worked and seemed right, but she was always planning to change her dimensions. "Whatcha got?" She peered into my tote. "Oh, sure," she said. "No wonder you don't worry about your weight."

I had three slender eggplants, those wild mushrooms, a head of elephant garlic, and four tomatoes. I was already experiencing mild postveggie *tristesse*, but in a mean-spirited lack of sisterhood, I didn't let on. Wendy wouldn't be around when later tonight I'd curse myself for not having bought cake or the fabulous exotic takeout that was everywhere around me.

She suggested we have a drink of something, and I realized how thirsty I was for both drink and the comforts of companionship. We found a spot at the Down Home Diner's counter. Behind us, the splendid old jukebox played a Fifties tune with lots of *uh-oh*s as lyrics. I couldn't believe any teens had ever liked such a stupid song.

I'm not sure why I thought this would be time out, a respite from the confusions of late. I'd bumped into Wendy before around town. Apparently, real estate wheeling and dealing didn't occupy all day every day, and Wendy loved to shop for almost anything. So in the past, we'd had enjoyable drinks of coffee, wine, or as today, iced tea. I expected only that. Normal schmoozing. Wendy ordered a cruller along with her drink. "I hate to occupy a seat for such a pathetically small purchase as an iced tea," she said. She'd said something along those lines wherever we'd taken our breaks in the past.

Normal.

We weren't more than three or four sips into our tea when Helen's name came up. However, that was within the realm of normal and ordinary. Helen was part of what bridged the two of us, and she was on both our minds.

Wendy leaned forward. "Listen," she said, and because I was already listening, I knew we were leaving the predictable paths. I didn't know *where* we were headed, but I knew we weren't staying on familiar turf. Good-bye normal.

"I don't want to sound like a gossip, or be catty," she said, "but there's something you should know, given that we're trying to piece together what was real and what wasn't about Helen. Trying to understand how she could have done it."

"*If* she did it."

"I wasn't going to say that," Wendy said even more softly. She gnawed on the cruller, waiting until she swallowed and drank more tea before continuing. "It sounds—it suggests stuff I don't want to think about."

I waited.

"So you're probably talking to everybody."

"I haven't," I said. "In fact, I haven't contacted anybody yet. Happened to bump into Roxanne yesterday when I tried to—"

Wendy sighed and nodded, as if that's what she'd expected. And dreaded. "Roxanne," she said. "You know, I love her. I love how she dresses and thinks, and I don't want this to sound the wrong way if I say you'll have to take whatever she said—whatever she might say—with a grain of salt. With a whole shaker of salt."

She was going to tell me those rumors about Roxanne and Ivan, and I didn't want her to. If Roxanne had been right about the ruined partnership, then maybe Wendy had things she'd as soon keep hidden, like a grievance against Helen, who'd squelched the deal.

Wendy looked embarrassed. "I'm sorry. I'm being . . . I just hate saying these things, but look, the thing is, I think Roxanne and Ivan Coulter may be more than friends again. You know they were an item in college, don't you? I know that was long ago, but those things happen."

"Why would you think that?"

"People talk. And Roxanne's so desperate and needy this past year, and she mentions Ivan all out of proportion to his being her neighbor, or a piece of her past."

"They're friends. They were all friends."

"True. Except . . . how friendly? She's a woman alone, and those things happen."

"You mean her husband traveling so much?"

Wendy sat back and looked at me, wide-eyed. "I can't believe you bought her story," she said. "I mean everybody knows."

"Well, I don't."

"I feel as uncomfortable as you do," Wendy said. "That's why I did that song and dance before I started. But this isn't gossip, Amanda. This is fact."

"What is?" I glanced at my watch, then counted out coins and put my collection on top of my receipt. It had gotten damp at the edges from my iced-tea glass.

"Don't rush away. I promise I'm not . . . let me ask you this. What do you know about Roxanne Parisi?"

I zipped my purse, thought fleetingly of the vegetables heating up in my tote, becoming ever less appetizing, and I shrugged. "That she's a freelancer. Writes well. I've seen her articles in the *Inquirer Magazine* and elsewhere. That she's got her own sense of style, her own way of painting her surroundings. That she has no kids and Larry travels a great deal for business. That I suspect her favorite color is peacock blue and she likes books that deal with women's issues. But what does that say? How could I do that for anybody, truly describe them, say what I know? How could I do it for you?"

"Well, for starters, if you were describing me, you'd know I was engaged, but not married, right?"

I nodded.

"Roxanne is neither engaged nor married. Larry left her a year ago. He isn't in Saudi Arabia. He's twenty-five minutes away in King of Prussia. With another woman. People have spotted him. At least three people in the book group that I know of."

"But . . . she . . . the updates, the letters she mentions?"

Wendy shook her head. "He's filed for divorce. She's heartsick, and I think by now she may honestly believe he's really far away. And that makes her much more desperate."

"How could—if people saw him, if people knew she wasn't being honest—why didn't anybody ever say a word?"

Wendy smiled, rather wistfully. "Because we're friends. Because we like her and this is part of her mourning process. Nobody's saying it's healthy to be in this degree of denial, but what good was it going to do to tell her secret? She knows that I know. I've suggested she go for counseling, but I don't know if she has. She needs to do this, Mandy. Right now, she needs to believe what she needs to believe. It won't matter—she'll be divorced soon whatever she pretends."

I had a lot to learn about friendship, not to mention what I had to learn about reality. And about who spoke truly and who twisted the facts to fit.

I felt dizzy. The iced tea had gone to my head.

"You should keep notes," Mackenzie said after dinner. We sat happily satiated. The plates that had held my version of pasta primavera were empty, and only I gave a thought, I'm sure, to the surplus veggies that were, even now, facing fuzzy futures in my fridge.

Mackenzie wasn't thinking about redundant produce. He was contemplating the tidbits I'd fed him along with the pasta—Roxanne on Helen and Ivan, Wendy on Roxanne, and Gretchen on me, with mention, too, of Ivan and the unknown book club member who made Helen uncomfortable. "Given that they're all contradictin' each other, write down precisely who said what. Need to know the source before you know its worth, and soon, it'll blur all up."

I knew he was right. I was already less than totally sure who'd said what, or whether any specific piece of what had been said mattered.

"Decide later if it's important. For now, note it all down. If it's a rumor or hearsay, note that, too."

I sighed. "It's a puzzle, this portrait of Helen. I thought it would be less depressing. I mean of course it's depressing— it's dreadful. She's dead and that's all wrong. But now it's more than that."

He held up the wine bottle, offering a refill, and I nodded. "I'd think you'd enjoy the process, based on my past observation of you."

I shook my head. "Those were different. Those were other people's secrets."

"So's this one."

"Not really. Those were other people's people. These are my people, my book group. Mine. That makes every-thing anyone's said so far disheartening."

"Why so?"

"I want to believe people are what they say. I want to believe that Helen and Ivan Coulter had a good mar-riage, that Roxanne's husband really does travel too much. I wanted to believe—"

"In the sanctity and public face of marriage? Of arrangements? With your book group as the shining ex-ample of wedded bliss?"

"Don't start that up again. We've done this, Mac-kenzie." Ever since his dinner with the much-married idiot friend, Mackenzie had been searching for antimar-riage evidence. This morning, he'd read me an item about a man who'd blasted his wife and children into eternity, then turned the gun on himself. When I commented that such stories were lamentably common, he'd said, "How true. My point, in fact."

I forced us back on topic. "I want to believe in who people say they are. How they behave. How they react to what they read. I want to believe the evidence of my eyes and ears. I love the book group—and love what I thought was the feeling we have for each other. A warm respect and enjoyment. Bookfriends. Something pretty wonderful. Now, I don't know what to think. Is my image of every single person going to turn out to be false?"

"Maybe not false. But somewhat created," Mackenzie said. "We all wear public masks to some extent. Except for this guy," and he chucked Macavity under his graying chin.

The cat occupied one of the chairs around the oak table. Biding his time, I knew, in the hopes a scrap would be left behind when I cleared the table—forbidden territory, but only when I was looking. "You're a carnivore, dummy," I reminded him. "You're in for a big disappointment tonight."

"The cat is what he is, and he's delighted about it," Mackenzie said. "And he expects that you are, too. Therefore, there's no reason whatsoever for a secret." They were ridiculously good buddies, my two Macs, forever purring at or praising one another. "But," Mackenzie added, "cats are in a class by themselves."

"So what are you saying? That I should teach my cat to read and form a feline book circle?"

"I'm sayin' that what I've learned out there is that pretty much everybody has something they'd rather gloss over or bury. A secret. Except me, of course."

I laughed. "You! That's rich, Chaim! Oh, no—wait, I meant Canute. Hey—maybe your parents stuttered and that's both your names—Canute Knute. It has a distinct

zing and rhythm, although I can see why you'd keep it
your secret."

"You have secrets, too, don't you?"

"Me?" I was without guile. "I'm the sucker, that's
what makes me so angry. I'm the fall guy. An open book.
I believe people."

He raised one eyebrow. "No secrets, then?"

I thought of my hideous new understanding that I was
becoming my mother, those Mackenzie hot flashes, un-
shared bursts of resentment about his skewed take on
marriage. I wondered how many other secrets I had.

"Like I was sayin', take notes. At some point you'll see
things that fit and things you should forget about because they're one person's gossip, not corroborated."

"What about that *liar* graffiti outside Helen's house?"
Canute Knute beat a pleasant rhythm in my brain.

"I'm sure they're makin' note of it."

"But what? What are they making of it?"

"Not my department. Not in fact a homicide case, at
least not yet. Isn't that what's got you going? Isn't that
the point of exposing those secrets?"

A sudden realization produced a nervous mix of jubila-
tion and anxiety. He wasn't saying stop what you're doing
and leave those secrets alone. He was, in fact, prodding a
bit, urging me to keep good notes, to remember the purpose of gathering information about Helen. "You aren't
discouraging me, are you? You're actually, in your fashion,
encouraging me. That isn't like you, Mackenzie. What's
the story?"

He grinned. Add that happy, almost catlike self-satisfied
expression to that list of assets. "Isn't a man supposed to
be supportive? Aren't those the current rules?"

I brushed that away. "A person's history matters.
Whether or not it's admissible in court, the past helps

you decide who they are, maybe predict what they'll do. Am I not correct?"

"You most assuredly are." Macavity, an oversize, over-weight lump of dust-colored fur, was by now on C. K.'s lap and purring so loudly he seemed a background refrain.

"Well, your history is clear on one thing—you do not approve of my curiosity."

"Snoopin'?"

"Intellectual curiosity."

"Not trustin' public servants such as yours truly to do the job?"

"Whatever. You don't approve of it. So why change now, unless you think it's a harmless little expedition, that Helen did commit suicide and I won't and can't do any harm. You're probably humoring me. Is that it?"

He smiled again. Macavity, without being able to see the smile, nonetheless upped the purr to a small roar.

"Come on," I said. "Tell me."

"Nope," Mackenzie said. "That's my secret."

Fifteen

THE PHONE RANG. IF IT HADN'T, WE MIGHT STILL BE SIT-ting across that oak table, eyes squinted at each other, searching for secrets that weren't about to be found.

But the phone did ring.

"Hey, it's Susan," she said, sounding remarkably chipper. "Where've you been? You never write, you never call. What kind of a partner are you?"

"I don't have much to offer yet."

"How are we going to crack this if you don't keep in touch?" Her tone made me queasy. "Guess what," she said. "Guess what, guess what?"

"Judging by the way you sound, you must have discovered the cure for cancer."

"The *book*! I have it!"

The book. As if there were precisely one such object on earth? "Which book? Yours? You've finished your book, is that what you're saying?"

"*Helen's* book. See, Clary's name was on the list for this thing."

"Back up. I've had wine or I'm just stupid, but Helen wasn't writing a book, and what's this about Clary? In fact, what's *this thing*?"

"Okay, listen. It's Helen's notebook—the one she wrote her suicide note in. I have it because our firm's doing work for—do not scream—Roy Stanton's election campaign."

I did not scream. I did not make a sound. Silently, I disapproved.

"I don't like his politics either, but I do like paying the rent and keeping my job. He has this fund-raiser tonight, and our firm does that kind of thing—the lists, the celebrity speakers—you know the drill. Denise tossed the business my way, and what was I supposed to do? Say I didn't appreciate her money? Say my boss didn't really appreciate me more because of her money? I mean . . ."

At least she no longer sounded giddy. But then something else struck me. "Hold it—Clary's name was on the list for the fund-raiser? Our Clary?"

"Uh-huh."

"Clary supports Roy Stanton Harris?" She of the fiercely feminist views on independence, on choice, on self-determination?

"The business bought a table for his dinner. Her business."

Used to be hers and Helen's. I didn't correct Susan, but I thought sadly of how quickly a person begins to disappear. I shook my head in disapproval, even though only Mackenzie could see me doing it. He pretended to be engrossed in tempting Macavity with a feathery cat toy even though the cat wasn't having any of it. What Mackenzie was doing was eavesdropping.

"You know," I told Susan, "if Helen weren't already dead, this alone would kill her."

"She knew. It was a sore point between the two of them."

Knowing Helen, this sore would have been septic and festering. A major bad thing.

"In fact, Helen insisted that *only* Clary's name and the name of the business be listed. Helen thought it was a disgraceful use of their funds, but Clary thinks it's smart to cover all possibilities, no matter her own emotions. Never hurts to have a friend in Washington, she says. Besides, he's the probusiness candidate—"

"And the antiwomen one, as well!"

"She says, 'Personal feelings,' and I'm directly quoting now, 'don't enter into this.' Her vote remains her vote, and private."

I understood the pragmatism, but it still annoyed me. That's how evil flourished, by people being "practical," tolerating the intolerant, putting on blinders for selfishly pragmatic reasons.

But Clary's ability to juggle opposing opinions for the sake of business—and for that matter, Susan's—were not why Susan had phoned. "The book," I said. "Helen's note. You really have it?"

"I have a copy of all the written-on pages."

"How'd you get them?"

"Clary copied them for me."

"She has it, not the police?"

"It isn't evidence of a crime, Amanda. They've been through it a thousand times, and it's what it seems to be—a sort of doodle pad. And it doesn't have much that's particularly gripping except for that so-called suicide note. Meanwhile, I asked, and she did it, once I saw her name on the contributors' list."

"You blackmailed her."

"I'd prefer not to call it that. I merely acknowledged what she'd said, that business is business. Let's be honest—neither one of us has any morals. Besides, she didn't want the thing. Nobody does. She said even Ivan didn't want it around. It bothered him."

"What do you want with it?"

"I don't think other people have read it—read into it—the way we'll be able to."

Now I understood the manic glee. The return of Susan the mystery fan and writer, giddily expecting clues, a hidden code that she or I would recognize and crack on the spot. I wished I hadn't gotten myself into this.

"Anyway," she said, "I have it with me right now, so why don't you come over?"

I checked the clock. Seven-thirty. Dishes still to do.

"I've read through it," Susan said. "Now you should. We could compare notes tomorrow. I have to be in Delaware all day, but we could have an early dinner with our men. Introduce them. Come get it."

"Where are you?" I asked. "At home?"

"No. A short walk away from you. Come on—it's a beautiful evening. I'll provide the properly mysterious atmosphere. Imagine it. Night falls on the waterfront, on the river and the pier. A woman passes information. All we need is a foghorn, right? Except there's no fog."

"Where are you?"

"At Roy Stanton's fund-raiser. I thought I explained. At the *Moshulu*."

Now at least the talk about rivers and piers made sense. The *Moshulu* was a handsome old sailing ship now serving time as a restaurant on the river.

"I'm making nice to the one thousand Philadelphians herein gathered," Susan said. "You should see it—the deck's tented and the ballroom's splendid. Very grand. I have had worse assignments, trust me."

"It's too late."

"It's seven-thirty! What kind of slug are you? Take a romantic stroll along the river. Have a drink. We can hang out."

"With Roy Stanton's friends? No way."

"We'll go in the bar. Nowhere near them. Or don't have a drink. I already talked a little with Clary about the stuff—"

"She's there?"

"I told you, she bought a table."

That didn't mean she had to be there, did it?

"Don't you want to see the pages? The note?"

Only mildly, to tell the truth. And not enough to rouse myself into action. Susan sounded as if she were playing a game that I had never agreed to. As for me, I was having a temporary bout of sanity. Probably the after-effect of an overly healthy meal. But a walk in the summery evening air did sound good. I covered the mouthpiece. "How'd you like to take a walk down to the *Moshulu*?" I asked Mackenzie.

He, too, looked at the clock and didn't find it an acceptable excuse, although I could see he wanted to. We had become stay-at-homes. Old marrieds without ever being newlyweds. "Sure," he said with reluctance.

He hadn't asked why. More points in his column. Or should I be suspicious of what was going on?

THE WALK TURNED OUT TO BE A GREAT IDEA I WISHED I'D thought of myself. I felt a resurgence of my earlier determination to eat vegetables and live the healthy life. Now I embellished that happy fantasy with a nightly long walk after dinner. We'd walk, we'd talk, we'd grow ever closer until our glow of health and emotional perfection reached halogen intensity.

I flicked away half ideas of our various schedules, of how infrequently Mackenzie was even around, of how often it would be raining, muggy, frosty, or windy. Add to that the fact that I am an exceedingly lazy human being. For now, this was the plan, and I could see my entire future, under my control, sane and close to perfection— linear at last. Also predictable and boring.

On Market Street, we took the pedestrian walkway over I-95. The traffic sounds receded as we neared the waterfront, which, only steps away, felt far from the city with its own, distinct atmosphere.

There's something about being beside a body of water that pulls the mind beyond its familiar boundaries. This works even with the Delaware River on a spring night. There should have been an ocean liner pulling out to sea, or mist above the water and the foghorns Susan had mentioned. Instead, there was a clear, but slowly thickening dusky light. And our nondistant horizon was Camden, New Jersey.

But even so, with the aroma of the water and perhaps a soupçon of drifting exhaust fumes, we walked the red brick pathway past white tents left from some recent celebration, past permanent posters, which I examined because I feel compelled to read any print in my vicinity. The reproduction of an old print was titled *Penn's Unterhandlung mit den Indianern*. I looked all over, but there was no explanation of why a painting by George Gilbert of Penn's treaty with the Indians was titled in German.

As we walked on, past the excursion boat docks, our talk slowly floated on its own course, lazily expanding and circling and redirecting itself in ways it seldom did at home. We passed a young girl huddling on a bench. The evening was balmy, but she looked chilly and as if she were waiting for the next bad thing to happen to her.

"She makes me think of Petra," I said. "And Petra makes me feel so useless. What should I do? Is there anything I can do? What would *you* do? What if she were your daughter?"

Mackenzie was quiet for a while as we slowly walked; then he spoke. "I'd hope to God that by that age, she'd know she could trust me, that she was able to tell me her troubles, whatever they were. I'd hope she knew that I cared, and that I had her present welfare and future happiness at heart. And given that, when she'd talk to me,

I'd ask her what she wanted, and we'd consider all her options, find her the best way."

His vision of parenthood floated into the night air and sweetened it. But Petra couldn't talk to her father and expect comfort or help, and the law blocked other choices. There was no one, in Petra's words, who was a safe adult or a safe harbor.

Our talk drifted away from the conflicts that had grown out of my work, to Mackenzie's workday conflicts.

He doesn't often talk about work, except in generalities. He does talk about the sillier cases he hears about— seldom if ever homicides, which are too horrible to qualify. However, there are exceptions, like the woman who filed a malpractice suit against the hospital for not saving her husband's life. The fact that she'd worked hard to end that life—shooting him four times before calling for help—apparently didn't seem relevant to her.

A few days ago, he'd told me about a trio of women who were robbing stores. Their modus operandi was alarmingly simple. Two of them bared their breasts. While the cashiers were thereby distracted, the third emptied the cash register. What was appalling was that it had worked three times now.

Another bare-flesh con involved a Midwestern woman who convinced men to undress in her truck, then get out and rub snow over themselves. While they did, she drove away with their clothing and cash.

Those are the crime stories I hear, the exceptions to the rule, the ones that produce at least half a smile. Those and generalities. He isn't supposed to talk specifics, anyway. But on this walk, his talk was very specific and obviously painful, and I realized how heavily it had been weighing on him.

Tonight, by the water, he moved outside the barriers he'd set up, and talked about having to notify the parents of an elementary schoolgirl found murdered in Fairmount Park. I'd heard about it while I was making dinner and the TV droned behind me. A fifth grader, reported missing on a class outing and found within the hour, dead, identified by her classmates. The question of who could have been that close and have acted that quickly was terrifying. And that's as far as I'd been willing to think about it. I'd turned off the TV.

"I can't tell you," he said softly. "Walkin' up those front stairs, knowin' what I'm about to do to their lives, their hopes, their hearts . . ."

"You weren't doing it. You didn't do it. You tried to make it as bearable as possible. I know that," I said.

He looked sideways at me, almost with pity. "When a bomb's dropped on your head, it doesn't matter how delicately the bomber's touch was on the release lever." We walked past the retired flagship *Olympia* in silence.

"I'm goin' stale," Mackenzie said after a while. "They come too fast, too many . . . an' I'm never going to forget that father's face. Got there just when she would have, if she was comin' home from school." I heard his deep intake of breath and slow exhale.

"Maybe you need a vacation."

"Maybe. Or maybe a more permanent change of scene."

Was I what would be changed? Was that what the anti-marriage business was about? Or was it just his job, not that that wasn't a major decision in itself. He'd mentioned going to law school when we'd first met, but he hadn't mentioned it since then.

"What do you think?" he asked.

I thought . . . what I thought was that he cared about what I thought. Law school meant years. Years of us together?

And so it went, touching lightly on possibilities and

problems. We neither solved nor resolved a thing, but still, our voices in the evening air made the issues feel less impenetrable. And then, we were at the *Moshulu*. Susan had told me how to summon her. I handed a note to a plainly dressed man at the entry of the ballroom, and he disappeared into the crowd of elegant women and men.

We meandered into the boat itself. I looked around, orienting myself. The centerpiece of the entry was a dramatically handsome staircase with a bannister of carved brass. "Want to peek upstairs?" I asked. "I think the crew's quarters are up there."

We walked toward the staircase, but before we reached it, we found ourselves face-to-face with a familiar face.

"Amanda!" Denise the smiling candidate's wife said. "I never—" She caught herself, but of course she was right. She would never have imagined I'd be at an event for her husband—unless it was celebrating his defeat.

I smiled. The truth was, I wasn't actually there, and our jeans and cotton sweaters were surely a clue that we were passing by. "We just stopped by to get something from Susan," I said.

"Amanda, Susan, and I are all in a book group," Denise said to her friends. Perhaps my inclusion in her social circle needed explanation. "We've just had a tragic loss in the group, a woman Amanda was particularly close with."

I wondered why she kept saying I was Helen's close friend, but it didn't seem worthwhile or diplomatic to contradict her.

"So sad. Are you still gathering information about Helen?" she asked. She smiled and glittered at the small group around her. "Amanda has a nose for crime, you see."

"Not really," I said. "And it's not truly an investigation.

We're simply pooling what we already know. Very in-formal." I smiled because she'd made me feel uncomfort-able about what we were doing, as if I were playing Nancy Drew. I wondered if that was so.

Denise flashed a rueful smile. "I do wish I'd known her better." Then she must have decided that talk about a dead woman wasn't likely to delight campaign contribu-tors, and she waved, expansively, at her surroundings. "Isn't it the most glorious evening?" she said. "We've been on the deck. It's absolute heaven, isn't it?"

I suspected that people like Denise had weeks filled with this painful time-passing inane chatter, and I won-dered how they avoided being carted off screaming.

"Oh, my! I haven't introduced you all," she said. "Forgive me! This is Amanda Pepper, a friend of mine, and her . . . oh, I can't believe I've misplaced your name." She lowered her gaze for a moment, a hint of a frown creasing her forehead between her brows.

"C. K. Mackenzie," he said to one and all. "Glad to meet you."

Denise smiled with relief. "And this is Stefan and Di-anne Stoverman, and Millicent Delucca, and Roy Stanton's son and right-hand man, Zachary."

"We've met before," Zachary said. I hadn't recognized him. He was groomed and tailored and smooth, al-though his unsmiling expression was still sullen. I real-ized he looked a lot like his father, and I wondered if his thuggy personality was also a genetic inheritance. He shook hands with Mackenzie and me.

Denise beamed at her other guests. "Amanda's a teacher at Zachary's alma mater," she said. "They did something right there, because we'd be lost without Zachary. He's been this campaign's biggest asset." Denise was every bit the politician that her husband was. Perhaps more. I took her praise of Roy Stanton's son for what it was, bright and meaningless conversation.

Zachary had been a senior my first year of teaching, and I'd never had the displeasure of trying to teach him, but I'd heard a great deal about him, and none of it was good. From time to time since then, I'd heard more tidbits about him, and again, none of it was good.

But politics obviously agreed with him, had galvanized him out of his torpor. Maybe kids actually did mature. Maybe an apprenticeship as thug and bully was useful to a career in politics.

Denise seemed unsure of whether it was permissible to leave us yet, and she was still making chitchat and probably weighing her options when Susan tapped me on the shoulder. She clutched half a dozen shiny plastic envelopes. Pink and powder blue and green and yellow. I saw handwriting through the top clear one. I had obviously missed a major stationery revolution. Everybody had these envelopes except me.

Susan looked surprised to see us all together, but then greeted us, one and all. The couples Denise was shepherding around must have been major players if Susan also knew their faces and names.

Finally, Denise's group drifted off, and Susan walked us over to the bar, a pretty room of woven wicker and inlaid woods that made me feel as if the ship had docked at a tropical port. We sat at one of the tables, and she had us order drinks, then told us that the drinks were on her.

We refused, till she said the drinks were on the candidate and that she was *so* sorry she'd made us come out. That she'd hoped and expected to have a drink with us, and talk about Helen's desk diary because she thought there was something to it, but one of the special guests— in fact, *the* special guest, a Broadway star with a definite right tilt to his politics—was having a tantrum about the seating chart.

We made a dinner date for the next night. She handed me the clear plastic envelope, took a deep breath, and darted back to the fray.

We turned to our drinks but, within seconds, heard Susan's voice once again. She was back. "I couldn't resist," she said. "I realized that—you know how I said we'd talk tomorrow?"

I nodded.

"Well, then, if this were a mystery, I'd be in trouble, because before I could ever tell you what it is, I'd be dead."

"Excuse me?" Mackenzie said.

"I heard you were a reader," Susan said to him with a mock frown. "You know. Books. That's what happens in them. There's a phone call, a promise that the next day you'll find stuff out, except boom! You don't because the caller's dead. There's always a second corpse. It's kind of a requirement."

"Luckily, this is real life, not predictable, stale fiction." I wondered if she was a little nuts, if writing mysteries all those years hadn't warped her mind.

"You're right," she said. "But it was a thought. And a funny enough one that I lost my headache for a minute. I'll tell you, it's possible that death is preferable to that egotistical jackass on the dais. I wish *he'd* said he had something to tell you—tomorrow."

And she was off, and not much later, so were we. By taxi this time. Enough healthy stuff was enough.

Sixteen

AMAZINGLY, THE NEXT DAY BLOOMED WITH PURE spring essence again. Philly's so often stingy with its favors, doling out one good day, then changing its mind. We're ruled by a weather goddess with attention deficit disorder, so we've all learned to carpe the good diems.

But today, we were being given a second helping. That was evident even up in our loft, surrounded by city and few green things. You could tell. The light from the skylight and front windows was different. I knew it would smell pale green and feel silky.

A perfect day to go to a garden, a spectacular garden, to live like a Du Pont without having to work with chemicals. We were both smiling as we locked the door behind us. Then Mackenzie stopped. "We're meetin' Susan and her husband for dinner, right? Doesn't make sense to come all the way back here first, but we never looked at the stuff she gave you."

We'd found better ways to occupy our time when we returned home last night. The Delaware may be unfabled, but it can be sufficiently romantic.

"Maybe we should take it along—look over it while we're there. Or better still—we'll get to the restaurant early and give it a look. Sound informed, okay?"

"Didn't you say it would be worthless?"

"I did indeed and I still believe that to be the case. But

it still seems polite to give it a look. She bein' so excited about her find and all. Just so we don't sound totally ignorant."

I went back and found the clear envelope and tossed it behind me into the minuscule backseat, which seemed designed for plastic folders, not human beings.

We were taking my car, top down. Driving a '65 Mustang, no matter how lovingly maintained, can make a simple outing a major adventure. The old darling can't have that many miles left in her. "Do you realize," I said, "that when this car was made, you weren't supposed to trust a *person* over thirty?"

"Good thing you weren't born yet." He adjusted the driver's seat back into a more comfortable position.

"Not me," I said. "This is a *car* over thirty, and we're trusting it."

"I'm sure you have a reason for saying that," he murmured in a tone you'd use only if the person you addressed was foaming at the mouth. "We aren't exactly going into the wilds. We're going to Kennett Square. If we get stuck, we could almost walk to Wilmington, so don't worry."

"I was making conversation." I could see how we'd be if we were together for years to come. One of those silent couples in restaurants, enduring each other in a masochistic marathon. Probably living with a single goal—to outlast the other one.

But of course, we wouldn't be together for years to come because things do have to move in one direction or the other. That includes relationships, and ours did not seem destined to move forward. Together. Because of the marriage-phobic driver.

I heard myself.

No. I heard my mother playing ventriloquist with my thoughts. I shook my head.

"What's that?"

"Nothing. A mild and fleeting headache." I patted his hand, and we were on our way to Chester County, near Wyeth country. "How come Pennsylvania was graced with Longwood Gardens?" I asked. "Why would a Du Pont leave Delaware?"

"It's a stone's throw," Mackenzie said. "And it was an arboretum before Pierre had it. A family named Peirce owned it from 1700 on and, about a century later, started planting specimen trees. Pierre bought it early this century so as to save the trees."

I should have known he'd know. "The wisdom of the immigrant," I said. "You know more about my home turf than anybody I know."

"I like that stuff."

And on we drove, on the outskirts of commercial areas, business for the very non–Du Ponts in often crumbling towns, until we were near the former residence of Msr. Pierre. "Money can do real nice things, too," C. K. said. "Like this place. Some of the trees were here, sure, but he created the rest."

And quite a rest it was. I'd come here as a child, once or twice a year, and had always loved its profusion, excesses, and astounding colors. Once, we'd come on a frosty winter day. The magical expanse of snow and icicle-laden greens in sharp winter light has stayed locked in my mind ever since.

We started with the Flower Garden Walk because, "That's what we always did," I said.

"Great reasoning," Mackenzie said, but he didn't mind. Every inch of the thousand acres of gardens was a good place to be. Besides, I knew the walk would be breathtaking at this time of year, and it was.

"Eighty thousand bulbs," he said as we walked between explosions of yellows and oranges, then masses of

white blossoms, then clusters of pinks and purples.
Tulips and daffodils and crocus and I don't know enough
about plants to say what-elses. But beautiful. Over-
whelming, in a fashion no garden I'd ever cultivate could
hope for. I silently thanked Mr. Du Pont.

At the end of the walk there's a stone bench. Its arm-
rests, on either end, are carved into mythic-looking
birds. The bench had been one of the wonders of my
childhood. "Sit there," I said, pointing at one end. "I'll
sit at the other end. Whisper into the bench back and I'll
hear it."

I listened as a very slow, Southern voice said, "Whoever hears this, I love you."

"I heard that," I whispered into the stone.

"Then I guess you're it," the stone said. I stood up.
"Magic, huh?"

The whole day felt that way to the point where I won-
dered if I should move to some green and open space, if
I'd always feel this contented and at peace in the country.
At least, in this expensively elegant form of country.

We wandered through the peony and wisteria gardens,
both in full bloom. The wisteria vines, heavy with
blossom clusters in white, purple, and lavender, had been
trained to tree-shape but were lovelier than any tree I'd
ever seen. We strolled through part of Peirce's woods,
trees canopying us and the azaleas that bloomed everywhere, and I felt removed, rejuvenated, and almost on
vacation.

"Let me show you the part of this place I fell in love
with first," I said, taking him into the conservatory to the
Children's Garden, where a topiary rabbit with floppy
ears stood taller than the children running through the
plants. Inside a kiddie-sized maze topped with flowers,
small people giggled and shrieked.

"You loved a maze," Mackenzie said. "This is probably the origin of lots of your problems."

"Want to see the orchids?" I asked, and then, as if the image had been a delayed-action development on my retina, I did a double take and turned to look again at the two figures who'd just entered. "That's Ivan Coulter," I said. "And Gretchen. What would they be—"

"I suspect the same as you. A trip down memory lane. She's a bit old for the scale of this room."

I turned sideways, trying to be inconspicuous. Even though I'd been here first, I was sure they'd take my presence as a further intrusion, that they'd resent me, whether or not that made sense.

"You were sayin' about orchids?"

"The um ... the ... Mackenzie, are they looking at me?"

"Absolutely. The girl's all but pointing."

"What should I do?"

"Tell me the next place to go. They're talkin' about you, Mandy, not to you."

But that felt wrong. Not simply unsociable, even rude, but almost as if I were, truly, guilty of making everything worse, as Gretchen had said. For a moment, I watched them, thinking about how long and how powerfully Helen's death would last and change the future of all those close to her.

Nothing would ever be the same for any of us. None of us would ever feel as confident about what or how well we knew anyone else. None of us would take a tomorrow quite as much for granted.

And Gretchen. I watched Ivan and Gretchen talk softly, full of sorrow for them. Actually, full of sorrow for her. My Ivan-sorrow was in reserve, pending clear information about where he'd been and what he'd been doing.

I walked over to them, leaving Mackenzie to examine the topiary. "Gretchen, Mr. Coulter. I'm glad to see you both in such a lovely place, and my sympathy to both of you." I introduced myself, sure he wouldn't remember me from the time Helen had once introduced us. I felt as if I were saving face by pretending I didn't know they'd been talking about me.

Ivan Coulter was gracious. He kissed his daughter's forehead and told her to go ask the guard right outside the conservatory about how late lunch was served in the Terrace Restaurant. He'd be right along.

"I thought flowers, a totally different environment," he said without preamble. "We're in limbo, and Gretchen . . . she's having a hard time of it."

"Understandably."

"I worked on a shopping center not far from here," he said. "Years back. Got in the habit of coming to this place whenever I could. It's therapeutic." He seemed almost defensive.

"This is one of my favorite places, too. A good place for Gretchen."

"She's a little old for this part now," he said, "but she wanted to revisit it. As a grown-up, she said." He managed a small smile.

"So did I. That's why I'm here, too."

"Since we've bumped into each other," he said, "do you have a minute?"

I nodded, reluctantly. I had all day, but it had been such a good day till now.

"Gretchen's upset about this project you—"

"No. Not me. The book group. Because we were fond of Helen. We wanted to do something *for* Gretchen, gift her with a sort of group portrait of her mother. Memories. Anecdotes—"

"Now you know it's somewhat beyond that," he said. "I gather you came to the house about it—"

"Not about that. About my raincoat."

He looked as if not only didn't he comprehend, he didn't care, either. "I gather from Roxanne that you—collectively—don't feel it possible that Helen ended her own life."

He said it in a way that held the words away from him, at a distance. If they'd been objects, his arms would have been stretched to the limit, the words dangling from his fingertips.

"Roxanne shouldn't have said—"

"Roxanne is a dear friend," he said. "I would consider it a breach if she didn't tell me things that were important."

"I'm sorry if anything has caused you or Gretchen problems or pain," I said softly. "That was the last thing anybody . . . we simply wanted—we want—to know her, because it's obvious we didn't while she was alive."

He looked at me appraisingly. "True. Because one thing you didn't know was that Helen was subject to depressions. There are people like that, and you wouldn't necessarily know it about them. They say most comics are depressed people. Things that other people bounce back from could flatten her. Everybody has their heart broken. Helen dated countless men. People said she dated every Tom, Dick, and Harry. I joke that she married me because I didn't fit, I was the only Ivan.

"She must have broken lots of hearts, and you'd think she'd roll with the romantic punches, but she didn't. Life could do her in. She was coming out of a depression when I met her, and she had another bad one when she had problems getting pregnant." He shook his head in small, tight back-and-forths, saying no to the memory. "It was terrible, to tell the truth. Of course, eventually,

Gretchen happened, and the bad time was just a memory."

"Were there—that was a dozen, thirteen years ago. Were there any more episodes since then?"

"Not as bad as those. No. But she's—she was—emotional. Moody. And lately, she hadn't been herself."

"We saw her the night before—she didn't seem depressed, or lethargic, or apathetic, or any of the symptoms I'd think were to be expected."

"People can mask their true selves. Helen had a public face. When everybody left, however, the facade would collapse."

"That Monday?" As soon as I'd said it, I regretted it. Ivan hadn't been there. Ivan couldn't know that answer.

He had to know how ugly it looked that he hadn't been where he was supposed to be. He had to know that I knew, that all of Helen's friends did. So if he'd clear up the confusion, clear away the suspicion—

Instead, he breathed deeply, straightened his posture, and tightened his lips. "I'd appreciate it if you would not further bother my daughter."

"I didn't ever mean to bother her." Roxanne had done this, and damn her for it. And him, too, for being so evasive. My friend was dead and I didn't believe the story and he infuriated me. "Where were you Monday night and the next day?" I asked in as noncombative a voice as I could muster.

He scowled. "I was where I needed to be. And I was surely not on that roof with my wife, if that's your secret scenario."

It hadn't been, not really, until he said it. I'd accepted the idea that he was out of town. With somebody he shouldn't have been with. That was the guilt I'd imagined. But now . . . Helen would have gone up to the roof with him. And then he could have disappeared. That wouldn't be difficult.

"I accept the idea that some misguided form of mourning for Helen has driven you to this . . . this whatever you call it. This quest, this . . ." He waved away whatever the end of that sentence would have been. "I'm asking you to respect our mourning and to stop adding to our misery. To Gretchen's misery. Stop it right now."

"But I—"

"I have nothing more to say. There in fact is nothing more to say. Have some respect. Have some compassion. She's a child and her mother is dead. Decency. That's all I'm asking of you."

"But—" And then I looked across the bright and charming room and saw Gretchen, who couldn't have looked more out of place. The slight girl was the one dark spot in the cocoon of green leaves and flowers, her shoulders slumped and her expression, fixed on me, heartsick. She looked helpless against the force of me.

I had become the villain of the piece, the source of pain, the problem.

Ivan Coulter turned away from me, toward his daughter.

I felt kin to every hypocrite who said she "meant well" while she worked her evil. Like something the groundskeepers here would spray into oblivion, something predatory and without value.

So that was it. Another damn learning experience. I was finished with this well-meant but hurtful pseudo investigation. I wasn't really going to unravel the secrets of a life. People were too complex to read in reverse this way, and Helen could no longer explain herself.

All I was going to accomplish or had accomplished was to hurt that girl more.

Let Helen rest in peace, however she had come to her final rest. Let her loved ones rest peacefully, too.

Sometimes, as Sigmund said, a cigar is just a cigar. Sometimes, the official interpretation of what happened is as close to the truth as a human being can get.

I wasn't going to forget Gretchen's tortured expression.

I felt as if in doing nothing from now on, I would finally be doing the right thing.

Seventeen

"WHAT WAS THAT ABOUT?" MACKENZIE ASKED WHEN HE rejoined me after Ivan Coulter had gone.

"I'll explain, but later." I wanted a longer time of flowers and plants and beauty.

Later, after a day of horticultural delights, we returned to the car. Mackenzie spotted the forgotten envelope on the backseat. "Will we have time to read it before the Hilemans get to the restaurant? I feel like a kid who forgot to do his homework."

"Doesn't matter, because—"

"How 'bout you read it out loud while we drive."

"I don't think so."

"Carsick? You never have been before."

"I think I'm out of line, making the Coulters' situation worse."

I sat facing forward, not looking in Mackenzie's direction, but I felt his glance turn to me. "That what Coulter said?" he asked.

"Sort of. And he's right. He told me she'd been depressed—I mean clinically, for real—at least two times before that he knew of, and somebody told me that she said she was going through a bad time, so . . ."

"You think she jumped?"

"It still doesn't make sense, but nothing else does, either. Including me. I mean think about it—how stupid was the idea that the book group could find the real Helen and turn her history over to the authorities so that justice was done."

He drove on.

"I'm glad we're both seeing Susan. With two of us there—"

"She'd object to callin' it off, you think? I mean if we weren't both there?"

"She has these enthusiasms. Maybe I got carried away with her excitement. She loves mysteries. Loves reading them and writing them and thinking them. This is too much of a game for her, but I think if we emphasize that this is causing pain, she'll back off. Besides, I don't know if there's any real basis to our suspicions. Maybe we hate the idea that Helen might have killed herself, but being uncomfortable with it doesn't mean it wasn't so."

"There's that Dumpster graffiti."

"But I don't know when that was written. After she died, but beyond that, anybody could have done it at any time for whatever sick reason."

And for the rest of the hour's drive, we spoke of other things—almost anything besides Helen Coulter.

We found a parking spot within hiking distance of the White Dog Cafe—quite a feat on Penn's campus, but Mackenzie has parking karma. If I'd been behind the wheel, we'd have circled another half hour, but when Mackenzie approaches a congested area with a desire to park in it, people feel compelled to drop whatever they're doing, rush back to their cars, and clear a space for him.

Before locking up, Mackenzie pulled the envelope out of the backseat. "Let's return it," he said, and I agreed. Walking the few blocks to the restaurant, I felt nostalgic and old. A century ago I had been one of those incredibly young and untroubled-looking undergraduates. I knew they were facing finals, that life issues loomed large, and that their lives were as fraught with grave matters as mine was.

But I didn't believe it. I was awash in mental mush about the good old days, and my false nostalgia was underlined by the time we entered the café's homey—not my homey, but a semimythic lace-curtained bric-a-brac kind of homey—atmosphere. The restaurant was in a row house that had once been owned by Madame Blavatsky, founder of the Theosophical Society. Once, she had a leg so infected, it was scheduled to be amputated, but it was cured, apparently, by a white dog lying upon it. In appreciation and homage, white dogs were everywhere represented—in china figurines and on prints and paintings.

It was a comfort to know that we were in no danger of having our limbs amputated while dining there.

Our table was ready, so we opted to wait there for Susan and Joe, instead of at the impossibly crowded bar.

"Well, here's to you and flowers and a fine Saturday," Mackenzie toasted when our glasses of wine arrived. And here was to us, and then to us again, and finally, Mackenzie grew tired of toasting and waiting and picking at the bread tray the waiter had put down, and he opened the plastic envelope. "Why not?" he said. "Just so I have an idea what . . . It's not as if we'll do anythin' with it. Here, take half."

I couldn't think why not, either. It was better than being annoyed with Susan and Joe's late arrival, although reading in the dimmed light was annoying, too. Oddly, the restaurateurs hadn't planned on having dinner guests read in lieu of eating.

Helen's "note" was in my portion, and I read it carefully out loud, but softly. The tables were very close, and the couple next to us looked bored with each other and in search of stimulation elsewhere. I leaned forward and whispered.

Helen's handwriting was jagged, with lots of spiky letters. Combined with the pale light of the little lamp on the table, it was almost illegible, but what I made out was:

Hate to do this—
upset family—
disrupt lives—
everything in me says no, don't—
battled with this long time—
hypocrisy is a true sin—
can't see other *honorable* course—[*honorable* had been inserted, then doubly underlined]
if could, would—
hope and trust family—anybody else who cares—
understand, forgive.

I read its cryptic, incomplete staccato phrases twice, then showed their arrangement to the cop and waited for a reaction. He had his chin pushed forward meditatively. "Odd," he said finally. "She didn't talk that way, did she? So vaguely? Disjointedly?"

"Not at all. Besides, why leave such a note in a loose-leaf book at the office? Who was supposed to find it?"

"Well, I've got my own mystery here," Mackenzie said after fanning his pages and picking a few out. "Do you know somebody named—" He lowered his voice still more. "—Polly Baker?"

It took a moment for the name to connect. I could almost feel my brain scan files—people I worked with, was in book club with, knew socially, went to school with years ago. But just as I was ready to say that I absolutely did not know such a woman, I remembered. *"Polly Baker!"*

"Shhh."

"Sure. Well, not know her, but know of her."

"Sounds like a piece of work. Listen: 'Prosecuted for fornication having borne her fifth bastard child.' Where is this? Have things degenerated further than I knew about?"

"She's—"

"Apparently, the father of her first child abandoned her and the child. And look here, a quote: 'Where there is no law, there is no transgression. Take away therefore the law, and you take away the sin; for 'tis none against nature.' "

The man was in love with his own voice. Even his own whisper.

"Doesn't say who said that about the law, but she—Helen—underlined it. And then it says—"

"Mackenz—"

"Oh, it's historical—I see now. The trial was in 1747." That intensified his enthusiasm. Anything historical does. If I were a few hundred years older, he'd have been paying attention to me.

"Conan?"

He barely took time to shake his head. "Let me finish. The woman's really something. She defended herself so well—including the fact that her first seducer had been a judge—that one of the judges married her and they had fifteen more children. Talk about a good closing argument!"

"Caedfel! Chauncey!"

He turned the page toward me. "What's this with the arrow pointing to *RvW* over here? You see that? Obviously important, but—"

I let my voice reach normal restaurant-dining decibels.

"Polly Baker never lived. She was Ben Franklin's hoax. He loved practical jokes."

I had Mackenzie's full attention now, and what a kick to be teaching him history for a change. "For two—nearly three—hundred years, people believed the story and used it for their own purposes. Voltaire referred to her and so did Balzac. Others used her case to advocate legalized prostitution. Some for men leaving women alone on issues of sex. Some to contest how the courts work. Franklin claimed he just wanted to fill space in his paper, *The Pennsylvania Gazette*. The point of what happened with it was how many versions it had and how far it traveled—the point is how history gets written."

"How do you know all this?"

"Because Susan is using Polly in her mystery, and Susan talks about her to the point of stupefaction."

His jaw was pushed forward again as he thought. "But still . . . why did Helen write all this down with underlines, question marks in the margins, a big arrow pointing at the thing about laws?"

I shook my head. I had no idea.

There wasn't much else. Susan had given me about twenty-five pages. "Think this really is all there was?" I asked.

Mackenzie sighed. "Worth double-checking, if we were checking anything, but my guess is this is all of it, because even most of these are doodles. Recipes." He passed the pages across to me, and I flipped through them and mine. I've been told that everyone has her own instinctive doodle shape, and I now learned that Helen's had been spirals. Large and small spirals, spirals with highlighted sides, spirals that were squared off to become almost mazelike.

I wondered what she'd been thinking about while her hand drew the ever-widening arcs.

I could tell what Mackenzie was thinking about. "I am starvin'," he said. We'd failed to have lunch. "And your friends are one half hour late. Do you think we could check whether they've left home yet, 'cause I'm ready to order without them, or is that too crass for words?" He took his tiny cell phone out of his pocket.

"Check the menu while I call them." I hate it when people flip phones in a public place. Hate to have their conversations intrude on my dinner, so I gestured to Mackenzie that I was taking the phone outside, and he nodded.

First, I phoned home to see if there was a message from the missing couple, but there was not. I then dialed Susan's house ready to leave a message because I was sure that they were en route.

"Okay, people," Susan's message said. "It isn't like answering machines are a new invention. Speak up."

"Susie," I said. "This is Amanda. We're at the restaurant and you're not. Guess you got tied up in traffic, so say we'll wait another . . . we'll be here, okay? But we might go ahead and order—we're starving. When you get here, we'll keep you company while you eat—hurry up!" I was squinting in the dim light to see the END button when the phone squawked with a male voice.

"Amanda? This is Joe. I picked up because—first of all, I apologize. I forgot about tonight."

"Well, that's okay," I said, not meaning it for a split second. "We'll just go ahead and—"

"Listen, I forgot and we aren't there because . . . the thing is, I just brought Susan home from the hospital."

"She's sick?" I had visions of one of those horrifying new viruses. "She seemed so healthy last—"

"She was . . . she was assaulted. Mugged," he said, sounding as if he had to force himself to speak. "Last night, after the event. She was going to her car—it was parked on the street, not the lot, but close by—and some-body came up from behind and . . . walloped her. With a stick, they think."

I could barely breathe. "I can't believe . . . I—how is she?"

I heard his loud exhalation. "Not great. She was con-cussed, and she has a big egg on her head, plus broken ribs, and the way she fell, she smashed part of her jaw. She'll be fine, they told us. But she doesn't feel that way now. She'd tell you so herself, but it's hard for her to speak."

"They—who—he?"

"She isn't sure. All she saw, before she was hit in the ribs, was a beige raincoat, she thinks. And pants. Could be anybody."

"That's all the person did? I mean that's awful, and I'm glad that's all! But it must have been a lunatic, to whack her with a stick and run away. Somebody in-sane." The city was different now, better, safer, and how could anyone even do it with an enormous crowd—a thousand Republicans, for God's sake—spilling out of a ballroom? Why? Why her?

Of all the people at last night's event, Susan was surely the least affluent, the least bedecked and bejeweled.

"Somebody driving by honked and shouted that they had called the police on their car phone—and the person with the stick took off. Otherwise, I don't know what might have . . ." He didn't bother to finish the sentence.

"Thank goodness for that Samaritan. Did the person in the car see the mugger?"

"No. According to the police, only from a distance. Saw Susan being hit, is what."

"Is there anything we can do, Joe? Anything anybody can do to help out?"

He made reassuring noises that all was well, she'd be

fine, he'd be with her till she was up and about, and she was going to be back to work in a few days, as soon as she could speak clearly.

I heard her voice in the background, and then Joe chuckled. Not a happy laugh, however. "Can you hear her?" he asked. "She said—in a fashion I won't try to imitate—a lot of uh-buh-duh's—or tried to say that she won't have work to return to because the quote damn mugger took all the records she was carrying. Her contact list—even her calendar. She actually didn't say all that—those are the accumulated facts she has shared today."

Her envelopes. That was too ridiculous. I mean I, too, lusted for them, but nobody goes berserk over stationery.

"She didn't notice till she was helped up, and then she realized he'd grabbed them when they fell on the ground. One truly stupid mugger. There is nothing of worth in any of them—except to Susan."

"Did he take her pocketbook?"

"No. She had it strapped across her chest, you know that way. Maybe if that driver hadn't shouted . . ."

I felt shaken and couldn't help but remember Susan laughing last night, invoking a mystery cliché, wagging her finger and saying that if there'd been a crime, then she'd be the obligatory second corpse.

I felt wobbly as I made my way back to the table. All I could hear was the word *mugged*, which didn't sound as brutal and terrible an act as it actually was. Bones broken, face injured.

And for what? Colored plastic folders that held business trivia, that meant nothing to anyone except their rightful owner.

However, there had been another folder. The one I now had. A folder you could read right through. Was it possible that's what he—or she—wanted? Only Susan,

Mackenzie, and I knew that folder was no longer with Susan.

I'm sorry, I silently said as I made my way between the tables. I'm sorry, Gretchen. I'm even sorry, Ivan. I really meant to back off, but things just changed.

I felt like the paving contractor on the road to hell, toting all my good intentions, but now, there was no doubt in my mind that Helen's death warranted—required—questioning.

It hadn't been Susan's overactive imagination that had walloped her across the head last night.

Eighteen

"I'M SURE IT WAS HELEN'S NOTES. THAT'S WHAT THE mugging was about. Why would anyone snatch lists of partygoers and invoices?"

Mackenzie worked on what was left of his chicken, carefully slicing a last delicious piece off the bone, chewing, and listening. He didn't look supercilious, he didn't interrupt, he didn't patiently explain why my thinking was all wrong. At least not yet.

This was so unexpected and thrilling, I got carried away and pushed at the theory. "Somebody obviously saw what she was carrying. You can see right through those envelopes, especially the clear one, the one Helen's notes were in."

"Who? When?"

I shrugged. "How would I know that? I don't even know when Clary gave it to her. Yesterday, sometime. Someone she met during the day."

"You haven't exactly narrowed it down," Mackenzie said. "Susan visits clients, works on the event itself—she must have gone a dozen places, seen who knows whom?"

I considered all this while finishing my grilled tuna. Also while our plates were whisked away. Also while we ordered coffee. "We could track where she'd been," I finally said. "It surely couldn't be that hard, then, to think of who had connections to Helen."

"Or how about to Susan? How about if somebody just plain wanted to hurt Susan for her own self?"

"Hate me for my own self and not because of anything else? A new credo?"

Our coffees arrived. Service was quick, but then we'd dawdled for so long, waiting for Susan and Joe to arrive. I couldn't really blame the restaurant.

"Isn't it possible that a mugger, out on his nightly prowls, randomly picked Susan, then got frustrated and grabbed whatever he could?" Mackenzie asked quietly. "When she fell, getting the bag with the strap across her would take more time than was available. Couldn't taking the folders be a desperate fluke with no meaning?"

He might have continued, but at that point, Mackenzie had gotten the unsubtle hint that we were preventing a second seating with our sluggishness, and so he asked for the check and we were out of there.

Back in the loft, I reopened the discussion, convinced that there had to be an internal logic to what had happened, whether we could see evidence of it or not. It was unbearable to think of these terrible things happening at random. Not that I normally believe in tidy cause and effect. I envision us like billiard balls—one gets poked and the rest of us are pushed into new and unexpected positions. My version of chaos theory. But now, I renounced happenstance. I became a devout cause-and-effect believer. I needed to.

"Let's operate on an as-if basis," I said after we'd checked the messages—none—and opened a bottle of wine. I put the duplicated pages on the sofa between us. Most had next to nothing on them. One had a recipe for moussaka, another, a funny drawing of a stick character apparently having a fit, with the comic-book signals for curse words—stars and asterisks and ampersands—in a balloon coming out of the figure's head. A few had dates scribbled without reference to what they were about, and almost every page had those intricate doodles. I tossed the packet down.

Mackenzie picked it up and went through it deliberately. "How compulsive a woman was she?" he asked.

"Not particularly. Not so I noticed. She paid attention to details, but I wouldn't call that compulsive. Why?"

"Was she forgetful?"

"Not that I ever heard or saw." I considered this. "No. Just the opposite as far as I could tell. She kept at least three tracks going in her brain at all times."

"I'm only half joking—but really, why leave yourself a reminder of where to be to kill yourself? Does this make sense to you?"

He pointed at one of her spirals. I hadn't noticed, but in its center, "Noon. Roof." The double os in both words had been gone over and over until they looked part of the design, not parts of words, which is why I hadn't noticed them before.

Noon. Roof. And the date she died.

An appointment with death.

He sighed and nodded. "This is what you've been sayin' all along, isn't it?"

It's terrific when the other person says "you told me so," but my elation was short-lived. So now he agreed with me—with what? We still didn't have much that made sense. I felt in the shadow of something I should have been able to decipher, that would explain Helen's death—and now, Susan's mugging. But shadows were all I could see. We sat in our own private clouds until finally Mackenzie stood and stretched. "Beats me," he said. "I'll think on this more. Makes no sense to make an appointment with yourself."

I looked up. "Maybe an appointment with somebody else. Maybe a real appointment."

"Wish we could tell. Police checked. Nobody there except the housekeeper, who was eating her lunch in the kitchen and watching a soap on TV, and who became so hysterical when she found out what had happened, she's never been considered a suspect. And who said she didn't think any workmen were there, but since they were always there, she thought maybe they were there. Maybe one. Maybe not. Which is to say, she went back and forth and was totally useless."

I remembered her. She was child-sized and would have had a hard time overpowering a tall woman like Helen or, in fact, anyone, and she was capable of being agitated beyond reason about a request to retrieve a raincoat. Roxanne had suggested that she was one of Helen's kindnesses rather than an efficient, competent housekeeper. "So somebody could have been there, somebody pretending to be a worker."

"But they were elsewhere, didn't you tell me that?"

I nodded. "Somebody pretending to be a special kind of worker, not one of the regular crew."

"Such as?"

"A landscape designer, a watering-systems man . . . I don't know. But not one of the contractor's regular crew. In fact, Roxanne thought she saw somebody in white overalls and a hard hat. It wasn't hard to know that construction was going on there—that Dumpster's been there for months. Maybe he—she—set up a phony appointment and was waiting up on the roof. Or met Helen outside. Housekeeper wouldn't even know with the TV blaring."

"If Roxanne's telling the truth. Bears further questions. When people talk about suicide notes, they don't mean notes to themselves, tellin' them not to forget when and where they're jumpin'."

"*Notes!*" I said. "That's what bothered me about the Polly Baker things. And the so-called suicide note. Those jumpy bits. They're notes. *Reminders.*"

Mackenzie sat back down. He looked as if he were willing to understand, if someone would translate me into his language.

"Why the Polly Baker stuff? That was the first question. Then why in that way? Why in there? Too much, too specific if you just wanted to tell your family about this story you heard."

Mackenzie gave a half nod. Mild encouragement.

"Those notes were to herself. Not to survivors or readers. The audience for those things was Helen herself."

"Why? What did she want them for?"

If I knew that, Sherlock . . .

"Speaking of notes—have you written down who's said what to you so far?"

"I—I started." A lie. I was behaving like one of my students. I hadn't written down a word yet, but I would tonight, I vowed. All of it.

"Good. So you were sayin'? About Helen?"

"She made notes on something the rest of us were groaning about. A two-hundred-year-old hoax. Why do you think?"

"I don't think much of anything. I'm still ponderin' that *RvW.*"

"Arvey W.? Who is that?"

"When last I mentioned it, you were speculating about my given name," he said. "Wonderin' if perhaps my Cajun mama had named me Chaim or the like. Perhaps that accounts for your not rememberin'. Let's go through it again. There's this wavy line from Polly's story to those letters, a fancy, decorated line."

It looked like an extension of one of her mazes, and I'd skimmed right over it. Thought it was another of her doodles. "Arvey?"

"Initials. You know, like *C. K.*? These are *R. V. W.* You're good with initials, so what do you think?"

"Somebody's Volkswagen? Rachel? Robert? Russell?" My brain felt made of soft, nonabsorbent material. "Who knows? Bad enough I have to do this with your name, but really, Mackenzie—"

"Hold on. Didn't give you all the info. Big *R*, little *v*, big *W*."

I thought of branding irons. Of Big D, as in Dallas.

"Versus," he said.

"Poems?"

"Versus as means 'against.' As in the *RvW*, Roe *v.* Wade, I think. Helen was connectin' Polly's persecution by the judges and—"

"Of course! That quote about laws creating crimes. Clever you!"

He nodded agreement. He doesn't bother with false modesty.

"Roe *v.* Wade! That's great! That's . . ." And that quickly, the moment of elation passed because—once again—so what? I didn't even have to say it. It was there in the air, a gigantic, inflated *So what?* Something had to connect to something else. This entire exercise hadn't brought us one inch closer to explaining what really happened to Helen—or to Susan, for that matter.

"Why would anybody want this?" I asked. "I kind of forgot the basic question. What's this about?"

"Notes," Mackenzie said. "So what sort of event could they be meant for? Something where she's making a logical argument for something. Was she giving a speech or writing an article?"

An article about Polly Baker? I couldn't remember her

ever doing something like that or even talking about doing something like that. An article? The small hairs at the back of my neck went on alert—not *an* article. "The *article*, Mackenzie. The *article*."

"I admire your enthusiasm, Amanda," he said. "I'm intrigued by your air of discovery and revelation, an' you're cute when you go crazy this way. All the same, I'd be happier still if you made yourself clear. What article?"

"The one she set up with Roxanne. A feature, she hoped, for the paper or the magazine. Helen said she had a big announcement. Roxanne assumed it was about the new internship program. But maybe it wasn't. Of *course* it wasn't. Helen told Roxanne it would be a *scoop*. That has the sense of an exclusive, of breaking news. Maybe it was about . . ." My mind sputtered again. Polly Baker? Roe versus Wade? A manufacturer of high-end children's clothing on historical hoaxes or legal precedent? What sense would that make?

"What if . . . what if the so-called suicide note was more of the same thing?" Mackenzie said. "It reads the same way. More prepping herself, reminders of talking points. Reread it. Listen to it. Think of it now as notes for an apologia—an explanation. So that she made sure she told the reporter—and the world, and her family— that she's thought this through."

I read it again, out loud: "Hate to do this; upset family; disrupt lives; everything in me says no, don't; battled with this long time; hypocrisy is a true sin; can't see other *honorable* course; if could, would; hope and trust family— anybody else who cares—understand, forgive."

He looked as apprehensive as I felt. "So either we have just another typically stupid mugger," he said slowly, "or we have somebody who didn't want anybody seein' those notes. Maybe the somebody thought there was more, and more specifics—things worth killin' over. Things that weren't to be said or known."

"The Dumpster, remember? 'Liar.' We're right. It was about something she said, or was going to."

He looked at me with those eyes that were so intensely blue they should be cold, but weren't. They were thoughtful. Concerned.

I wondered if he was thinking what I was. That whoever wanted the notes enough to attack Susan still didn't have them.

I did.

Nineteen

"WHO KNEW SUSAN HAD THAT FOLDER?" I ASKED RHE-torically. Mackenzie was engrossed in his book again, as was Macavity, who considered any volume a potential bed. The cat kept reengineering himself onto it, and the man kept gentling him off it. Neither seemed bored by the predictability of it all.

"Clary knew," Mackenzie said without looking up. "Yet another example of my amazing powers of deduction."

"You think she gave it to Susan just to look as if she didn't care about it? Talk about convoluted motives. Okay. She's on the list, but who else? Susan had meetings all day. In fact, she had lunch with somebody from the group—"

"And dinner with another, right? That Republican thing."

"I didn't think of that as her 'having dinner with,' but yes."

"Tight group you have there. If they were all male, you women would be outside picketing about exclusion."

"Untrue. And not true of the group, actually. But everybody in it is close with one or two other women, and I guess anybody who was thinking of a PR firm might think of Susan. At least consider her. That's what I think the lunch was about. But I'm blanking out on who it was."

"Save needless mental strain an' ask Susan when you see her." Mackenzie sounded finished with the topic, at least temporarily, and two seconds later was back into his book about recent Philadelphia history. I wanted to point out that I was in fact a part of recent Philadelphia history and so was this discussion. But it would be futile. Mackenzie doesn't consider wheel spinning valuable exercise the way I seem to. When he had more data, he'd regear. Until then, what we did know was filed in a compartment of his brain, and he was operating as a happy camper, complete with cat and book.

Still and all . . . "Are you going to . . . ?"

He slowly looked up, as if a hand were dragging his head into a position of attention.

"I don't know how these things work."

His brow slightly crinkled. My vagueness puzzled him, but not pleasantly. I wished I could be more blunt, but I was frankly nervous as I tiptoed onto his turf.

"In a case like this, I mean where it isn't actually a criminal case but you have suspicions . . . nothing definite, but . . . do you . . ."

"Would I suggest we look at it some more?" he asked mildly. "Is that what you're gaspin' over?"

"I mean, it's none of my—"

"We should have a sofa pillow embroidered with that," he said. "But the short answer's yes. And the longer one is, let's give it the weekend, see how it sorts itself out, and then, yes, if it seems to warrant it, yes. What bothers me is that Ivan Coulter hasn't said somethin' along those lines. That in fact bothers me a lot."

"He bothers me, too. And if I made matters worse, so did he. I still have no idea where he was when Helen died—and why wouldn't he just say it? Why keep it mysterious?"

"Could be immoral, not illegal," Mackenzie said. "Wouldn't want his daughter to know if he was with another woman at the time."

I had a horrible thought. "What if Helen really *did* jump? And it was *because* of another woman, a break in the marriage?"

"Was she that type?"

Much as I wanted to believe in this last scenario because it explained Ivan's cryptic silence, I couldn't. Besides, it's my observation that in real life, men are the ones who have romantic histrionics—often involving the death of the "beloved." Women, after a teary spell, mostly pull themselves together with a minimum of dramatics. Women are pragmatists, even though men don't like knowing that.

"It also bothers me," Mackenzie continued, "that her business partner and supposed best friend has also not said word one about the possibility that it isn't a suicide. That's the route it most often would come to us. That's what happens when there isn't any initial suspicion."

"You're saying Clary? . . ."

He'd kept his finger in his place in the book, almost promising it that he'd be back quickly, and now he looked at me, then toward the heavens, then back. "I'm not sayin' that at all. Not either of them. Necessarily. Because an equally good hypothesis is that Ivan and Clary believe it was a suicide. That they know Helen way better than you do." And having effectively shut the door on further open-ended speculation, he returned to the chronicled problems and triumphs of the city.

I felt a reflex twinge of annoyance, but then I reconsidered. He might have temporarily lost interest, but on the other hand, Mackenzie wasn't squelching or disputing me. He wasn't telling me to stop thinking, acting, doing anything. In fact, in his own fashion, he was behaving like a partner. But he was also suggesting that we'd reached a good stopping point, until we had more information.

He was undoubtedly right, and had experience on his side to boot. But I felt agitated, wanted to do something. I'd anticipated a pleasantly long evening with Susan and Joe—perhaps a movie after our early dinner, or a walk through the city with a stop for drinks, or coffee and talk back at one or the other of our homes. Now, the evening stretched ahead. It was early. Lots of stretching ahead.

I rolled my head to uncrick my neck. I looked at my stack of unread books, all titles for which I'd yearned. I looked at my pile of *New Yorker*s. I drummed my fingernails, such as they are, on the table. I paced.

And finally, I did what I'd known I was going to do all along—I phoned Clary Oliver. But I did it from our bedroom.

"Oh!" I said when her voice and no prerecorded message responded. "You're there! I expected . . . it's Amanda, and I—"

"Because it's Saturday night? I have no life," she answered. "But then, you're the one calling me, so you can't be kicking up your heels, either."

"Not exactly."

"But I bet you aren't watching an infomercial for hair weaving."

I had to laugh. "You are bored, aren't you?"

"Actually, I'm not doing that either. Wanted you to feel sorry for me. I'm catching up on bills and mail, listening to music. It's soothing to do busywork after a bad week."

"Listen, Clary, this bad week just got—"

"Mandy, did Susan give you the stuff I copied for her?"

"That's more or less why I called."

"I take it that's a yes?"

"Yes. But—"

"I'd like them back. I'm sorry I gave her the material. I thought it'd set everybody's minds to rest—there's no secret message in there—but still, they weren't mine to duplicate, and it certainly didn't set Ivan's mind to rest. He's furious with me."

"Why?"

"I don't know. I mentioned it in passing, and he blew a gasket. Everything's getting to him—as well it might. Just give them back—or burn them, and I'll say you gave it back, okay?"

In the age of the copy machine, what did it mean if I either burned or returned? I could make a dozen more copies. So this was all an idiotic formality. There seemed no point discussing it.

Or raising the question of whether Ivan wanted it back so much he clubbed Susan in order to get it. "I'll put it in the trash tonight," I said. "Shredded, if you like."

"I know it doesn't make sense, but I think Ivan feels so out of control—the rug pulled out from under him. All that. So whatever I can do . . ."

"You can do something for me. You can tell me precisely when you gave the pages to Susan."

There was an overlong silence.

"Clary?"

"Yesterday," she finally said.

"What time of day? And where were you when you handed them over?"

"Mandy? Are you and Susan still playing spies? What is this?"

"Please."

She exhaled directly into the mouthpiece, making sure I registered her irritation. "Probably ten-thirty in the morning. At my office. Give or take a half hour."

"Thanks. And were all the pages in the notebook copied?"

"Yes, but why does it matter?"

"And finally, when did you tell Ivan that you'd done it?"

"Oh, Jesus, Mandy, enough's enough!"

"Please."

"Hell. He called about . . . actually shortly after Susan picked up the pages. That's why they were on my mind and I mentioned them. I cannot believe such a fuss is being made about doodles and notes relating to nothing in particular. I think the group should lay off, leave this alone. There's no conspiracy to unravel, but if you keep probing and searching and pushing, things may come out that will be of no use to anybody, except to make things worse. Gretchen is already beside herself."

"Things about Gretchen?"

"No, no. Things about . . . business. I'm not going into detail. We aren't a megacompany, and I'm sure Helen needed a short-term loan and would have put the money back shortly, but maybe she was afraid she wouldn't be able to, and in any case, she couldn't. She died. So what good would it do if you poked around until somebody here in accounting tells you that? Just as an example."

"You're saying that's what the note was about?"

"That's all I can figure. Isn't it enough? If we didn't own the damn business, if we were a public company— then it would have to be revealed. But it doesn't have to be, so let it . . . let it all stop here and now with you. Unless you and Susan and whoever else think this sleuthing around is fun and gnaw at it until Gretchen finds it out. It isn't the nicest thing about Helen, but it isn't as bad as it would sound to Gretchen, so why do it? It would just be another punch in the gut to her."

I was stunned. Clary might speak of it lightly, but in plain English, Helen had siphoned funds off from her own company. Without telling her partner and best friend. It opened new and unsavory prospects.

And questions. Hadn't Roxanne said something about a deal Helen had prevented—Ivan and Wendy Loeb? Were those events related? Had not having capital had anything to do with it—and was this her attempt to make amends by digging herself a deeper hole? Hadn't there been something about Gretchen wanting computer equipment and Helen saying things were too tough for that? I remembered, because Gretchen had felt responsible for her mother's plunge, thought it had stemmed from that.

Maybe that house had swallowed every cent they had, but even if so . . . "Wow," I said softly. That was all I could manage.

"What's the verdict?" Clary asked.

"I . . . my impulse is to say sure. No problem. Except—"

"Oh, please! No excepts!"

"Clary, listen. Susan was attacked last night. Ribs broken. Her face messed up."

"Dear God," Clary said. "Where? When?"

I explained the locale, I told her the time, Susan's injuries and prognosis.

"I was right there!" she said.

"I know." I left her politics and motives for another discussion. "The thing is, she'd been carrying envelopes. Four or five of them, in different colors."

"She had them when she came to the office," Clary said. "Keeps her organized, she said."

Maybe that eliminated Clary. She'd have known the

color of the envelope. She wouldn't have taken the others.

"The ones she was carrying last night had receipts and seating charts and things like that in them," I said. "And the one with Helen's notes, which I came by and took. Then I left."

I've noticed that half the time when speaking to my single friends, I edit Mackenzie out of nonessential descriptions, as if on some level, I'm ashamed of being luckier in life and love than they. I guess I shouldn't have felt the need to do it for Clary. She'd been married twice. She'd had her own guys to edit out with a vengeance.

"She was hit with a club or a stick, from behind, right up from the restaurant on Columbus," I said. "When she fell down, the envelopes went flying. A driver shouted that he'd called the cops, and the mugger fled—after he took all the envelopes." I waited for a response, but got none. "Clary? You still there?"

"Here," she said.

"I'm convinced there is something about those notes," I said. "Or at least, somebody thinks so."

"I understand."

"So about your request? That nobody pay any more attention to who Helen was or what was going on?"

This time I expected an angry blast and had the receiver out from my ear by the time I finished my sentence.

"Be careful," Clary said, not at all angrily. "Be very careful."

I wasn't sure if she was wishing me well or giving me a warning.

Twenty

I DON'T MEAN TO ANTHROPOMORPHIZE, AND I KNOW
Mother Nature doesn't program based on my moods,
but the next day was as gloomy as I was. The air outside
looked the color and texture of mustard, and I knew that
the second I left the air-conditioned loft, the humidity
would cover me with its slobber-doggy kiss. The thought
was enough to wilt my hair and send me searching for
excuses not to visit Susan.

Of course, I knew I would. Not visiting a friend who's
been as physically insulted as she had been wasn't an
option.

Besides, I had questions about who had seen the envelope or knew Susan had it, although their numbers were
ever-increasing. Clary knew, and Ivan knew, and who
knew who Ivan had told? Roxanne—and Gretchen—
seemed to know whatever peeved Ivan. And Denise
could easily have seen it during the evening or when we
were all talking and Susan came over. Who else?

And how had it happened that the most innocuous
people—my book group, readers, book lovers—now
seemed a potential den of murderers? It was ridiculous
and hateful. Everybody loved Helen. She'd been easy to
like. I'd never heard of a squabble. But suddenly, half the
group seemed to have hidden motives for murder. Roxanne to eliminate a romantic impediment. Wendy and

perhaps Clary, too, to eliminate a business impediment. And even miserable Louisa, on behalf of her overprivileged children and their preschool educations.

And while I mentally spun in circles, in mazes as tight as the ones Helen had doodled, another entire brain category said, "Are you forgetting Petra?" Where was she? How could anyone help her?

Talk about feeling useless.

The shroud my own mind cast over the day was even worse than what was outside.

I whipped through the Sunday paper, reading book reviews, the magazine, and little else. The news section had a long feature on Roy Stanton Harris. I studied his generic good-looking face. There was even a photo with his son, Zachary, and I studied that one, too. Roy Stanton smiled more than his son did, or was further along in his politicking and knew enough to twinkle for the camera.

Enough of them. I flipped past, cranky and bored.

Unable to concentrate, I began the day finally doing what Mackenzie had suggested a while back. I wrote down whatever I'd been told, and by whom. My first attempt produced an incomprehensible jumble. I pulled out a fresh piece of paper and wrote HELEN in the middle. Then I drew circles.

Beginning with the ludicrous: Louisa fought with Helen about whether she had kept Louisa's kids out of a nursery school on whose board Helen sat. She said she repeated "rumors" to Helen, but refused to say what they were. I drew a line between Louisa's circle and Helen. And dotted lines—possibly the rumor—to Wendy's "news" of an affair between Roxanne and Ivan, to Louisa's sister Clary's suggestion that Helen had secretly borrowed funds.

Susan had said there was strife between the partners

about supporting Roy Stanton's campaign. I drew another line between Clary and Helen.

Roxanne's balloon said: Helen and Ivan were going through a bad time—or Helen was. Or Helen's business was. Helen had freaked out about money. Helen had squelched a deal where Ivan would have been in a partnership with Wendy.

I drew lines from Roxanne to Helen, made a new circle for Wendy, and connected her to Roxanne and Helen and the new circle for Ivan, too.

Gretchen said her father was upset. That Roxanne was their conduit for all news. That somebody—no line to draw—in the book group made her mother uncomfortable.

Gretchen's bubble sat out in space with a lifeline to Roxanne, but that was all. I drew wiggly, unconnected lines from her to remind me that I didn't know who that "someone" was.

The *R.I.P. Liar* was out on its own.

Wendy's bubble said that Roxanne and Ivan were probably an item. That Roxanne lied about her husband's whereabouts and her own marital status. I realized, rather belatedly, that Wendy had been full of news about Roxanne, but not about Helen, and not a word about herself.

Ivan had said that Helen had a history of depression. About love, about fertility problems. Ivan's line was short and bonded to his dead wife's circle.

Near the Dumpster's graffiti, I put the *RvW* and *Polly Baker* as reminders, too.

And that was about the sum of it, circles and lines and missing links. Dollar signs and hearts and tears.

"I use those little skinny notebooks," Mackenzie said when he ambled in and found me glaring at the page, making arrows and connector lines. "Easy to juggle the little pages."

"I thought this would be graphic in some revelatory way."

He studied the names and the facts while he drank coffee.

"It's depressing to have nice, ordinary people suddenly seem suspicious," I said.

He grinned. "Probably because they're just what they seem—nice, ordinary people. Guilty people work at hiding the truth, maneuvering around it. They have careful alibis, but ordinary people don't have reason to think in that direction."

"But it's such a muddle. Missing money—"

"Real life is messy. Maybe Helen's done that before. Maybe even Clary."

"Why'd she mention it? Pure honesty, or something else?"

He shook his head and had more coffee.

"There are lies all over the place," I said. "Not just on that Dumpster. To lie about whether you're still married, for God's sake!"

"Oh, right—Roxanne. Means we have to change the stats on the book group, switch her column."

"I'm not keeping statistics," I snapped. "What is it with you? You seem desperate to gather antimarriage material. You have something against the institution? These people are trying their best!"

My mother again—and now, coming right out of my mouth! Audibly!

He pulled back, looking astounded. "I think—I thought my opinion of marriage was the same as yours. I was stating facts about that particular cross section, is all. You told me they're as bad as your mother, or you seemed less than in love with their nagging, too. That's why I paid attention to what their romantic lives are like. Consider the source."

He had a gift for freeze-drying the long harangues in my mind until they were flaky bits that blew away. I'd had a whole lot to say—and now, nothing. So I looked back at my stupid chart. "What do I know about Helen?" I asked softly.

"That she was complicated. That people liked her, loved her—and probably envied her. All of that affects what they'll say about her, or about Ivan, or about life in general."

"Then whatever's here"—I waved at the two pages of notes—"is pretty much—"

"Nothing. The death's suspicious for me because of the graffiti—though God knows any crazed kid who heard what happened could do that out of spite."

" 'Liar'?"

"Who knows what that means? Maybe she said something to one of Gretchen's friends. Or fired somebody. Or picketed somebody. It's as vague as the other stuff."

"I would like to know who in the group made her so uneasy that she considered quitting, and—"

"Hold on. Those two things aren't necessarily related. Maybe she was tired of the books you read, too busy. You don't know enough."

There was an understatement if there ever was one. I didn't know anything. Not even what I'd have said I knew a few short days before. Before Helen died.

BY THE TIME I WAS ABOUT TO LEAVE FOR SUSAN'S HOUSE, the cloud cover was a few inches off the pavement, and midday was as dim as dusk. It was going to pour. On me, she who lacked a raincoat, and even though Helen's house could be on the way to Susan's, I would not willingly face the Coulters again this weekend. I was rummaging through the closet in search of an umbrella when the phone rang. I grabbed a small red umbrella that I was afraid was broken, and caught the phone before the service picked it up.

"Amanda," a cultivated voice I immediately recognized said. "This is Denise. I hate to bother you on a Sunday. Forgive me."

I made all the soothing no-problem sounds I could muster.

"I wondered if we could talk at some point soon."

"Well, I . . . sure. We could talk right now."

"I wish . . . but we have a church service in Chester County we have to get to—a special service—and we're already running late. I was afraid we'd get back too late for me to make this call and . . . I wouldn't bother you if I didn't think . . . it's a matter of import."

She sounded like a politician lately. The whole family was infected. "I'd like to talk with you," she said.

"About this? About Helen?" Denise wouldn't call without something tangible to report. Something more than rumor.

"There's a situation. She was in touch recently." I heard someone in the background. "I have to run. Zack's calling. We call him our wrangler lately, herding us here, then there. An absolute slave driver!" She trilled a laugh that sounded anything but sincere. "Do you have time this evening? My schedule—this election makes life impossible. We'll all be on Rittenhouse Square tonight. I could duck out while Roy Stanton's speaking. Could you possibly meet me somewhere nearby for a few minutes? I think you'll agree it's . . . not trivial."

I didn't want to meet her at all. She worried me. Sounded furtive. "Tell me where and when," I said.

*   *   *

I BROUGHT SUSAN LOLLIPOPS AND ICE CREAM. I PUT THE
ice cream in the freezer and talked briefly with Joe, who
looked haggard. I told him he could trust his wife to my
keeping, and after asking me half a dozen times if I was
sure of that, he looked dizzy with relief, and murmuring
something about a game on TV, he wandered off.

"No scars," Susan said with minor difficulty. Her jaw
was wired. In the thirty-plus hours since the injury, she'd
learned to speak around it and sounded as if she had an
unfortunate accent, as if she were a great deal less literate
and verbal than she is. "Dey pahmise."

With a little work and concentration, she was intelli-
gible, which was a relief. My visit didn't have to be a long
performance monologue.

She was sitting in bed, propped at an angle with a pile
of pillows that lessened the pain of the broken ribs and
the bump on the skull. "What you learn?"

I'd brought along my yellow notepad full of the circles
and lines. I not only thought it would intrigue Susan and
make this convalescent visit less onerous, but I thought
that given her war wounds, she deserved full knowledge
of whatever had gone on—whether or not I understood
it. I gave her back the copies. "You have to destroy them
later. Clary's request."

"Copieth!" she said. "Whoth playing spy gameth
now?"

"I know it's stupid, but I promised."

She shrugged, then winced.

"Cool it with the body language for a while," I suggested, and she nodded, the humor momentarily gone
from her face.

She spoke slowly and deliberately. "I think." It sounded
like "Uffing," but translation was becoming easier with
each word. She tapped her jaw. "Wanted kill me." She

nodded lightly, and I could see how she was still trying to understand what had happened.

I squeezed her hand and felt tears smart on my bottom lids. "Thank goodness for the person in the car, whoever it was. Now, at your own pace, what were you going to tell me? Remember? About the notebook pages."

She almost frowned in concentration, but those muscles also apparently hurt. "Not soo-cide."

"Me, too," I said. "Convinced me it wasn't suicide."

"Article. Polly, too."

"Precisely! That's amazing—we're 100 percent in synch."

She shook her head—very gingerly—and pointed at her jaw. "Where's yours, then?" she asked. She pointed at my messy chart, which I'd explained, and said, "Whoth least likely?"

"Least likely what?"

"Killer."

I sat back. It was confusing how well she'd interpreted the notebook pages, how logically, and then how her mind put her on ridiculous detours. "In real life, it's the *most* likely who does it. Ask Mackenzie."

Susan looked at the list, then added the rest of the book group's names to it. *The Not Yet Heard From* she wrote in block letters beneath their names.

She pointed at Denise's name. "Leatht likely."

"Interesting. She called as I was leaving. I'm meeting her tonight. She has something to discuss. She said Helen had been in touch with her recently. Do you have any idea why? Aside from book group stuff, which she wouldn't have mentioned."

Susan's eyes were wide. "Cweepy. Bad. Don' you know ayfing? Perfn sayth tell you later *dieth* before can tell it. *Always.*"

"I thought you'd fulfilled that prediction already," I said.

"I here."

How many muggers and batterings would it take for the woman to know when enough was enough? "Get a grip," I said. "Denise had to go to some mix of church and state. I'll see her in a few hours. This is nonfiction, Susie. I don't mean to be harsh, but you make a game, almost, of what is definitely not—look at you! Bashed up, in pain, can barely speak. I don't have to tell you this is for real."

"No game."

I opened my mouth for another stab at introducing Susan to reality, but she—and I, perhaps—were saved by the bell. The doorbell, in this instance.

Twenty-one

"TESS!" I'D GONE TO THE TOP OF THE STAIRS TO SEE who'd come calling. My surprise was honest. "What—"

"How is she?" Tess looked anxious in a therapist sort of way. Concerned, but not hysterical about it. She held an artfully arranged spray of daffodils and tulips.

Joe waved up at me and returned to his game. "I thought you were at the shore," I said as I walked downstairs to greet her. Once again, I felt that unwelcome wave of suspicion that any unexpected behavior or words by any member of the book club—or anyone associated with it—produced in me lately.

"Was. But the weather's disgusting so we came home this morning. And there was a message on my machine from Faith."

"Really? Did Clary start a telephone tree?"

"Guess so. And I more or less had a found day, so I thought . . . you know, most times you wish you could do certain things, but you can't. Clients lined up, sick child—something. But today . . ." She shrugged and smiled and gave a small wave of the flowers. "Her timing worked for me, I guess. So how is she?"

"Bones broken, bumped up, but she'll be fine."

"Her body, you mean," Tess said, being Tess.

"Of course. The trauma . . ." I shrugged. I didn't know how I was going to be about all of this, either. "Go on up. I'll find something to put these in and bring them up."

Susan's kitchen was a lot like her, with humor wherever possible. She had a collection of perfectly dreadful cookie jars atop the cabinets. My pick was the Mona Lisa, whose eyebrows served as the lid's demarcation. The spoon rest was Elvis, hips swiveled at an angle. The clock had its numbers running backwards. The canisters looked like haphazard arrangements of children's building blocks.

But her vases were straightforward. I could see them through one of the cabinet's glass panes. I wished I knew how to arrange flowers in the manner they deserved, but settled for what I could do and carried the results upstairs.

It was interesting watching Tess fill a comfortable space between friend and therapist. She was drawing Susan out—not that getting Susan, wired jaw or not, to talk required great skill. I watched as the mugging was replayed, in as much detail as its victim could summon. Tess nodded encouragingly.

Susan's lips looked dry, and I realized the glass next to her bed was empty. I offered something to drink—tea, ice water, whatever I could find below—and once again descended the stairs.

They'd both opted for iced tea, which needed to be made, but as I waited for the kettle to boil and pulled out the extra-thick mugs Susan had promised would not crack when hot fluid and ice were both in them, I caught myself again in the suspicion zone. It would be incredibly easy for someone like Tess to find out just how much Susan had seen or recognized. When precisely had her family left for the shore? Friday night or Saturday morning?

Which was so bizarre a thought I knew I'd gone over the top and was now as bad as Susan. Upstairs, a kind woman was being a friend, and I was reading under-handed motives into it. I'd become warped.

On the other hand, Helen had become dead and Susan had become seriously banged up. Somebody was out there.

It seemed forever before the water boiled and I added half a mug of it to the glasses, let it steep, extracted the tea bags, added ice and sugar, found a tray—Susan was thoroughly organized. I thought of the plastic envelopes, everything in separate compartments, and realized I should have expected that.

They were laughing, Susan holding her face so as not to hurt it and making odd sounds, somewhere be-tween a cough and a snort. "I was telling Susan about this pathetic neighbor at the shore, who—" Tess waved away her words. "Oh, never mind. I can't bear going through the whole thing again." Susan gave another cough-laugh-snort.

Then we grew more sober. My yellow pages were still on the bed, and Tess moved her head in their direction. "You've been busy," she said. "But even if somebody harmed Helen, isn't your—our—scope a little narrow? I mean these are all book group people."

"Plus Ivan."

She waved that away. "What I mean is that these are people we know. But Helen knew lots of people. She operated in the business world, and—again, this is rele-vant only if there's real reason to believe somebody hurt her—"

Intriguing that the shrink who wanted Susan to talk it through couldn't bring herself to say the word *killed*.

"—then I'd think any real investigation would have to consider that world, too. Plus her social life. Old friends. Et cetera. We're looking at her life through a very tiny keyhole, only at the part we were in. Besides, there really is no evidence, is there?"

"The Dumpster," I said.

"Cruel, but have you looked at most walls, corners, and street signs? Give a malicious kid a spray can, and anything is possible."

"But *liar* is such a specific accusation."

"Well," Tess said, sipping her iced tea and stirring it with the straw. "Maybe that's my point—not that the accusation's true, but that somebody she knew socially, or in business, or even through golf—who knows?—thought she lied about something. And that somebody could have had nothing to do with Helen's death, but could simply be spewing nastiness, saying in essence, good riddance, dreadful as it sounds."

"But if," I began, "if we come to believe—if there's convincing evidence, ever, that someone pushed Helen. Murdered her." Tess winced at the word, but it felt important that it be said. "We still have the enormous obstacle about who and why would she have gone up to the roof with anybody if there was discord between them."

"Thumbody she liketh," Susan said.

"Roxanne thought she saw a workman." Except I wasn't at all sure Roxanne didn't have cause to lie.

"Helen's entire crew was at my house," Tess said. "Redoing my porch. Helen knew that. In fact, Helen arranged that when she couldn't use them."

"Fake workman?" Susan made a muffled sound. A strangled yawn, I thought, wired inside.

I stood. We were exhausting her. "Time to go. I'll stop by after school tomorrow again. Have Joe call if there's anything . . ."

Tess also stood. "Rest up and heal," she said. "Maybe having visitors and talking isn't the best thing for you, after all."

Susan made polite if garbled protestations, but she did look within seconds of sleep.

Downstairs, we said good-bye to Joe, again made offers of help, and walked out together onto the Hilemans' old-fashioned porch. "I didn't mean to cut your visit short," I said. "I thought if I left—"

"I would have gone in a minute anyway. Being slammed around that way, hurt as much as she is, exhausts the body, not to mention the emotions." She took a deep breath and looked at me speculatively. "Besides," she said. "Besides . . ."

I borrowed her act. I nodded and smiled and looked encouraging, but said nothing.

"I need to say I'm uncomfortable with this whole . . . investigation thing."

"It isn't an investigation."

"What would you call it?"

"A . . . an exploration. An active discussion. A finding out how little any of us know anybody else."

Tess's grimace eloquently suggested that I was playing with words.

"We're searching for the question, not the answers," I said. "We're trying to find what most likely happened, and if there's reason for a criminal investigation. We're looking for leverage, for definition, through who Helen was."

"Fair enough. But whatever you're calling it, I have reservations about it." She gestured at the metal glider on the porch. I remembered when Susan found it in a junk store. It didn't look much better now, even painted multicolored pastels and given homemade pillows, but it beat standing out in the rain.

"I met Helen, years ago, when we were both college-age—different colleges—but we had summer jobs waiting tables at the same seafood restaurant." Tess seated herself and so did I. The glider creaked and rocked slightly. I had the sense of a long story starting.

"I was a year or two older than she was," Tess continued, "but we had more in common with each other than we had with anybody else there, and we were instant, if temporary friends, because we didn't cross paths again for half a dozen years at least. But that summer with Helen is probably why I decided to become a psychologist."

I waited for an explanation.

"She functioned all summer. Seemed normal. But when I got to know her, I got to know how depressed she actually was. Talking about suicide, in fact. She terrified me, and finally, I didn't know what to do except read all I could about mental illness, then research psychologists and steer her toward one. My interest in the subject, especially depression, began with her. Until then, I thought I was an art major."

She gazed out at the street, at a small boy in a slicker and boots. He jumped into five puddles while we watched, and each time, his mother, two steps behind, said, "Don't jump in the puddle, Jason. You'll get all wet."

Tess cleared her throat. "I'm trying to say that Helen could very well have chosen to end her life, and in fact, I assume that she did. She had an unfortunate tendency to be overly hard on herself. It may have helped her succeed in the business world, but it surely didn't help her be happy."

"I'm not sure why you're uncomfortable about this," I said. "Nobody's trying to pry into areas that would *hurt* Helen. Just the opposite!"

"But her family. She would hate it if you dredged up things she'd never want her daughter to know about."

"Like what?" Tess wouldn't know about the missing money. "Helen, to all accounts, was a model citizen, a committed, good-hearted, outspoken woman. What are you talking about?"

Tess closed her eyes and took a deep breath. "What a person considers shameful isn't taken from some table of standard shames. I'm not saying she ever did anything wrong. But she thought it was wrong. That summer, she'd just ended an affair with a married man, one of her teachers, and she was incredibly ashamed of having been involved with him. That's all I know, nothing more specific. But she talked about it in terms of a disaster, spoke of guilt and retribution and shame. I never understood why, but that wasn't the problem—the way she was flirting with the idea of death was the problem. What mattered was how it felt to her.

"Another sort of woman might go on national TV and joke about mistakes made in her youth, or not joke at all—might lambaste the married man for his role in it, the teacher for his unprofessional lack of ethics. But Helen wasn't either sort. Years later, when we'd become friends again, she referred back to that summer as if it still haunted her. She always called it our secret. Even Ivan didn't know about whatever it was, and surely, Gretchen didn't. Under that business suit, Helen was something of a Puritan. You know how she was—when she thought something was wrong, she spoke up about it. When I first met her, she thought she herself was what was wrong, and she seemed half-ready to don the scarlet *A*."

I was reminded of Helen's notes. The words *hypocrisy* and *sin* and *honorable*. "Ivan told me she's been depressed—seriously—twice," I said.

Tess nodded. "Funny thing is, when we met again, she was in that second serious depression. She commented on how I seemed to appear when she was in the dumps. I never knew if that was an insult or a compliment."

"Did she explain why she was in the dumps this time?"

"Well, this time she'd gone to get help on her own. I just think it was a hard time for her. She was trying to conceive and having a bad time of it, and that can be emotionally grinding for anyone, especially somebody as hard on herself as Helen was. She acted as if this were punishment for her sins, divine retribution. But once again, if you'd met her at a party, you'd never suspect how desperately unhappy she was."

"Suicidal?"

"Possibly. The point is, being shocked that she jumped off her roof is one thing. Deciding it can't be true because she didn't give you advance warning—that's not a logical assumption. And so pushing and probing for the secrets she kept to herself feels like a humiliation beyond the grave. A needless, futile humiliation. She had it in her to be extreme, and she had it in her to mask her desperation. Why hurt her family's memory of her by spilling secrets she didn't want shared?"

"No problem."

Tess looked relieved. "Good. Nobody wants to further upset the family. And speaking of families, I'd better get home to mine, then," she said. "Thanks for listening."

Upset the family. I'd heard those words before. My mind tracked them—upstairs, inside the house on that sheaf of pages I'd given to Susan. The words were part of Helen's own notes.

Nobody wanted to or intended to upset Helen's family.

Nobody but Helen, because, according to her own notes, she'd felt obligated to do just that. Had perceived it as a necessity and the only honorable course.

Twenty-two

I WAS TURNING MY KEY IN THE DOWNSTAIRS DOOR WHEN an unfamiliar voice said, "Excuse me?"

I turned and found an equally unfamiliar young man in front of me.

"Are you Miss Pepper? Are you a teacher at Philly Prep?" He was well dressed, in the sloppy way that well-dressed college-age kids can be these days. He didn't look crazed or frightening. Off-putting, perhaps, because of the tilt of his stance, separating himself from me even as he introduced himself, and his barely contained expression of distaste.

"Why do you ask?" I put my door key between my middle and index fingers. It's a handy weapon in that position. Just in case.

"My name is Ethan. I, um, know Petra. Does that answer?"

It certainly did. But my house? "What—how did you know where I—"

"Some girl named Bonnie who goes to Petra's school. Where you teach, she said. She wouldn't tell me her last name, or her phone number. But she gave me yours. I called and got your machine. Didn't want to leave a message. She's been driving me crazy the whole past week. She said she saw a list of the faculty addresses. Something in the office, something about summer. I don't know, but that's how she explained it. I'm not here to do anything except get her off my back, and since she said you're part of it, to call off your troops. You're making things worse."

"What troops? What are you talking about?"

He looked around. "Can we talk a little less . . . publicly?"

We certainly weren't going into my house. The idea of walking wasn't overly appealing, either. The rain had subsided, but it was obvious it would start up again, soon. Meanwhile, a wet wind rustled my clothing.

"It's not like I'm any kind of threat," he said. "You're the threat. To me. And to Petra, if you have to know."

I had to know. "Let's walk." We headed toward Independence Mall, toward tourists. I didn't mind being near people. Just in case. "Why would you say I'm a threat?" I asked. I had taken on evil powers this week.

"Involving cops."

I thought he meant Mackenzie. I couldn't understand why, however, and I shook my head to show my incomprehension.

"Look. I admit I made a major mistake in judgment. I thought she was older. I thought she—I thought a lot of wrong things, okay? But to act as if I'm a criminal—"

"I never—"

"Bonnie said you called the police. About me."

I took several deep breaths.

"I could have ignored her, if you want to know. Petra. When she called—I could have so easily fanned her off. Most men would."

Men, indeed. There's a major difference between being male and a man, or at least, I want there to be.

"I barely remembered her. I was pretty far gone that night. And so was she. I am amazed she remembered my name or where I lived. I didn't remember her name." His voice almost pulsed with emotion, and he gesticulated, his hands arcing as we walked. "Then I was only home that one night Petra called because of my grandparents' golden wedding anniversary party. That was the only reason I ever talked to Petra again. It was all pure chance."

Just like the pregnancy. "Chance affects a lot of things," I murmured.

He glared. "I don't know why you and that Bonnie treat me like scum. I mean it took two people, didn't it? And I behaved *honorably*. I didn't *have* to, is what I mean. Don't you understand?"

Honorably. Honorable. The note. But that was Helen's, not Petra's. The two of them were merging, blurring boundaries. "I'm not sure I do, Ethan. I'm worried sick about Petra, as are her parents, as is her friend. So far, I wouldn't paste the word *honorable* on much of this."

"Bonnie! Call her off, would you? I don't want my parents hearing about this—Jesus, that's the last thing I need right now. I wasn't supposed to use the house that way, for a party, in the first place."

"You're in college, right?"

He nodded. "Freshman. I was home that weekend, for a friend's birthday. My parents were on vacation. They didn't even know I was in town. I'd rather they never did, thanks." He walked silently, gesturing as if he were having an argument with himself; then the words burst out of him again. "What is that Bonnie, insane? What the hell *was* all this about?"

"Petra's missing. The police are of course involved. Is that what you mean? Her parents—"

"I don't mean that. I mean telling the cops I murdered her!"

"Who ever—"

"*Bonnie!* Why do you think I—why would she even think that, let alone call me about it three times? The first time, I called her from school, the night before my last final. I hung up on her. After that, when I was home, I had my mother take messages until I got scared that Bonnie would tell my mom what she told me. For God's sake—I could imagine it, 'I'm calling because Ethan murdered my friend. Would you give him that message?' She called me three times in the last two days. What's wrong with her?"

"She's scared. Her friend is missing." And maybe she's nuts, too. What if there truly had been foul play? What kind of high school student would mess with a killer—if she really believed that—and more to the point, what kind of student would then give the killer my home address? "It has happened, you know, that a father, an unwilling father, harmed a woman."

"Jesus! Not now! Not ever, for me—I'm not like that! I didn't hurt her. She called me last week and at first . . . okay, I admit at first, my impulse was to tell her to get lost. I thought she was making it up. I thought . . . look, the party was at my house. My parents were away. I— they have a pretty large house. Impressive, I guess, to some people. Petra seemed impressed, all right. I guess I mean I thought she was trying to . . . I thought she thought I was rich, and maybe she wanted money."

That's what he thought at first. And then? "Where is she?" I asked. "You know, don't you?"

We'd rounded the corner and were at Elfreth's Alley, the cunning street where you could believe you'd been transported back in time. Its claim to fame was as the oldest continually inhabited street in the U.S., and the narrow houses were precisely as they'd been when the city began. And up on their second stories, small mirrors, "busybodies," tilted out from the brick, spying on two centuries of passersby. I was sure that countless times, they'd reflected people like us having this same conversation about this same dilemma on this same street. Some things don't change.

"She wouldn't come home, and I couldn't stay," he said.

"Where is she?"

"I could go to jail. Don't you understand anything? She's underage and we didn't get parental permission."

Which meant he'd taken her out of state where she had options on her own, where she still had choice. However, making that decision on her own was a crime in our state. Transporting her elsewhere to make that decision was a crime. I understood Ethan's reticence, the need to talk in something akin to code. "Okay, I won't push, but I need to know that she's safe."

"I was with her, then after, I left her with my cousin. I have a summer internship starting tomorrow. I couldn't stay even if I wanted to. Even if I knew her. I'm not going to tell you names or addresses. When she feels ready, she'll come back. I gave her the fare. I paid for everything. My cousin will make sure she's okay. Her parents can just think she ran away for a while."

"Just!"

"Yeah, she told me how it is with them. She'll be in big trouble, but not as bad as if . . ."

I hoped not. Now I could talk to Rachel, present my plan. We would talk to Petra's father about almost all of her dilemma. About her running away. About the psychological danger she was in. Of how his daughter felt about her home life. Of her suicidal talk. Maybe that would galvanize him into action on her behalf. I felt a flutter of hope for Petra.

"She's safe," Ethan said. "Isn't that the thing? The whole point? She's safe and she's . . . she's okay."

"Thanks. It's good knowing that. I had some pretty horrifying images of where she could have wound up. One thing—I want her to call me. Reverse the charges. Tell her I think I can help."

"Why? You don't believe me? You think she really is dead?"

"No. I have a plan for her. I think there's a way to make things better at home. I want her to know about it, to feel safe."

He nodded. "So would you call off the dogs?" he asked glumly. "Tell Bonnie to stop? I don't want her calling my house. I don't want her talking to my parents. And I do not want the cops involved. I could go to jail because I helped her."

"I don't think the police were contacted about anything except that she was missing."

He glared at me. "This was a hoax? What was that, blackmail?"

"Ethan, you're a little bit paranoid, and you're still taking all of this too lightly, as an irritant to you. It's lucky that you had the financial resources to see this through, but just because that part was relatively easy doesn't mean this wasn't a serious situation. You still don't seem to understand how worried people were— still are—about Petra. And that includes her friend Bonnie, who overreacted and maybe said something that wasn't overly bright, but only because she thought she was protecting Petra by frightening you. We're talking about a missing fifteen-year-old who's desperate and ter-rified and feels she has no safe place on earth. Maybe, while you're doing your internship, you should think about the big picture more seriously than you seem to. This was not about your being pestered or annoyed. Do you even begin to get it?"

He raised both hands in a classic image of supplication

to heavenly powers. As if I were incomprehensible, a burden he had to bear. He didn't begin to get it. "I have to go," he said. "Have to catch the train."

I nodded. So be it.

He left. I walked to midblock, where I turned and entered Bladen's Court, an alley off the alley. Not many people knew about its small courtyard, and it was a place I liked when I needed solitude. Of course, it was more enjoyable when breathing didn't feel like inhaling through a wet sponge. On good days, I'd sometimes take papers to mark, and sit on the bench in the circular courtyard and see the "spinning porch" of the house facing the community well. That's where the women sat and worked through the hot summer, although the enclosed courtyard must have been unbearably oppressive as the temperature rose.

And on that porch, I now thought, they must have talked discreetly, perhaps more obliquely than even we had, of the same troubles.

I sat down. Sooner or later, I would be rained upon, but the warm blustery air was not unpleasant, and this had proven a good place so many times. A good place to think, which is what I did, in no particular order, my mind overfull of the drama and events of the past few days, and of today alone—the visit to Susan, the talk with Tess, the encounter with Ethan.

And of Petra, somewhere, as safe, I hoped, as he'd implied. But alone. What a mess it all was, and she still had an angry family to face. I wondered how she'd be, long term, because of all that had happened to her.

Anger, guilt, pain. What a roil of emotions this Sunday had held. Petra's. Helen's.

And then I sat very quietly as the two women blurred, blended, superimposed themselves, one on top of the other, in my mind. I thought about Helen's secret, her unhappy love affair, the depression when she couldn't conceive, her sense that the infertility was punishment for her love affair with a married professor.

Tess saying I should back off, be more discreet, that there were things Helen would not have wanted Gretchen to know.

The notes in the daybook about hoping to be forgiven.

Polly Baker and her illegitimate brood.

Petra's pregnancy.

RvW.

The quote about laws creating criminals.

I stood up quickly and walked double time back to the loft, and my pace had nothing to do with the impending rain, which I could smell in the air. It was a return to what I'd felt at the end of the visit with Susan, the talk with Tess.

I hurried to look again at precisely what Helen had written.

Yes, I had told Susan to burn the copy I'd given her, just as I'd promised to do. But first, I'd copied the pages that seemed important.

So I'd lied a little. Better sometimes to be a liar than a fool.

Twenty-three

I WAS BEYOND EDGY. MY MIND FELT LIKE A CITY UNDER siege. Thoughts about Petra and Helen torpedoed my brain. I reread Helen's notes in the light of what Tess had said about her puritanical ways. And then I couldn't concentrate on that anymore, so I reviewed the talk with Ethan and didn't get anywhere in particular with that, either. I needed to fill the yawning, agitated space ahead until something happened—Mackenzie came home, or I felt like preparing dinner, or it was time to go meet Denise.

I saw the tape I'd promised to edit. It wasn't much of a job. Most people, as I recalled, had said pleasant enough things. Only one that I remembered had been upset—a poor choice of words that she'd then changed. Cutting and splicing would be simple. Eminently doable.

I listened as Denise complimented Helen's values, more or less, and felt just as irrationally annoyed as I had when I'd first heard her cast Helen's goodness as a political plug. I was even annoyed that a fine word such as *values* had become code for something narrow and less fine. And I heard Roxanne be generous about Helen's beauty and radiance, and Clary pick up on how the boys had loved Helen, and the anecdote about dating every Tom, Dick, and Harry. Someone else had used the same expression with me, I remembered. Helen must have been incredibly popular. And Tess, so kind and sane, talking about Helen's joy at her daughter's birth and about Helen's principles, and then Wendy, talking about their early business relationship.

This was good stuff, a fine gift to Helen's daughter. A warm and completely positive portrait. We should do this for everyone while they're alive. Have their memorials while they can appreciate them and force us all to see more of each other than the slivers we observe in passing.

I heard Wendy say, "Turn it off!" Time for me to work.

I sat with the tape, the women's voices echoing as I cut and spliced out her unfortunate reference to a "happy ending for everybody." I wondered if anything on the tape was worth adding to my diagram that looked like balloons and free-flying trash and added up to nothing. So when the minor editing task was completed, I pulled my notes close and studied them.

You know how it is when a song gets trapped in your brain until you're humming it so incessantly you're annoying even your own self? That's how it was with the Helen/Petra/Susan clusters of words, issues, problems in my head. They refused to stop spinning, repeating themselves, until I could almost picture the interior of my skull with words zooming in spirals that matched Helen's doodles. Helen. Death. Beautiful. Helen the firebrand. Helen solo on a protest march. Morality. Ivan and Roxanne. Ivan and Helen. Where was Ivan. Clary works. Stresses. Hypocrisy. Family forgive and understand. Polly Baker. Petra hiding. Petra in trouble. Ethan. Pregnancy. Trouble. Big trouble. Parents. Shame. Guilt. Fear. Secrets. Family.

Helen falling. Denise making Helen a Roy Stanton

Harris kind of person. Denise. Roy Stanton Harris. Helen radiant. Every Tom, Dick, and Harris.

Harry!

A slip of the tongue because Roy Stanton's damn family values had insisted on being part of the babble in my brain. No need for Doctor Freud to stick in his two bits.

I nonetheless considered the slip.

Hypocrisy. That was the one word in Helen's notes to herself that most puzzled me. Was it about her business dealings? She had borrowed funds, but still . . .

When Helen thought something was wrong or immoral, she spoke up. Wasn't that what Tess had said? That or something that meant that.

The "announcement" via Roxanne.

Hypocrisy.

A scoop. Big news.

There's a feeling like a faint electrical shock when things begin to come to you. They aren't there yet, but there's a force field around them that you can feel, and I felt it then.

I went through the recycling pile and fished out this morning's paper.

And there it was, as I'd remembered. Before entering real-life politics, he'd studied and taught it. Poli sci professor at Penn State. Helen's alma mater. A professor. The years dovetailed. They were there at the same time.

Still, it was an enormous leap from there to . . .

Not all that enormous. Not when everything was considered. Hypocrisy. Honor. Rage about a contribution to his cause.

I considered the long piece, more than I'd ever before wanted to know about Roy Stanton Harris. This time, I read every word, and midway down the second column, under a subheading called EARLY VISION, I saw:

Harris's campaign manager has ties to the candidate that predate politics and that have bound the two as friends for several decades now. "They say you're who you're going to be by twelfth grade," Michael O'Malley said, "and I can say that 'Harry' Harris was a pain in the neck. We were all still walking around with no idea of where we were headed or what we wanted to do with our lives, except for Harry. Made the rest of us feel like he was the only grown-up. As long as I can remember, he had his eye on the flag, and he . . ."

Every Tom, Dick, and Harry. Was that possible? At least two people had said that phrase, had mentioned Toms and Dicks. Was Roy Stanton Harris really Harry the married teacher?

His wife had been sick for a long time, ultimately dying right before Zachary entered Philly Prep, a fact the boy used as an excuse for his bad behavior. Was that part of Helen's sense of shame? Not only a married man, but one with a dying wife and a child?

Words and ideas pressed and pushed at me. I spoke out loud, startling the cat and even myself a bit, but I felt as if I were preparing a case, a prosecution.

The loose puzzle pieces began locking together, making one coherent picture. Roe *v.* Wade. Polly Baker's babies. Fertility problems, depression. The law that created criminals. Hypocrisy. Honorable. And so I paced and told my case to the judge, in this case, a mildly bemused Macavity.

Mr. Family Values, the front-runner, had had an affair with a college student while he was married and his wife was ill. And then—it had to be—he arranged his lover's abortion. That's why she thought her fertility problems were a judgment.

But now Harris preached against everything he'd done, blamed the world's problems on such actions. Wanted the law reversed so that others in his situation would not have access to what he'd had.

That had to be the "hypocrisy" in Helen's note. His. His false morality. That was the only thing that made sense of it all.

Helen, who was hard on herself, felt guilt. About her own silence in the light of his platform rhetoric. And anger, about Harris's hypocrisy. No wonder she'd been furious about Clary's donation to his campaign. That may have sparked her determination to go public.

I was willing to bet her discomfort at the book group, the thing she'd said to her daughter, had to do with the presence of Denise, the candidate's wife.

Denise, who needed to see me. What had she said? "There's a situation. She"—meaning Helen—"was in touch recently." Helen had made contact about this, about what she planned, maybe in the hopes of getting Roy Stanton to own up, or ease up on his rhetoric. In either case, with that contact, Denise would have known that Helen was trouble.

Helen spelled potential disaster to that campaign. An upstanding, model citizen was going to come forward and say to the candidate, "You are a hypocrite and I am willing to tarnish my own reputation for the sake of exposing you." I looked at her staccato notes again and nodded. It all fit. Every bit of it.

Maybe Helen had warned them, or asked that they be publicly honest. It would have been like her to do so.

So you make a specious appointment, pretend to be a workman, dress like one, get entry into the house where a distracted and confused housekeeper dizzy with a year's worth of workmen barely notices you, and you wait for Helen.

The remodel was no secret, certainly not to anybody in the book group.

You didn't have to be strong to push someone who didn't expect such an act. The surprise of seeing a familiar face might have given the killer enough time to push and have it over. That quickly.

And then there was Susan and her notes. The book group knew about that, too. You didn't have to be strong to clobber somebody from behind, either.

I was out of breath, pulse racing. Somebody I knew could do something like this, to someone as good as Helen. And attempt to do it again with Susan.

I phoned Susan. I had to hear all of it said out loud. "No need to speak," I assured her. "Just listen. Grunt when you object, or hear bad logic—or anything."

I got all the way through without hearing a grunt. "Can't believe it," she said. She said it as if through a terry towel, missing letters and softening syllables, but I heard it as sharply as if each word had been polished to a point.

"Why not? Where am I going wrong?"

"Denise," she said. "So . . . proper. Not like us. Always earrings."

I knew what she meant. Garb for the book group was whatever anybody felt like wearing. Roxanne obviously got a kick out of costuming herself. Most of the rest of us wore whatever was most unlike work and most comfortable—jeans or sweats. Not Denise. She was ever and always a lady. A first lady in the Nancy Reagan mode. Little tailored suits. Stockings. Discreet earrings. "But you're always talking about the least likely suspect, right? I was the one who said the least likely is the least likely, and now I think I was wrong."

Silence for a second, then a long sigh. "Denise is *really* least likely. Prim!"

Pwim, it sounded like, but I got the picture. A pwim killer.

"Look, I'm asking you whether you see a hole in the argument. Nobody else makes sense, really. Even if Helen borrowed money without mentioning it, what would anybody at the firm gain by killing her? Even if Ivan was off somewhere where he shouldn't have been, what would he gain by killing his wife? Roxanne? I don't think so. I don't even know if the rumors are true at all. Men and women can be friends." I thought I heard a small "hmmph!" of disbelief, but I ignored it. "So where is the hole in the logic?"

"Figged out because slipped the tongue?"

"I figured it out through a slip of the mental tongue—but not completely. I was sure it had to be about sex, and about illegitimacy, abortion—something like that."

"Why?"

"Your painkillers have eaten your brain," I said. "The fact that she'd copied so much about Polly Baker. When we saw they were notes—probably for her announcement—what else could the forgiveness be about? The only sin, isn't that what she called it the night of the book club? A woman having sex without intending to procreate?

"Suppose it was only about this secret affair with a married man. That was long ago. If that was going to be her big announcement—so what? Excuses and apologies would be made. That's not worth going public with something she kept secret from her daughter and husband. There had to be more. Something that mattered on some public, civic scale. I'm sure she was going to make Polly part of her announcement—giving some historical perspective on women and their bodies and legislation. Look at those pages I brought you—at the arrow from Polly to Roe *v.* Wade. To whom do those ideas relate? And who's prominent enough to warrant a feature piece about this sort of thing?"

"Aaah," Susan said. "Mirmorty."

"Mr. Morality. Right. Only him. She could have blasted the man's entire platform, his holier-than-thou stance, couldn't she? Virtually destroy him, or at least injure him severely. But I don't think he'd do anything himself. I don't think he'd dirty his hands or be that obvious. Besides, would he know about workmen? Or your schedule?"

"You wery good," Susan said.

"Once you're off narcotics, some of the glow may recede." It no longer felt revelatory. It felt horribly, ploddingly obvious and logical.

Susan squawked. "Don' go! No meeting now!"

I laughed. "You mean like those idiots in books? The ones who run into the maniac's house to see what the screaming's about?"

She made clenched-jaw noises of agreement.

"Just because the old baseball bat would work as efficiently on me as it did on you?" I asked. "And because maybe there won't be a passerby this time?"

The door opened, and Mackenzie entered. Shuffling, just about. He looked as if he'd topple with one push. "God but it is good to be home!" he said before he was even in the room. That sentence apparently had used up his last reserve of strength. He walked over, kissed my forehead, and sat down on the sofa and started an exhausted-sounding monologue. He hadn't even noticed that I was on the phone. I covered the speaker side of the receiver with my palm and listened.

"This is all I wanted all day," he said. "All I thought about every minute. I am tired of crime and killings and sorrow. I am tired, tired, tired, and I jus' want to be with you and consider other life alternatives. Like becoming a street cleaner."

Poor man. Poor desperate-for-the-sanctuary-of-home man.

"Manda?" Susan said.

I took my hand off the speaker. "I'm not an idiot," I answered her. "I'm not going there alone. I'm going with police protection."

Mackenzie already had one shoe off, but he stopped in mid-removal of the second one.

"Who wif?" She waited a minute and, still blurry-lipped, said, "Wif whom?" We'd majored in English at Penn. A few bashes on the head aren't supposed to eradicate that.

"Guess."

"Oh. Fawt he was wurrgink."

I considered the poor man holding the shoe. I felt compassion, understanding of where he was emotionally and physically. I felt concern.

I realized, once and for all, that I truly, permanently loved him.

Which nonetheless coexisted with my need to see the mystery of Helen's death through as far as I could go.

Mackenzie still waited, his hand on his second shoe, his excellent features slowly contracting into an affectionate, but suspicious expression.

I put my hand over the receiver. "Might as well let that second shoe drop," I said. "Or I will. Because yes, the answer is: with you." I waited. This was a test, I realized. A grossly unfair one, just like in fairy tales. I waited with held breath.

"Out?" he asked.

I nodded.

"Again?"

I nodded again.

"Tonight?"

Another nod.

"In the rain." Not a question, but I gave him one final nod.

"Damn." He picked the first dropped shoe up. He didn't ask where or why, possibly because he was too tired for any more words. He merely shook his head slowly as if in disbelief and got himself ready.

"You pass," I whispered. "You permanently pass. No more tests."

Twenty-four

OF COURSE I EXPLAINED, IN GREAT DETAIL, AFTER I ended the conversation with Susan. I explained what all I thought I knew, and I explained it top speed, partly to cover up my nonanswer when we saw that the sky had fallen yet again and we were in monsoon mode.

"Where's your raincoat?" he asked as we were leaving.

"The umbrella will do," I said. It was only a little bit broken. "Anyway, the kid, Ethan, got me to thinking about . . ."

I watched his reaction. I waited for him to disbelieve, to stop me and correct my logic, but he couldn't. And didn't try. Instead, he seemed concerned—about me.

I felt a tenaciously held set of reservations—a series of nearly transparent scrims that I'd carefully placed between us—fall. They were gone. Disappeared. And there Mackenzie was. Clear as day.

He was no longer "the other"; he was a part of whatever I was.

I kept that late-breaking news to myself. The timing seemed off for a man who so recently rhapsodized about our lack of binding ties.

"IT MAKES ME SICK," I SAID AS WE SETTLED IN A BOOTH at the place Denise had specified. It was sparsely populated, with a lone man at the bar, and possibly others at the back, in booths, although I couldn't see them. They should be home, anyway. The rain was tropical, torrential, not at all the spring showers that bring flowers. This deluge smashed blossoms, flattened them to pulp.

The slick interior seemed designed for a life other than mine and even, perhaps, an era other than this one. Recessed lighting skimmed blue velvet seats and brushed stainless tables. A pianist played Cole Porter tunes, and I yearned, for the first time in two years, for a cigarette. It seemed a requirement of places such as this. Spare time and a hat with a veil that covered the top half of your face, leaving your mouth free for martinis and kisses.

"This place bothers you?" Mackenzie asked.

"I've never felt close to Denise, or overly fond of her, but she seemed okay. Not a bad sort. Ambitious, but then so are lots of my friends and there's nothing wrong with that. But to have your ambitions warp you that way. To . . ." It made me shudder. Or else it was the air-conditioning.

I could talk about it easily because I was with Mackenzie. Not that I could bear picturing myself a damsel in distress, waiting to be saved, and not that I believed he was my personal superhero, able to protect me from life's insults. But there was no getting around the fact that a tall, healthy male specimen of cophood was a plus on the arm.

Denise would have to do only what she said she was going to do—speak with me. Say what was on her mind, if anything besides walloping me was. If or when she tried to sneak behind me with a bat, or push me into traffic, or do much of anything, she'd get herself arrested and hauled away.

So I could settle into the evening, almost watch it reel by and admire it for what it was.

"You don' want to know about it, is that it?" he asked softly. "About Denise. About what people can do."

I considered this, and then I nodded. "Ignorance might not be bliss, but it sure beats looking at everybody—I mean everybody now—suspiciously. Being a little afraid all the time."

He nodded.

"That's what's getting to you about your job, isn't it?" I asked. "That bad feeling about humanity in general."

Carefully, overly carefully, he wiped a bead of sweat off his glass of beer. "After all these years, my view of the world . . . I don't think it's accurate. In fact, I know it isn't. It's skewed, bent from lookin' at the rotten pieces of the puzzle all the time. But all the same, it's what I see, pretty much."

"You used to talk about law school. Or science—forensics, some such," I said. "How does that sound now?"

He nodded. "Both worth thinkin' about, but it's a hard call with lots of factors to weigh. Includin' you, of course."

"Being weighed isn't my favorite thing," I murmured, and he smiled. "I think I could get used to places like this, though. Why don't we hang out in them more often? There's something about it that makes you want to talk about stuff. About life. Big stuff."

"It's called cryin' in your beer." He downed the last of his uncried-in beer and signaled for another.

I ordered another glass of wine and an assortment of tapas. *"In vino veritas?"*

"Possibly. But it's more who we are this particular night. Bars, cafés, whatever are only spaces, like the commons were supposed to be. The parks. Places to gather and become a community. Whatever kind it is. Sometimes, the only sounds in bars are mating calls. Lots of times, it's all about lies large and small. You and me, we talk here, but we talk at home, too. And in delis and restaurants and parks and in the car . . ."

I couldn't help smiling at him. Despite Denise and the reason I was here, I was enjoying myself. I felt worldly, on the town, out of my normal walls and spaces. "We've become fogies," I said. "Homebodies."

He shrugged. "Nice, isn't it?" He looked at his watch. "Where is she?"

"She'll be ducking out of another of his endless appearances. It's exhausting just to read his schedule, to think of how many times he must say the same thing. It must be hell on wheels to stand or sit there and smile at the same drivel, time after time after time. I couldn't do it." I envisioned Roy Stanton Harris, elegantly dressed, charming, disarming with the combination of classic features and deep dimples that flashed when he smiled. It was no mystery how and why a young girl like Helen— or anyone—could fall for him. I just couldn't understand how a grown, independent woman like Denise could tolerate his politics, let alone so absorb them that she could kill a friend and nearly kill a second one for their sake.

"What you couldn't stand, Denise seems willing to kill for." He checked his watch again. "We'll give her a few more minutes. It's nice here, anyway. She has good taste."

"Except in husbands."

Husbands. Silently, I repeated the word. Tasted it. Tested it. The man at the piano played "Always." Too corny to believe, except I suddenly thought: why not?

Why not now?

A good man is hard to find. You've found one. My mother again! She'd tracked me down.

Or was it me?

In any case . . .

"Mackenzie," I blurted out, "will you marry me?"

He had just raised his glass to his lips, and he sprayed out a light fan of beer. And laughed out loud.

My skin burned, then iced over. The future—including what had been a perfectly fine status quo—crumbled. *I asked him to marry me! The guy spouting bad marital statistics. The guy who's never mentioned the word, except negatively. Was I out of my mind?* "Scared you, didn't I?"

"Of course," he said.

"I was only—"

"I thought you'd never ask."

"—joking."

"Wait a minute," he said. "You're retracting the offer? I've heard of short engagements, but this is ridic—you were toyin' with my affections? Not nice, Amanda, not at all."

"*Yes?* You said yes? You meant yes?" I heard the squeak of disbelief in my voice. I'd lost my martini sophistication midproposal.

"You anticipated otherwise? Hoped I'd say no?"

"You've been preaching the happy nonmarried life as if it were the received word of God. What else would I think?"

"This is the weirdest—what are we disputing now? But still—if that's what you thought I felt—why'd you ask? Just to make me feel—"

"No, because I—"

"Wanted me to say thanks a heap, but no? Wanted *me* to be the problem?"

"Are you saying I am?"

"Of course. You're the high priestess of single. Every time your mother tiptoes near the subject of marriage, you erect new barricades, write new manifestos against it. What else would I have thought? Didn't want to rush or push you where you didn't want to be." His voice was kind, bemused, entertained as if he'd been watching a good show for a long time.

I felt a goofy smile force itself on my face. He laughed again, and then he raised his glass. "A toast," he said. Then his smile froze, he cocked his head, and he put his glass back down. "Hold on. Have to be sure. This has not been exactly a Hollywood version. Amanda, given our ability to poorly communicate, tell me so that I have it straight—what, precisely, would we be toasting? What was it you asked?"

"I . . . I . . . we . . . want to get married?"

He nodded gravely. "Tha's what I thought. And I said yes, and you said you were kidding, and then we—so I'm askin', are we on or off?"

On or off. I couldn't believe that prepositions would determine this most major of life changes. Shouldn't it be something grander? Something more heroic?

"On," I said. We clicked glasses.

So it was like that. Betrothed while waiting for a murderer to show.

The solitary drinker at the bar had been watching us, and he nodded and smiled, rather wistfully, I thought, as we toasted each other. Then he settled his tab and left.

"What happens next?" I asked Mackenzie.

He kept grinning. "Beats me," he said. "I'm new here myself. We'll have to play it by ear."

And as if that *ear* had miscued someone, ours were assaulted by shouts. The outside door was pushed open, and the man who'd just left stood there, shouting above the drum of the rain pouring on the awning. "Help! Call an ambulance! There's a—" At this point he probably realized that a certain level of histrionics wasn't necessary. He could deliver his news indoors. He stepped in and closed the door.

"There's a woman outside on the ground. I shouted, but she didn't budge. I touched her, she didn't move."

"It's probably old Bets," the bartender said. "Damn. She gets herself into a stupor and falls down and gets pneumonia—"

"This isn't any homeless lady. Call the police!" The bartender was already punching numbers on his phone.

Mackenzie was shaking his head. I could almost hear the thoughts inside: *This is the last thing I wanted tonight.* Insult added to injuries. Nonetheless, he was on his feet and in gear. "I'm police," he said, producing his badge.

It wasn't going to be Old Bets outside, I knew. I followed Mackenzie, hanging back a few steps, but I was the one who could identify the body. If it wasn't Old Bets.

It wasn't.

Even though I'd known it as soon as the man first shouted, I still couldn't believe what I saw. Couldn't fit Denise, sprawled and bleeding on the sidewalk, into the jigsaw puzzle I'd completed. I looked up, past her into the wet and empty street, past that to the empty sidewalk on the other side.

Denise wasn't the killer. I'd been wrong. She hadn't killed Helen or attacked Susan. My carefully constructed puzzle picture fragmented again.

Around us, sheets of rain, blued by the sign outside the bar, cascaded down the awning and off, making a wet crime-line barrier.

Who?

Anybody, the rain hissed as the night yawned around it. It could be anybody. You're back to square one.

Twenty-five

I WAS BEING WATCHED, OR WE WERE. I LOOKED ACROSS the street and saw a ragged man emerge from a doorway, newspaper his defense against the downpour. I felt a surge of hope—he could have seen what happened.

But even as I raised my arm and shouted, "Hey!" he lifted a sleeping bag and took off.

Mackenzie had been kneeling next to Denise's body. He stood up. "I feel a pulse."

I took a moment to be relieved. "That man"—he was turning the corner at this point—"he saw what—"

Mackenzie put his arm on mine. "I saw him when I first came out. He was asleep," he said. "Our noise woke him up and he cursed us. Incoherently."

The whine of a siren interrupted him. "Why don't you wait inside?" Mackenzie said. "That'll be the paramedics. I'll be two minutes."

I nodded and went and ordered a brandy. I brought the untouched plate of tapas over to the bar, then pushed it away. I sat nursing my drink and thinking about what a ridiculous question I'd been asking with my "if not Denise, then who did it?" Even that incoherent homeless man across the street would have taken no more than five seconds to answer that question.

Mackenzie came in, asked me to order him a brandy,

too, excused himself for five minutes, then came and sat next to me on one of the plush blue-velvet barstools.

"It's Harris, then," I said. "I was only wrong in thinking he wouldn't get his own hands dirty. He'd know everything because Denise would have told him."

"Maybe not."

"Maybe not know everything or maybe not that he did it?"

"Either or both, plus maybe you weren't wrong in thinking he wouldn't. Might be time to take a deep breath, drop back, and reconsider the whole thing. Look at it from a new vantage point. Start instead with the business of the husband, the missing money, the mysterious absence," Mackenzie said.

"The missing husband Ivan? What would he gain by doing that?"

"The money, maybe. And Roxanne." Mackenzie shrugged. "I always thought he was a more likely suspect than anybody else. The spouse, you know." He put both hands up. "I'm not sayin' a thing against marriage. Just that you always look at the spouse first. And most often, last." He sipped again at his brandy, and I did the same. I could feel the fumes warm their way down my body.

"Jiggle your thinking out of the way it's been directed," Mackenzie said. "Think in terms of Denise, not Helen. Maybe we've got all of this backwards. What could Denise have known or owned that made this person think she had to be stopped at any cost? What felt like life-or-death to this other person—another person who is not, by the by, her husband."

"Why not? It has to be him."

Mackenzie shook his head no, looking sad that he had to do so. "It lacks logic. Why would he hurt her? He wouldn't. Not ever. She's an asset."

"Not if she was going to tell me that he killed Helen."

"Tell you." His tone was noncommittal.

"Yes. Me. It was something important."

"Well, then, you could be right. Except you aren't."

I leaned close and enunciated each syllable, trying to be as obviously superior to him as possible. "Given that you found my theory convincing one small half hour ago, how can you *possibly* say with such *consummate* authority that this *small* revision, which does not change *any* of the principal ideas, is beneath consideration?"

He grinned. "Very good, your elegance! I can see how you might easily terrorize small children and the semi-literate, but I, despite being humble, have my own ways of knowing things, too, even words, and am not easily terrorized by a fine vocabulary and syntax."

"Avoiding the question, aren't you? Why is that? Because you don't have a sane answer?"

"You're going to regret your supercilious tone," he said in a mild voice and with just a trace of a smile. "I didn't avoid the question, just the hurt the answer will cause your ego, is all. The thing of it is, I talked to Roy Stanton. I myself can provide his alibi." He leaned back, basking in his superiority and almost toppling off the barstool, which for the nastiest slice of a moment would have pleased me mightily.

"When? What about? What does any of this have to do with—"

Mackenzie gestured toward the back of the bar. "Five minutes ago?"

"I thought—"

"I was answering a call of nature, when in fact, I was making an unnatural call. To turn a phrase, if I dare do so in your august presence."

"Continue. We are mildly amused."

"The man had to be informed that his wife has been in a serious accident."

"Accident? You mean whoever attacked her didn't mean to? The heavy object slipped out of his hand and onto her head?"

"Don' know it's male, Amanda. Or was that a sexist, knee-jerk response?"

"You're right. The attackperson's heavy object slipped."

"I had to tell Roy Stanton his wife was seriously injured. An' where they were taking her. He sounded unable to comprehend a word of it."

"That proves nothing. He must be a good actor to say the things he does with a straight face."

"The thing is, before I could get to him, I had to go through two other people, then wait, because Roy Stanton was windin' down, concluding his talk. I myself heard the applause, which went on forever. Way excessive. My guess is that Denise sneaked out at the start, thinking she'd be back by its conclusion and nobody would notice."

My shoulders sank so low, they rested on my pelvis.

"The man talks for too long."

Damn. Double damn. The ominous dark crept in still more, a frightening straitjacket waiting to be snapped around me.

"Furthermore, if I were to check back, which I surely will, if ever there is a clear and proven homicide, he will turn out to have been out in front of a thousand people when Helen fell."

"That was midday."

"A luncheon speech, or at least a meeting, you'll see. He's running hard and nonstop. As for Susan? You don't really believe the guest of honor, the candidate himself, could walk outside of an enormous fund-raiser and excuse himself to bean somebody up the street, do you? Know how many tagalongs there are? Aides and confidantes and yes-men and well-wishers and people like

Susan and . . . even if 99 percent of them were gone, his car would be right in front of the ballroom, waiting. He would not have been able to escape notice."

He was right, I was wrong, but I didn't like that at all. It is sometimes difficult behaving like an adult. "I feel as if . . . I feel endangered. Three people in my book group now. That can't be coincidence."

"Doesn't sound like it."

"It's . . . it's pretty . . ."

"Terrifyin'."

I wouldn't have been able to say that word out loud. Almost one-third of the group seriously, if not fatally, hurt. Who was next? Why? "What could anybody have against us? What could we possibly know or have done that could so infuriate someone? We're ordinary women. We don't even have that much in common besides loving books."

Mackenzie was shaking his head in that sad-but-true fashion of his. "Only way to find out is to ask," he said. "Maybe it's time for a real truth-telling session. Instead of each one comin' to you with her version and her bit, maybe everyone has to do what you were tryin' to. Toss their knowledge into a public, open pot. See what emerges. Answer hard questions."

"And meanwhile, the official investigators will do what?"

"Officially investigate," he said. "Startin' with yours truly."

"We won't survive this, will we?"

"You and me? Why not?"

I flashed him a look. "I meant the book group. As a group. Once people ask Roxanne about having an affair, or Clary says the thing about the missing money, or Wendy talks about the aborted deal, or Tess obliquely refers to Helen's problems . . ." I couldn't go on.

"You seem curiously out of the loop," he said. "You and Susan. The snoops."

"I dread telling Susan."

"Rough, comin' on the heels of her attack." He held up his snifter, visually measuring just how long he could make the last sip of cognac last.

"Undoubtedly, but I meant something else. She's mixing up real life and fiction, and she makes predictions, or warns against things, because of the way things happen in books. Maybe it's that blow to her head. But she was right this time. When I told her Denise wanted to talk tonight, she said that meant Denise would be killed."

"Denise isn't dead."

"Yet? That's good news, but that's luck, or chance. The basic thing's come true, and the point is Susan. It's too creepy that life is mixing up fiction and reality even worse than Susan does."

"You won't call her, then?"

"Of course I'll call her." I exhaled so forcibly the cocktail napkin rose from the bar and fluttered. "I'll call everybody." There wasn't any need to start a telephone tree. There were so few of us left to call.

Twenty-six

I HEARD SUSAN'S INTAKES OF BREATH AS SHE GULPED IN what I told her. "Now what?" she asked when I finished.

"Mackenzie suggested—and I agree—that we have to get the group together. We have to openly pool whatever we know or suspect or fear. If we don't find out what this is about, how do we know what to do? How do we even protect ourselves?"

"Why's somebody after us?" Susan said, echoing my earlier sentiments.

"That's what we have to find out. So for convenience's sake—yours—should we meet at your house tomorrow night or mine?"

"Mine," Susan said. "Ear pauking." Easier parking. Her pronunciation kept improving, so that she almost sounded like a lockjawed aristocrat. "Hey!" she said with almost her former vigor. "*Classic*. Gather all the suspects together—"

"This is our book group, not suspects!" I said. "Next you'll say we'll use the drawing room. Too bad you don't have one."

"Somebody's knocking us off."

"But not anybody who'll be in that room, Susan." Oh, how I hoped I was telling the truth. "There are other options."

"Who?"

"Ivan Coulter. Mysterious whereabouts. Having an affair. Helen might have been very much in the way. Somebody altogether else. Somebody we don't know about at all. Somebody who—are you ready?—doesn't like books, has never heard of a book group. It could be anybody."

"You fink ev'body tell truth? Right out?"

I thought about Clary and the missing funds, Roxanne's nonmarriage, Tess and the psychological history, Wendy, who'd wanted to be partners with Ivan. Private things that should have been able to die along with Helen. Private things that would kill the book group.

"All in liv' room," Susan said. "And we name the killer!"

No wonder she couldn't sell her book. "What's going through your injured skull?" I asked. "A Nero Wolfe flashback? That isn't how it happens—not even in books anymore."

"They had more fun back then."

We both sighed, I suspect for different reasons.

"So maybe instead . . . killer goes berserk and mows us all down. 'Cept the heroine. Who is the heroine of this one?"

I did not deign to honor that with a response.

"Okay," she said. "Just joking."

"It is good to hear that sanity has returned along with better enunciation. Six-thirty at your house tomorrow. Let people know. And I'll have time after school to pick up sandwiches. Everybody can pay me back."

"They never worry about food in books," Susan said. "Did Miss Marple have hunger pangs? Sam Spade?"

NEXT MORNING, DENISE WAS HANGING ON, HER CONDItion somewhat less perilous than it had been the night before. The papers were full of the news of her attack, and in addition to the sorrow, the worry, the fear, and the confusion, what really rankled was that Denise's attack served as free PR for her husband. I saw him on the morning news before I left for work, and there he was, son Zachary by his side like a younger reflection, both of them sorrowful but statesmanlike. However, Roy Stanton's voice did break when he said the words *my wife*. And he did not use the opportunity to talk about our weakened moral fiber or any of the other campaign rhetoric he could have easily adapted to the situation.

Much as I still wanted to, even I would have had a hard time believing him guilty of anything except grief. Even without knowing that he was standing in an auditorium in front of a crowd when Denise was attacked.

"So how does it feel?" Mackenzie asked as I headed for the door.

I had no idea what he meant.

"Goin' off to work for the first time as an engaged woman!"

I had forgotten. All it takes is attempted murder, and like that—my betrothal slips my mind.

He winked. "Cinderella got her prince. Happily-ever-afters on the horizon. The story grinds to a close."

"That sounds fatal."

His next question made it clear that while I may have popped the question, he was asking the crucial question. "When you going to tell your mother? Or did you diabolically plan this for the one time she's inaccessible?"

How could I have forgotten my mother, for whom this would be her core experience? "She knows," I said, listening to her purr in the background. "Trust me."

"All the same, maybe we could pretend this happened after they get back. For the record, for the official announcement. Tell you what, next week, when they're home, I'll propose. My turn. I'll even ask your father for your hand."

"And the rest of me, too, I sincerely hope." I heard my mother chuckling. "You're perfect," I said, and then I really did have to leave, betrothed or not.

My marital status didn't make a lot of difference in the teaching of how to use the semicolon or even in finishing *The Scarlet Letter*. Of course, it would make a considerable difference to the odds of my ever needing to wear a scarlet letter. I had a fleeting image of Hester Prynne walking down Walnut Street today with her scarlet *A* sewn on the front of her overalls or T-shirt. Amusing, except that it led to thoughts of Petra Yates, who might as well have been required to wear the letter. And of Helen, who in some sense had secretly worn it all those years.

At lunch, I knocked on the school counselor's door, and Rachel and I talked for the entire hour, planning the Save Petra Yates campaign. We weren't going to lie to her father, but we weren't going to break Petra's trust, either. Instead, we'd tell her father half the truth, the whole half the truth, and nothing but the half the truth. Emphasis on her despair, loneliness, and suicidal thoughts. He needed to hear the appalling stats on teen suicides. Rachel was going to call him immediately.

As for me, I'd called the book group about tonight's meeting, and I also called the hospital four times during the day. Denise was still in critical condition and unconscious, but by some measure, still also "improved." She was holding her own.

I wished I knew what she'd intended to tell me.

In the hopes of seeing at least one thing to completion, I sent messengers looking for my missing editor in chief. Cinnamon had to be told that her revisions were farcical and unacceptable. Together—and I'd be at the meeting this time—we could forge a final edition of the *InkWire* that wouldn't be mortifying—even by Philly Prep's low standards. But the deadline for copy was this week, and Cinnamon was not to be found. This might be a battle I lost.

At three P.M., Rachel sent me a note. "Amazing! Mr. Y. came in immediately—solo. Agreed to fam. counseling! Keep fingers crossed—looks hopeful!"

It might actually work. Obviously, the man cared. He was weak and needed strengthening. He simply hadn't wanted to see, to challenge his second wife and alter their dynamics. But now, his daughter was missing and he had to look. He had to see. It sounded as if he would. I breathed a bit more easily on behalf of Petra Yates.

Giving up on finding the evasive Cinnamon, who was undoubtedly off on some fashion quest, I packed my briefcase at end of day. Then I realized that I needed to take care of a few administrative chores, and I had the time to do it then. I had over an hour before I'd pick up sandwiches for tonight. I needed two student addresses and phone numbers—their failure warnings had gone unacknowledged. Time for a desperate last-ditch conference with the parents. Havermeyer's philosophy of education was simple and to the point: If the families pay the bills, the children pass. We were allowed to set pedagogical standards—as long as we set them as low as it took to pass everybody. But they had to at least prove they were breathing. They had to go through the motions, and these students weren't doing even that.

I went downstairs reluctantly—I always go to the office as reluctantly as a child in trouble with the principal. Dealing with the malevolent secretary, Helga, was never a joy.

The school was settling into quiet, with only isolated sounds here and there. I approached the walnut office door when it swung open and Ivan Coulter emerged. We stared at each other.

"Mr. Coulter! I—what brings you here? Is Gretchen well?"

"I'm taking her out of school early." He looked in pain. "For the term. She'll miss a few weeks. I came over to make sure her teachers cooperate and don't penalize her. She's been through enough."

I nodded.

"I'm taking her away. Really away. The problem with day trips like Longwood is that you still have to go home again. Now, we're visiting her grandparents—my parents—and then, I'm not sure. I'm afraid for her. I don't know what's going on, but too much is. I'm hoping her teachers will allow her to write papers in lieu of final exams. Or base her grades on what she's done so far."

I was surprised he would bother explaining himself to me, but maybe Denise's attack had made him rethink some things. Maybe I was no longer an archvillainess.

"I'm sure the staff will cooperate. You know, I'm not one of Gretchen's teachers. You don't have to even request anything of—"

"I know that. Your only relationship to her is that you keep sending the police to her door!"

Guess I was wrong about having been pardoned. "I never—"

"Your *boyfriend* did," he said. "Same thing."

So Mackenzie had decided, after the weekend, to push for a criminal investigation. Good for him. I didn't express my pleased surprise, or inform Ivan Coulter that it hadn't been my *boyfriend* who'd suggested to his fellow cops that a visit to the Coulters was a good idea. It had been my *fiancé*.

I had a moment's pride in Mackenzie's ability to make things happen. In the quiet way he took care of things.

"I was sure Helen had jumped. Why wouldn't I think that? It never crossed my mind that anyone would want to harm her, and the truth was, we were in the middle of a bad time, a very rough time. Not that I expected any such thing. But I didn't believe she could have had an accidental fall because I couldn't imagine why she'd be up on the roof on a workday at noon—leave work for the rooftop—unless she meant to jump."

"The workman—"

"There were no workmen."

"Roxanne thought—"

"I know. And now I think so, too. But then, what I knew for sure was that there were no workmen there. None of ours. I was right—and at the same time, wrong. It's increasingly obvious that somebody was there. Somebody probably pretended to be involved in the roof project, and made an appointment with Helen. She was forever running back and forth from the office to check up on things. And our housekeeper's peculiar command of English—if somebody spoke quickly and with authority, she pretended to understand. She'd let a person in if they had a convincing act, and she was easy to convince."

I nodded. This was pretty much what I thought. This made sense.

"So I'm back to square one," he said, "except that two more people have been seriously hurt and I can't understand any of it. I want out of this. Most of all, I want Gretchen out of this. We're leaving for an indefinite time. I can do my work from a distance."

"But—"

"I've informed the police. I had nothing to do with any of this, do you understand? I know you meant well—all of you meant well—and in fact, you were right, apparently, and Helen was . . ." He shook his head. "But your efforts haven't felt benign."

"I apologize again."

His voice softened. "I know it was out of love of Helen and concern for Gretchen." He sighed. "But the maniac isn't going to harm any more members of my family. I don't even want Gretchen to know about it if anything more happens."

We shook hands. It was quite odd. We hadn't known each other, but our good-byes were heartfelt. As he took his hand from mine, he put it up, one finger pointing to the ceiling. "I forgot. About Roxanne. She's got problems that she doesn't want public yet, and I'm not giving any details, but instead of spreading rumors—"

"I honestly never—"

"Somebody is. My question is—why aren't you all kinder to her? Your group is supposed to be friends. That's what Helen and I were trying to be to her. Friends. Good neighbors."

I thought of the women who had kept Roxanne's secret. "We did try. We do. Please," I said. "Even if it's another woman—whatever it is, please say where you were that night. Because if you don't, the police are probably going to keep visiting."

"A threat?"

I shook my head. "An honest request. It won't go any further. I promise. Where were you?"

Annoyance twisted his features. "The police know where I was. Your boyfriend probably knows. I was with my family. My parents."

"Why be so mysterious about it then? Why not say that right away? You had to know it would throw suspicion on you."

"It's not against the law to have secrets. To respect privacy." His sigh sounded near exasperation. "Do you have brothers or sisters?"

I nodded.

"Have you wondered what you'd do if they got into serious trouble?"

My sister Beth is the upright, solid sister. I had never thought of her in trouble, though I wouldn't be surprised if she'd thought about me that way, and more than once.

"You'd help." He didn't seem to require confirmation. "But what if your sibling had done something so stupid—out of fear and confusion—so incredibly stupid that he was in danger of being locked up for it? Would you still help? I don't actually care what your answer is. I would. I did. My brother is a good man, but he got desperate and did something idiotic. Understand that I in no way condone his act. It was criminal and wrong. It's messed up my life and it was messing up Helen's. Aside from the emotional toll, particularly on my parents, it prevented me from being part of a venture that would have required my capital."

The deal with Wendy. Helen hadn't stopped him, and it had nothing to do with Wendy's unsavory fiancé and his underworld alliances. Ivan wasn't who I'd thought. Nobody was.

"It's taken time to undo it, and we were just ahead of the posse, so to speak. Helen was amazing. Astounded me how supportive she was. She didn't have to be. Finally, we—I—she—got together the balance of what he owed, and now all of it has been returned. I was taking care of that last part of the mess the day she . . . the day it happened."

The missing money Clary had mentioned. A loan to bail out Ivan's brother. I felt still worse.

"We had to call a halt to the remodel. It wasn't missing material, it was missing funds. That's why I was so positive nobody was there that day. Nobody was going to be there for a while. Charges were going to be pressed against my brother anyway. My parents are old and fragile. The shock of having their son . . ." He shook his head. "I was doing the right thing by my lights, making restitution, but it was a less-than-legal act. Helping him out and helping him away." He waved his arm at that last word, and I realized he'd also helped his brother evade the law, probably by getting him out of the country.

"The irony of it—that he'd committed the crime, he'd embezzled the money, and I'd kept him out of jail—but that I'd be the criminal and I'd be jailed for aiding and abetting when I explained—was forced to explain—where I'd been. Forgive me for not wanting that scenario, although I now have it."

"I don't know what to say."

"What's done is done. There's a chance I won't be in trouble with the law about it. Maybe not even my brother, now that the money's back in place. We're all negotiating. In any case, Gretchen and I are leaving, so watch out for yourself," he said. "Tell the book group to do the same. Somebody crazy is out there. Don't turn your back."

Talk about unnecessary advice.

Twenty-seven

I watched him leave and I felt sorry for all his burdens, and all that had happened. But I also knew that caring, perhaps too intensely and too actively, was the book group's—and my—only "crime." No longer suffocating under a sense of guilt, I was ready to face the office witch.

The outer office was empty, the door to Havermeyer's office closed. Helga's desk looked unused as usual, and the place was eerily pleasant without her scowling presence. She must have stepped out to the ladies' room, although I doubted that Helga had any natural functions.

Green paper folders were stacked on her desk. Her in-box was empty. I'd once heard it said that if ever a person's desk was totally cleaned up with not a thing left undone, the person dies.

I guess it wasn't true.

I couldn't remember why I'd come in here, then I realized I was holding the second-warning notices for two students. I needed their addresses. I stepped behind the long walnut barrier that demarcated Helga's kingdom. There was no actual NO TRESPASSING sign there, and no reason the staff shouldn't be allowed access. Nothing but the memory of Helga's witchlike scowl, but that was enough. Entering her turf gave me an illicit thrill.

Such are the highs of my professional life.

I spotted something unsealed, undone. A human flaw for Helga, hidden so the mere mortals on the other side of the barrier wouldn't know. Next to her desk a carton sat, flaps open. An untaken-care-of item, probably her amulet against that desk-death. I peered in, hoping for something delicious, like sample textbooks that publishers send and Helga refuses to distribute because then we might want them. Or supplies that hadn't yet made it into supply room purgatory. Instead, the carton contained statues, Roman centurions. A small army of them.

The graduation awards. For each grade's Athlete of the Year in the least athletically outstanding school on the Eastern seaboard. Fittingly grandiose and absurd trophies. It figured.

But everything except the carton was indeed locked up. I know this because, although I had nothing specific in mind, I tried the door of the supply closet, imagining its wrapped reams of paper, boxes of pens and pencils, stacks of lesson plan and grade books. The large room's shelves remained well stocked because Helga refused admittance to one and all and made staff members feel positively Dickensian as we begged, "Please, Helga, twenty-five sheets of paper for the copier?"

I rattled the door, but it was locked tight.

As were the drawers in which I might find the needed addresses. I tried the top row and should have been able to generalize from that, but I hoped that maybe this once, Helga had forgotten to shield every inch of her kingdom. I needed Alicia Wortham's address. She was way at the bottom, and maybe Helga's back hurt her, so she skipped the bottom locks. I squatted behind the divider and tried the drawer. It didn't budge.

"Guess you like staying after school a whole lot more than I ever did," a male voice—most definitely not my principal's—said. "But then, I never liked this place," he continued. "To put it mildly."

And then I knew who it was, and why he was here, even before I stood up and saw him.

I stifled the impulse to duck back down again. Every organ in my body slipped lower, sank. My heart made a death-defying *tha-whump!* and a shrill voice inside my brain screamed, *"Run!"*

I didn't bother to answer it because all I could have said was *"Run where?"* I was behind one barrier, and if I'd gotten out of it, Zachary Harris would provide another and even more formidable one. He stood there, tall, muscled, still wearing the smooth veneer I'd seen on TV this morning.

It was difficult keeping my voice at normal pitch. "What are you doing here?" I asked. "Back to make up classes?"

He leaned on the other side of the walnut divide. His sneer looked so natural, it must have been encrypted in his muscles. "What am I doing here?"

People who repeat questions instead of answering them really annoy me. Zachary, I thought. His father's clone. Zachary Harris, the former pain in the butt, petty criminal, and sluggard, who'd fallen in love with politics and potential power. Surely willing to do the dirty work. Zachary Harris, who had precisely as much as his father had at stake.

I'd thought about his father. I'd thought about his stepmother. Why had I been too blind to put Zachary on my mental screen?

"What are you doing here?" My turn to repeat. I needed time. Maybe that's why people like Zachary repeated, too.

"What am I doing here? Beats me," he said. "This is

about my least favorite place. Being here was like being in hell. Or jail."

"So I heard."

"You heard? So my reputation outlasted me, I guess." His smirk intensified.

If you won't run, then at least think! the brain-screamer howled. *Think of something!*

Prissy voice. Why not come up with a plan instead of carping?

Zachary's smile was an upturned sneer. He certainly wore a different face when he was out politicking with Dad. He straightened and paced back and forth the length of the room, trailing a finger over the polished countertop, like someone inspecting for dust. "The only day I didn't hate this place was graduation. Good thing you guys graduate everybody who's able to stand up and grab the diploma."

We are a tolerant school, and we cater to children who don't fit in the larger systems. But as I recall, when Zachary Harris graduated, his teachers all but danced in the streets. One, a Brit, called him "bent," and it always stuck with me, that image of a boy who hadn't grown straight up.

"Well, in that case, it's amazing you've chosen to come back," I said. "Given your feelings about your experience here." *Where the hell was Helga? Surely she could affect him as lethally as she did me.*

And where was my headmaster? This made no sense. Ivan Coulter had spoken with someone about Gretchen. I'd met him as he exited from the office, and nobody else had followed him out. There were no alternate exits from here that I'd ever heard of. It was hard to believe in secret passageways or trapdoors.

Damn peculiar. Wherever Havermeyer and Helga had

wandered, for the first and only time I could recall, I wanted them near me.

And if they brought along a militia, that wouldn't be bad, either.

Like Zachary, I, too, paced, running my hand along the back of the divider, bouncing it off all the drawer pulls. And then I found the switch, a small toggle, and followed it up, to a wire, to the microphone.

The damnable Philly Prep PA system. Primitive, annoying, and disruptive. Loud and squawky. Precisely what I needed. I flipped the toggle and kept moving.

"I wanted to come to your room. Certainly never wanted to be in this office again, that's for sure. But you split, and then I had to wait till that guy left."

He'd been in the building for some time. Watching. Waiting to pounce. And he wanted me to know that.

I figured the only weapon in my armory was Zachary's hated high school experiences. The wrath of teachers. The repeated chewings-out. "You shouldn't be here, Zachary," I said loudly, aiming my voice for the microphone. "You know the office is off limits." *Where are you, Helga? Don't you hear me? Your turf has been invaded by the barbarians. Hurry!*

"And yet I am here," Zachary said. "Life is interesting, isn't it?"

He was very calm, with a smooth sound to him. It was much more frightening than any show of emotion would have been.

"Times have changed since I was a student," he said. "I thought this place would have changed, too."

"In what way?" As if I cared about his observations. *How long was I going to have to do this? The PA reached every crevice of the school—except the room we were in. Can't you hear us, people? Aren't our voices deafening you wherever you are? Mr. Hall! The janitor had to be* somewhere. And where was the principal? Had Ivan Coulter killed him? Left him dead in his office? Because if not—where was the man?

I didn't want to use the microphone to openly call for help. Not yet. If nobody was listening to it, it was worthless, and all that would do was make Zachary still more dangerous.

"In what way did I think it would change? I'm talking security," Zachary said. "Don't you people read the papers? Don't you realize the things that go on in high schools these days? Don't you *learn* from others?"

"How did you get in?" Did he have a gun? Was he planning to mimic recent school atrocities? Or was he doing it his way—with a club, one by one.

"How did I get in?"

He was never going to make it in politics. It wouldn't be the murdering that kept him out, it'd be that tic of repeating the questions.

"I walked in, Miss Pepper," he said. "That's what I did. All nice and politelike. Somebody came out that back door. I said, 'Could you hold it there?' He did, and . . ." He shrugged. "I thought for sure there'd be a cop in the halls. What is wrong with you people?"

"We assume decency." It probably was a big mistake. We had locks and a security protocol, and because of the recent hysteria, all of that was supposedly going to be upgraded during the summer break—along with the PA system. But Philly Prep, like the schools and churches and synagogues that had been defiled by violence, wasn't, no matter how Zachary felt about it, a prison, so of course it was breachable. Parents, students, teachers, and administration needed flexibility about meetings and conferences. There weren't gun towers from which all approaches were covered. There wasn't a central list on which each person's calendar and appointments were coordinated, and so the doors weren't locked instantly after the last student left. There'd been plenty of time for Zachary to enter the building.

"Looka me," he said. "Following the rules for once. I'm checking in at the office, just like it says at the door."

I imagined his voice crackling and hissing static through all the empty rooms. Maybe I hadn't made it clear that this was bad trouble. "You aren't supposed to be here," I said. "This is illegal. Leave the office right now."

"Don't talk to me that way!" he shouted. "Don't you dare talk to me that way! You aren't my teacher! You never were my teacher! Don't tell me what to do—I'm here, see? And I'm staying as long as I want to. As long as you do. We're leaving together."

Now they'd know. Anybody hearing that would immediately leap on a white horse and come to my rescue. Surely.

And somebody had to have heard it. Two somebodies.

I asked my question again, more loudly, looking him directly in the eye. "Why are you here, Zachary Harris? You know you shouldn't be—and people will be back in a minute. The principal—you remember Dr. Havermeyer, don't you?"

For a split second, his lashes fluttered and he looked down at his feet.

I moved my vocal cords into Nightmare-Teacher Mode. "You're in big trouble, young man," I barked.

He looked startled, almost stepped back from the divider, but caught himself.

This place must really have felt like hell to him.

And so it was beginning to feel to me. How could I be all alone in the office? And why did I keep thinking I heard elevator music?

I looked again at Havermeyer's office, locked and

dark. It had a pebbled glass window through which I could see nothing.

I looked in the other direction, at the solid wooden supply room door, a door I'd rattled earlier. No window on it, no way to see through. No way for anybody to see in.

I shocked myself with my own thoughts, but where else could the two have disappeared into? I'd spoken with Ivan Coulter for some time. They must have thought he was the last person in the building. . . .

I couldn't believe my own logic. Maurice Havermeyer and Helga the Office Witch . . . a couple? Trysting to elevator music in a supply room? It was too ugly to imagine.

Zachary pounded the countertop with his fist. Just once, but it sufficed. "You know damn well why I'm here."

He wasn't that schoolboy anymore. He was a political aide. He had status, he could look ahead to power. Just as long as his Daddy's coattails were still flying.

"My condolences about your stepmother," I said. "How is she? Seems you bungled that job along with the one you did on Susan." I got as close to the mike as I could without alerting him to the fact it was on. "You didn't kill either one, did you? Tried to, but you couldn't get it right. One out of three tries. Bad stats, Zachary."

Do You Hear Me Out There? This Is a Killer!

That had to be what Denise was coming to tell me. She'd found out what Zachary had done—for his father, for himself. She'd fed him all the necessary information—inadvertently, I was sure. Table talk, maybe, including the misconception she had that I was very tight with Helen. Table talk and, perhaps, more than that. A quarrel, a heated discussion once Helen had called and Denise knew her husband's complicated history.

All Zachary had to do was listen. He'd know about the remodeling, about the gathering after Helen's death, about what was said and planned.

He'd even been with Denise at the fund-raiser. He'd been standing there, part of the group when Susan appeared with the folders. He'd been around all afternoon and evening, as far as I knew. He could have seen what was in the folder, could have read some of it right through the clear plastic.

Besides, hadn't Denise asked me about "gathering information" about Helen? And then I'd made it clear that I was there to get something from Susan.

And the Dumpster. The stupid, petty graffiti. How had I not realized that an adult wouldn't have done that?

"You and your lying friends are not going to ruin everything. You are not going to destroy my life!"

"How do you know what my friends and I might do, Zachary? How could you possibly know that?"

"When somebody is stupid enough to threaten my father—to write him letters—then I know. I open my father's mail. Sort it. Who can he trust more than me? So I knew. Like my father knew, and Denise knew. Only Denise never thinks I know anything. Denise . . ." He shrugged.

A letter. Helen had written Roy Stanton a letter of protest. Helen had behaved like a citizen of a democracy. I felt so sad, for the innocent and honest impulse, the sense of fairness that had led Helen to write the candidate and request the completely unrealistic.

No wonder Helen had no longer felt comfortable in the book group. I'd seen the strain in her snapped responses to Denise that evening, but I'd had no way of imagining how serious it must have been, or its reasons. Looking back, I was sure that Denise had shown up only because she was the presenter, and Denise met her obligations.

"Letters," I murmured.

"Threats, more like. 'If you don't speak up, I will have no choice.' Blackmail. I don't stand for blackmail."

I listened hard in the small silence that followed his words, listened for any sound of life in the building—a voice, a chair scraping, a door's creak and whine. Even, revolting as the thought was, sounds of lovemaking from the supply room. But it was only the occasional snippet of music—so soft that I could have been imagining it—I heard. That, and my own pulse pounding in my ears.

"It isn't blackmail when you ask somebody to tell the truth and your threat is that if they don't, you will," I said. Whenever I tried a direct stare, his eyes flitted to the side, away.

"You mean *her*? Those were lies! She's a liar! Have you ever *listened* to my father speak? Do you think that while my *mother* was dying—" He pounded a fist on the counter again. Even his fingers had muscles.

"Did your father tell you to do those things?"

His face colored. "I'm not a kid anymore. I'm an adult—I can decide what has to be done on my own."

"Who did you pretend to be?" I asked him.

"What?"

"How did you get that appointment with Helen?"

A glint of cold amusement sparked in his eyes. "An inspector. A building-permit inspector," he said. "I had to check the progress of the work on the roof. I don't even know if there are such things, but Helen sure made it clear she considered herself a good citizen, all right. I knew she'd say yes." He paused, as if waiting for me to congratulate him on his cleverness. When I didn't, his voice changed into a low growl. "Now get out of there," he said. "We're leaving."

I gave up on anybody riding to my rescue.

"It was really immature of you to spray-paint the

Dumpster," I said. "Like a signature. Advice to the police: look for somebody who'll never grow up. A *big baby*! *Now you get out of here!*"

He didn't listen. Never had, never would. Instead, he came closer. He looked around the room, spotted the swinging half door that was official entry to Helga's hallowed ground.

I felt my pulse in my neck, heard it pounding.

If he came into this space, I was trapped.

If I left this space, I was trapped.

If I went outside with him, I wouldn't make it past the first quiet spot, where I, too, would be made to look mugged.

Which is to say, I was trapped.

I couldn't believe this lout, this miserable excuse for a man, was going to protect his cushy, unearned future by making me his fourth victim. My blood roared in my ears, drowning whatever he was saying, whatever else was around, except—I couldn't believe it—a snip, a fragment of "Feelings" drifting out of the supply closet. I thought to go pound on its door, but what good would that do at this point?

It was over. I have nothing to lose, I thought. Nothing.

Which was when the office doors were flung open and Mr. Hall, terrified, jumped into the room. The custodian, a frail man in his sixties armed with a mop, braced himself with one hand on the wall. He raised the mop. Its wet gray strands flopped. It looked like he was toting a sharpei on a stick. Mr. Hall, with his limp and his arthritis.

"Leave, Mr. Hall!" I screamed. "Get out—call the police!"

But Zachary had wheeled around and was hell-bent now on getting poor Mr. Hall, who looked as if he'd just suffered a stroke. He stood, motionless, gulping, his mop straight out in front of him. My own Don Quixote.

He'd distracted Zachary. That was enough. "Just a *minute*, young man!" I bellowed, hoping it would activate high school nightmares. *"What do you think you're doing?"*

While I shouted, I ducked and grabbed one—then two—of the hideous brass trophies. When I popped up with them, I saw Zachary, his back stiff, stuck between wanting to go after that teacher-voice and go after poor old Mr. Hall, as well. Blessed criminal indecision.

I hurled a centurion, praying that Zachary's bulk made him the target, not the quavering man with the mop.

Zachary ducked and the trophy crashed into the wall.

"Again!" I screamed—and to my amazement, Zachary stayed down and put his hands over his head—

—at which moment, Mr. Hall raised the mop and solidly landed it on Zachary's thick skull. And then did it again for good measure.

I dialed 911. I knew that even if I didn't get to say a word, the police would come. So I left the receiver on the counter and raced around, and as Zachary Harris, murderer and would-be murderer, climbed back up to his feet, I raised a knee, and in a most unpedagogical fashion, I gave him a much-deserved what-for. He doubled over and I pushed him from behind till he was sprawled on the floor; then I sat down on his back and patted the space beside me. Mr. Hall, who still hadn't said a word—he simply gulped—joined me. "The police are coming," I said.

Mr. Hall nodded.

"You're terrific. You saved me. Saved both of us."

Mr. Hall nodded again.

I didn't think Zachary, who was hurting in several body parts, could toss both of us off before the police arrived. I drew my first semieasy breath. I looked at the mangled centurion and thought about victory. I didn't feel any of it, just relief. Too much had been lost, starting with Helen. If this was victory, it was bittersweet indeed.

Just then, the supply room door opened, and out came Helga and Dr. Havermeyer.

Both feigned surprise that anyone was there. "What's this?" Dr. H. said. "Mr. Hall? Miss Pepper? What are you doing here—and who is this? What's going on here?" He was revving up into his supercilious role, but was still too flustered to lapse into his usual unintelligible jargon.

They must have been listening in terror when I jiggled their love nest's door in all innocence. Now I imagined them in the dark, surrounded by shelves of supplies, and then I gave it up. I love stationery and wasn't about to sully its status in my heart by associating it with them. Imagining these dreadful people joining forces—joining anything—was too ludicrous to contemplate. Did Havermeyer use pedagogical mumbo jumbo as love talk? Did Helga ever remove her omnipresent cardigan? Did they know that they deserved each other? That they were fitting punishment for their collective sins?

"This is Zachary Harris," I said. "A Philly Prep alumnus. He killed a friend of mine. Tried to kill two more of them, then came here to kill me, but Mr. Hall and I—"

"We were taking inventory, you understand. The door there is solid. That must be it. We didn't hear a thing . . ." Dr. Havermeyer's jowls looked mottled. Bits of him were blushing. "Imagine! If I'd known anything was going on . . ."

I looked at him, keeping my expression blank, something akin to "that look" with which teens wither adults. More pink blotches appeared on his chins.

"The trophies!" Helga screamed. "Oh, my beautiful

trophies!" She rushed over and lifted a decapitated centurion and cradled its torso to her breast. "Look what
you've done!"

I heard the sweet music of police sirens and I smiled.
Maybe it was relief, and just a touch of hysteria, but I
suddenly felt so good I thought perhaps I'd never stop
smiling. I'd turn into a Have a Nice Day button. Because
it was all too funny, this part.

"Look what I've done?" I asked sweetly. "Oh, no,
Helga. Look what *you've* done! Your skirt's on inside
out!"

Another bittersweet victory, true. But a victory
nonetheless.

I was willing to bet I'd have no trouble getting paper
supplies in the future.

I wondered if Helga kept raincoats back there, too.

Twenty-eight

MACKENZIE MADE ME POPCORN. "THANK YOU, *FIANCÉ*," I said. The word gave me the giggles.

"No luxury is too great for my intended, my betrothed," he said.

I was bone tired. I'd answered several sets of questions to what seemed the police's satisfaction—at least for today. The book club's emergency meeting was canceled, which had given me a bonus evening with my *fiancé*. I wanted to do nothing more than sit back, eat popcorn, and stare at something amusing.

"Look what's on. How good, how appropriate." Mackenzie held up the TV page of the paper. "You'll never guess."

"Absolutely true. My mind is gone, so don't torture me; tell me."

"*The Philadelphia Story*. My very favorite, too."

Right. Appropriate not only because of its locale, but because Mackenzie had told me that he'd grown up in a household run by Katharine Hepburn and Cary Grant fanatics. His mother even collected their movie posters. Well, it would do. Anything would do that didn't require thinking. I needed a break. I needed to regain my breath and my strength. My parents were returning to Florida the next day.

"She's going to ask, you know," I said.

"Who? What?"

"My mother. Your name."

"Too tired for full sentences?"

I nodded.

"No problem."

"Easy for you to say, Caesar."

"You're funny. I like that in a wife."

"Guess I'll see the entire name on the marriage license."

"Guess so."

"That's reason enough to go ahead with this."

"But if it turns out not to be to your likin', you're amazingly creative at renaming me. That'll come in handy when we have kids. Don't want to use my parents' system."

"Which was what?"

"Obviously derivative," he said. "But my mother was a small-small-town girl. In fact, where she grew up wasn't even big enough to be a town. She learned about the world from the movies. Hepburn and Grant were like nothing and nobody she'd ever seen, the epitome of glamour and sophistication. She didn't know they were like nothing and nobody anybody'd ever seen offscreen."

"Yes, and?" I asked.

He gestured toward the TV screen. The movie had started. His family narrative would be continued later. I sighed in contentment as the credits filled the screen, right at the beginning in that nice old-fashioned way, so you didn't have to sit through the whole movie wondering who was that actor playing so-and-so.

"Wait a minute!" I said as the credits disappeared. "Wait—what did that say? Roll it back!"

"This isn't a tape, Mandy. I can't."

I watched Hepburn toss Grant—her first husband, Dexter—out of her house and life, and then cut forward two years to her impending second marriage. Maybe I'd imagined what I'd seen on the credits?

And then, minutes into the film, when her handsome ex is mentioned, Katharine Hepburn said the name I'd thought I'd seen in the cast of characters. "Mother," she said, "if I never see Mr. C. K. Dexter Haven again . . ."

I looked at my C. K., my mouth slightly agape.

He smiled and nodded. "Those glamorous people's names—not even theirs, not Kate and Cary, but the names of the characters they played, people who lived in mansions and were clever with words—that was something special she could afford to give her children. In fact, just about the only thing she could afford."

"Your name is C. K. As in C. K. Dexter Haven."

"I thought you knew. Named for a fictional and feck-less playboy," he said. "Can you believe it?"

"Your name is C.K.?"

"The Dexter Haven's silent. And aren't we glad she left it off? It sounds like a rest home. After all, like I told you, one of my sisters got Bunny, a name she has hated since age two. And another is Lutie, which isn't much better."

"C. K. stands for C. K. I cannot believe it."

"You're kidding, right? I thought you just enjoyed the jokin'. The game."

I looked at him, open mouthed.

"How clever you could be with alternative names. The weirder the better." When I didn't say something clever or alternative, he shook his head in wonderment. "It's *The Philadelphia Story*, after all. What could be more appropriate? It's part of the reason I wandered up here in the first place. Saw the movie so often. I thought it'd be just like that. Mansions and all."

I burst out laughing. I guess nothing could be more ap-propriate, even if it was going to take me a long time to get used to the fact that the name by which I knew him was in fact his name.

The mystery was solved.

I laughed again, then settled closer to my fiancé-with-an-entire-name to watch somebody else's Philadelphia story while I enjoyed my own.

This story was born of affection for my book group. Obviously, in crafting a mystery, I had to change the peaceful real-life atmosphere of women discussing books to one that included the violent death of a member. It was a plot requirement; it was fictional; it was acceptable.

Then one of the group was killed in a tragic accident.

I put the manuscript aside. It felt wrong—and impossible—to forge an entertainment out of grief. But the mourning process made me realize with new force how much the group meant to me, and I decided to try to put that, and the great sense of loss, onto the page.

And so, with hopes that some of that came through despite the necessary mayhem surrounding it, and hopes that none of the pain and loss was trivialized, I dedicate this to all those who join together to celebrate what books can do and mean, to all book groups, but in particular to my engaging, talented, interesting book group (none of whom are depicted in these pages!): Kate Baker, Sharon Bass, Dorothy Breiner, Carol Burnham, Karla Clark, Betsy Cutler, Judith Ets-Hokin, Laurel Feigenbaum, Peggy Harrington, Ann Jeffrey, Kay Matan, Bunny Petroff, Ann Rivo, Ann Turner, Alice Steinman, and with special love and grief, Ann Neeley, who is missed every time we meet, and in between times as well.

Don't miss any of the
Amanda Pepper mysteries:

CAUGHT DEAD IN PHILADELPHIA
Winner of the Anthony Award for
Best First Mystery Novel

PHILLY STAKES

I'D RATHER BE IN PHILADELPHIA

WITH FRIENDS LIKE THESE. . .

**HOW I SPENT MY
SUMMER VACATION**

IN THE DEAD OF SUMMER

THE MUMMERS' CURSE

THE BLUEST BLOOD

ADAM AND EVIL